A Benedict Aberthorp Mystery: Book One

FOR MURDER PRESS 3

P.M.A. HAYES

CRANTHORPE
—MILLNER—

Copyright © PMA Hayes (2022)

The right of PMA Hayes to be identified as author of this work has been asserted by her in accordance with section 77 and 78 of the Copyright, Designs and Patents Act 1988.

All rights reserved. No part of this publication may be reproduced, stored in a retrieval system, or transmitted in any form or by any means, electronic, mechanical, photocopying, recording, or otherwise, without the prior permission of the publishers.

Any person who commits any unauthorised act in relation to this publication may be liable to criminal prosecution and civil claims for damages.

This book is a work of fiction. Names, characters, places and incidents are either products of the author's imagination or are used fictitiously. Any resemblance to actual events or locales or persons, living or dead, is entirely coincidental.

First published by Cranthorpe Millner Publishers (2022)

ISBN 978-1-80378-063-4 (Paperback)

www.cranthorpemillner.com

Cranthorpe Millner Publishers

Chapter 1

Antiques shop owner found stabbed to death on back lawn

On the afternoon of May ten, the body of thirty-six-year-old Francine Roydon (of Roydons' Antiques) was found by her next-door neighbour, Ms Lilac Browne, under an olive tree on the back lawn of her home in Korimako Street. She'd been stabbed in the chest with an antique dagger, still in situ. She is survived by her husband, Aldo, and a sister, Irene. The police are speaking to neighbours who may have seen something and are appealing to the public to come forward if they know anything at all about this heinous crime.

***

Monday 27th May 2024

In the small coastal city of Seagrove, on the east coast

of the North Island of New Zealand, a man of fifty-four was busy tidying away his breakfast dishes when his phone began playing a tune, called *Smooth Wave*. Having just completed a difficult surveillance case, this was his first day off. He answered the telephone. "Benedict Aberthorp. How may I help?"

He listened while the man on the other end of the line nervously told him he required the services of a private investigator. Usually, Benedict preferred to hear from potential clients via email, but this man sounded desperate. Benedict asked him the usual question: "Are you able to give me a rough idea of the area you require help in?" Typically, he handled cases relating to divorce.

"I-I'm sorry," came the stranger's voice over the line, "but it's rather delicate. I'd prefer to speak to you in person."

Mmm, okay. So probably a divorce situation, Benedict presumed. "I'm free this afternoon," he told the man.

"My shift at the café finishes at four p.m. I could come after that?"

"That's fine. Come to my office at number fifty-five, Rowan Street. It's in a two-storey brick building set back from the road. My office is up the stairs, first on the left. You'll see my name on the door – Benedict Aberthorp, P.I."

***

Afterwards, Benedict set out on his usual morning walk along the Seagrove waterfront, just two streets from his home. He loved to watch the crashing waves dashing onto the pebbly beach. On a fine day the sea would be deep blue, other days, a steely grey. It didn't matter to him either way. One way or another, the colour of the sea always reflected his mood. Today, his eyes travelled over the varied shapes of driftwood lining the high watermark and he breathed in deeply, savouring the fresh sea air.

Now that he had completed his last case, he had time to relax. He tucked a few loose strands of his straight, black hair under the edge of his cap. The breeze blew against his arms and shoulders, which were slimmer and toned since doing light weight training. Even his polo shirt and trackpants felt baggier than usual. After adjusting his dark-rimmed glasses, he looked up at the sky and watched a couple of gulls swooping over the water, hunting for fish as he pondered the phone call he'd just received.

Benedict liked the simplicity of his job. Clients came to him wanting to find out the truth about something. Is my wife seeing another man, or woman? Is my husband cheating on me? My daughter's gone missing. Can you find her? In each case, Benedict assumed the role of 'truth-gatherer.' Once he'd immersed himself in the job at hand, he'd write a report containing, what he hoped, was the truth. He'd also report on how he had come to that conclusion. Thus far, he'd fulfilled all his clients' requests. They either left his office smiling, frowning or deeply upset. Of course, he preferred them to be happy – then he was happy too. Yet their ultimate reaction was dependent upon the nature of the truth he presented them with.

The midmorning sun beat down, as he trudged along the coastal path; a wide strip of green grass, some pine trees and a busy express-way, separating it from the sea beyond. He was enjoying his temporary free time and experienced a sense of relief after the closure of a difficult case that had involved a cheating spouse. Benedict continued walking, trying to imagine what his next potential client might want him to do.

***

"I was scared – still am – scared to hell they'll arrest me for my wife's murder, when I had nothing to do with it. I suppose you've already heard about it – Francine Roydon?" He sat rigid in his chair, fighting to suppress his emotions of grief, shock and fear, his hands pressed tightly between his knees as he leant forward. He sniffed a couple of times as he spoke. Benedict was a little tense himself. He suspected that the man in front of him – Aldo Sherwin – wanted him to find out who had killed his wife.

"Yes, but take your time and tell me in your own words," he said.

Aldo was staring straight ahead, his eyes seemingly not focused upon anything. Benedict hoped he'd start telling his story quickly.

To coax him along, Benedict began telling him about a time in his own life in which he'd been fearful. "You know, one of the scariest things I ever did was go for a job interview at a large public hospital. This was before I became a private investigator. I'd been told one of the interviewers was an uncompromising woman with a history of putting people in their places. But somehow, I got through without allowing my fear to get in the way. They must have approved, because I got the job."

Aldo smiled and nodded. "I was asked to go to the Seagrove police station, and it wasn't a nice experience. Detective Finnegan, who interviewed me, had a face like stone. He stared hard at me all the time and I know he thinks I'm guilty. Maybe he's already decided it must've been me."

"Well, you're here now and you can tell me everything. It won't leave this room." Benedict had met Detective Finnegan before, and among his string of other unpleasant personality traits, had found him to be inflexible and intimidating.

"Someone's trying to frame me for my wife's murder," Aldo finally said, his eyes widening in fear. "For God's sake help me! I don't care what it costs."

His last words were like manna to Benedict: 'I don't care what it costs.' A light switched on in his mind, illuminating the word 'debt' that had such a hold over him. Now Aldo Sherwin's eyes became focussed, drawing Benedict in like a money magnet.

A pile of unpaid bills stared back from Benedict's desk. Essential car repairs had used up nearly all of his last client's payment. Aldo Sherwin's haunted eyes were still trained on him. "I'll do what I can," he finally said.

Aldo's mouth twisted into a grimace. "How do you charge?"

"By the hour. Fifty dollars plus Goods and Services Tax. I can give you an itemised account."

"Fine. I just want to clear my name."

Benedict picked up his notepad and a pen. "So, Francine kept her own name when you married?"

"Yes, she decided to keep it because she was expected to take over and run the business, Roydons' Antiques."

"Can you tell me what happened on the day of the murder?"

Aldo took a sip of the coffee Benedict had made him and then began. "We hadn't lived together for over a year, after I moved into our beach-house, which we both own. So, once a month we met for lunch at our main house, where Francine still lived, in Korimako Street, to go over our finances. The day it happened was one of those days. It was raining, and I was wearing a brown raincoat when I got there and I remember putting it back on again before I left the property. When the police came to the beach-house – where I live – asking questions, they wanted to see my raincoat, but I couldn't find it. I always hang it on a hook behind the laundry door. My guess is that someone came inside when I was out, took the raincoat, and have hidden it somewhere. The police seemed to think my missing raincoat was significant."

"Hold on a minute. Why were the police so interested in your raincoat?"

"Sorry, I forgot to tell you: a brown raincoat was found at the murder scene, beneath my wife's right hand. And of course, I'd already told them she didn't own a brown raincoat – hers was black, mine brown – so they asked to see my coat but I couldn't oblige."

Benedict sucked in his breath noisily. "And have they shown you the raincoat from the murder scene? The one they think is yours?"

Aldo frowned. "No, I have no idea whether it's anything like mine or not."

"Can you fill me in with some details about your marriage, and anything you think might be relevant concerning the death of your wife?"

"What I can tell you is that Francine was an adept yet sly businesswoman who made enemies through her line of work."

Aldo's gaze moved to the office window that overlooked Rowan Street. "Of course, you need to know someone's been following me. When I was parking just along from your office, I looked in my rear-view mirror. It's just something I do, because as I said, I'm convinced someone is trying to frame me. So how do I know they're not following me around too?"

His words came out quickly, and his gaze kept darting back towards the window.

Benedict decided on a matter-of-fact approach. "I take your point. But did you actually see anyone following you?"

"I-I'm not sure, but when I got out of my car and was

locking it, a car flashed past. It turned into the next street."

"Do you know who it might have been?"

"N-no, I have no idea."

"Were you still in love with your wife?"

Aldo paused, as if trying to decide how to explain things. "It was complicated. To start with I loved her – more than I've ever loved anyone before – but later when I found out she was unfaithful to me, I began to hate her. From then on, I had trouble believing anything she said. But she was good at reassuring me she still loved me and I suppose I hung onto that. She often met other antique dealers in bars and had drinks with them. I don't drink, so I guess I couldn't blame her for finding others to share a drink with. But I knew it wasn't just a drink."

He got up and placed the empty mug on the bench before standing by the window, looking out to the street. Benedict watched as he turned to sit back down again.

"Look, why don't we get down to basics; do you have any idea at all who might have wanted your wife dead?"

After looking up at the ceiling, he said. "God, I don't know. Francine was currently seeing a woman called Tegan, but I don't think Tegan would've had anything to do with it."

Benedict wanted to ask Aldo to explain about Tegan,

but decided against it, instead writing her name in his notebook for later.

"What time did you leave after you'd had lunch together that day?"

"One thirty p.m. I had a dentist appointment at two."

"Was Francine alone afterwards?"

"No. Astrid, her housekeeper, was still there, but she was preparing to leave too. She's there on Mondays, Wednesdays and Fridays."

Benedict looked at his watch. It was already five thirty. "I think we can wrap this up for today, Mr Sherwin."

He handed Benedict a card. "You can call me Aldo. These are my contact details."

"Thanks, I'll be in touch soon."

After he'd left, Benedict went to his whiteboard and drew a diagram featuring a house, a back lawn, a dead woman under an olive tree, a dagger and a shadowy figure, standing a little way off, looking back at the scene.

Chapter 2

Tuesday 28th May

Gail Hollingford wore casual slim-fit blue jeans and a blue short-sleeved shirt. She was tall and slender with short wavy hair, like the colour of pale straw. She looked up to see Benedict framed in the doorway of Coffee Mania. His amiable face was a welcome sight and she smiled, beckoning him over. Benedict was also slim, although a little shorter than Gail. He grinned back, and Gail smiled at the familiar glint of gold in one of his upper front teeth. Benedict's eyes, behind the dark-rimmed glasses he always wore, looked back at her in a way that told her he was pleased to see her. It had been a while since they'd last chatted.

They'd first met four years ago, when Gail had sought Benedict's help to find her niece; who'd gone to the South Island, to pick fruit for the summer. She had presumed everything was okay, until her niece failed to keep in touch. Benedict eventually found her, living with a drug addict, and fast becoming one herself.

Throughout this time, Gail and Benedict became friends. She admired the hard-working private investigator and liked the fact that he was always honest with her. So, while she was at home for a holiday from her contract nursing work in Australia, they'd arranged to meet up, which they had done ever since.

Gail remembered the first time they'd had a heart-to-heart conversation two years back, while she was on a break in Seagrove. That's when Benedict had confided to her what had happened to him after his wife, Bryony had died suddenly in 2014. Shortly after her death, Benedict had become agoraphobic, and as he explained to her how he avoided leaving the comfort of home, going shopping and even driving his car, she had listened patiently. Her nursing experience meant that she understood what being agoraphobic meant.

Benedict explained to her that he'd sought help and attended a support group for some time, because even when he thought he'd overcome the crippling fears he experienced, there were times, especially when he was stressed, that his symptoms came back and stopped him from carrying out his work as a private investigator.

There had been other times, when Benedict had called on Gail to do some fieldwork for him on days when he struggled to leave his house.

***

Benedict entered the café just after ten a.m. and joy welled up inside him when he saw Gail sitting at one end of a booth, near the back. "So how did you cope with the heat?" he said, knowing what it was like in the outback of Australia.

"I got used to it. Hate the bush fires though. It really gets to you, seeing all the homes destroyed and the animals trapped. Tragic."

Benedict empathised, as the news had reported the Australian bush fires daily, and the skies overhead were affected by them, causing the morning sun in Seagrove to turn pink during the worst of the fires.

He started telling Gail about his last case before moving on to his most current one. How the victim had been pinned to the ground by a dagger. It was so good to have Gail there to share things with again.

"Come round tomorrow afternoon," she said, and we can have a proper catch up."

***

After leaving the café, Benedict drove his car around to the Roydons' at 9 Korimako Street, where he'd arranged to meet Aldo at eleven a.m. Shortly afterwards, Aldo's car pulled up behind his.

The street was lined with stunning homes, and the Roydons' had a semblance of subdued grandeur. It was a two-storey, cream weather-boarded house, with an unhindered sea view, standing behind a low, orange- brick wall. Two pink flowering Manuka bushes enhanced the impeccable front lawn.

"Wait here, I won't be long," Aldo said, showing Benedict into the lounge while he headed down the hallway.

A vacuum cleaner droned in the distance. While waiting he lowered himself into a comfortable armchair and admired a mahogany coffee table in front of him. In the centre stood a square silver vase holding three yellow roses. There were books and magazines in neat piles on each end of the same table. Something hard was digging painfully into his left thigh. He slid his hand down the side of the chair to see what it was and his fingers closed around a small, square object. It looked like an address book so he quickly slipped it into his inside jacket pocket, thinking it might be a useful source of information.

"Astrid, this is the private investigator, Benedict Aberthorp," Aldo suddenly said, the two of them standing in front of him. They had come into the room without Benedict realising; their footfalls deadened by the wall-to-wall shag-pile carpet. Aldo was now standing alarmingly close to Benedict, who forced a smile to hide his guilt and took a deep breath.

"I'll make some tea while you two get to know each other," Aldo said, turning away, but not before his eyes roamed quickly around the whole room. Benedict's heartbeat took a while to regain its steady rhythm as he observed Aldo's demeanour, now subtly transformed into one of wariness.

Astrid had moved towards the far end of the room where there was a table and three chairs. Benedict joined her and pulled out his notebook and pen. She was wearing tight-fitting clothes, over which she wore an apron-like smock. Below the short sleeves, her bare arms were firm and toned; achieved, he presumed, from the physical work of her housekeeping position. Her dark hair was tidily arranged into a bun except for one lock, which fell over the left side of her forehead, partially concealing a ruddy and slightly curved scar. Otherwise, her face looked honest, accentuated by deep red lipstick. Benedict guessed she was in her early sixties.

"This is a beautiful place," he said, looking around and smiling benignly.

"You've come to find out what I know," Astrid said

abruptly. "So you might as well go ahead. I've just about had enough of this place, if you want to know the truth."

Her straightforward manner caught him by surprise. "Because of what happened?"

"Definitely, but I'll be honest with you: it's everything – from the moment I began working here. I'll be finishing at the end of May, and it can't come quick enough."

Benedict pursed his lips, clicked his pen a few times, and flicked through his notebook. "It's a difficult time for everyone when this kind of thing happens. But my questions won't take long and I want to thank you for being so willing to talk to me. I appreciate it, Mrs Lorning, I really do."

Her facial expression was one of anger. "I wouldn't be working here at all if Elroy was still alive."

"When…?"

"It was a long time ago. In March 2005, my husband, Elroy, was killed, trying to save a woman who was being attacked by two men. They were going to rape her. Unfortunately, the attackers turned on him and stabbed him several times."

"Were they ever brought to justice?"

"I'm afraid not, Mr Aberthorp. They've never been caught."

They sat in silence for a few moments and Benedict

noticed Astrid was no longer sitting so rigidly in her chair; now moving her shoulders as if trying to relax them.

"Anyway, I suppose we need to get back to what happened here on the day of the murder. The police grilled me for hours," she said.

"Did you notice anything different that day?"

"No, nothing at all." She answered quickly, looking down at the floor.

"Mr Sherwin came for lunch, didn't he?"

"That's correct."

"Was it raining much that day?"

"Yes, definitely. Look, will this take long? I'm busy." Her impatience failed to mask an almost imperceptible nervousness.

"Was he wearing a raincoat when he arrived?"

Astrid paused for just a second or two; long enough for Benedict to notice.

"I didn't see him arrive, but his coat was hanging up in the kitchen. He always left it there when it was wet."

He made a note in his book. "And was he wearing it when he left?"

"I don't know, I was busy doing housework at the time."

He noted the impatience in her voice, and said, "See any strangers lurking about?"

"Nope."

"All right. So, what time did you leave for home?"

"Right after Aldo. Around one thirty p.m. I live a few streets away, in Fernhill Crescent, so can walk back."

Benedict wrote everything down while Astrid watched, a grim half-smile on her clamped lips. He had to admit he was a little surprised at how quickly she'd replied to all his questions. He decided to keep the rest of the interview brief to see how Astrid reacted.

"Did Mrs Roydon have a man friend, by any chance?"

"I wondered if you'd ask that. The answer is no, but she did have a woman friend."

Benedict stood up and stretched his legs, to ward off cramp in his upper right thigh: something that happened if he sat for too long. "Her name?"

"Tegan. She used to arrive in a taxi, and after they'd had lunch, I'd hear Francine ordering another taxi and off they'd go."

He sat down again. "I see. So I take it Francine didn't have a car?"

"Correct, she always used taxis and had no interest in getting a car, although she drove one a long time ago and even used to work on it herself."

"Well then, I have no more questions right now, but thanks so much for your help."

Benedict smiled to himself. Astrid's expression was a sight to behold.

"Oh," she said, with a puzzled frown. "Are you sure?"

"Yes, unless of course there's anything else you'd like to add?"

She looked as if she was about to say something – no doubt, he surmised, from her list of pre-arranged answers, but then changed her mind. "No, I don't think so."

"If you do think of anything, please call me." He handed her one of his glossy business cards.

"I will."

Then, like a ghostly shadow, Aldo came in with a tea tray. Benedict got up. "Don't worry about the tea, I'm in a bit of a rush. Just popping round to your neighbour's. I'll be in touch."

"You can get there through the gate in the hedge," Aldo blurted, looking startled. "There's a path round the back of the house."

"Thanks."

Benedict suspected Astrid had had everything well-rehearsed but he hadn't given her the satisfaction of saying it all.

***

After walking along the suggested path in the back yard, Benedict found himself admiring a green, well-manicured lawn. There was a wooden gazebo to his left, where a large fluffy grey cat was asleep on a chair. To his right, just before he opened the gate in the hedge, he glanced over to where two mature olive trees stood and wondered which one the victim's body had been found beneath.

Lilac Browne looked fit and spritely, with fine, white hair styled in a short cut, combed forward, to give her face an elfin look. Her smile was like that of a shy school-girl.

"I'm Benedict Aberthorp, private investigator, working on behalf of Aldo Sherwin. Do you mind if I come in and ask you a few questions? It concerns the death of his wife."

She opened the door, which led into her kitchen. "Do come in, Mr Aberthorp."

She led him into a room just off the kitchen, where there was a dolls' house on a low table, with various pieces of tiny furniture arranged on a shelf behind it. Benedict spent a few moments looking at the handiwork before taking a seat in a straight-backed chair, Lilac leaning forward in hers, watching Benedict intently.

"Dominica's handiwork. She's been gone for almost

twenty years, but I've left everything the same."

"It's beautiful," he said.

"Er, I might as well tell you – Dominica was my partner and loved to make things." She inclined her head towards the dolls' house. The room seemed like a shrine to the absent woman.

Benedict nodded and tried to look empathetic. "Do you miss her a lot?"

A glassy film of tears filled Lilac's eyes and two drops fell, one rolling down each cheek, until her fingers hurriedly brushed them away. "Yes, and I think of her every day. I couldn't believe it when she ran off with that damned Aussie guy, from Queensland."

As he watched Lilac crying, a picture came to Benedict, of his father's stern face, when, as a child, Benedict had cried after hurting himself and his father had said: "Big boys don't cry. Now, come on, be brave." From then on, he'd learnt to hold his pain inside him and not share it with anyone.

"It must've been a hard time. Did you know him at all?" he said, as Lilac sniffed into a paper tissue.

"Heck no." Her facial expression was one of anger, at the memory.

Benedict waited for her to compose herself before asking. "I believe you were first on the murder scene?"

"Yes, and it was horrible." She sniffled and blew her

nose on a tissue.

"What did you see? And what time was it?" He leaned back as far as was possible in the stiff upright chair and stretched his legs out in front of him to ward off the possibility of cramp threatening again.

Lilac looked down at a low table where there was a packet of cigarettes and a lighter. "I can still picture the scene: it was around three p.m. She was flat on her back, her shiny black shoes pointing upwards, and a ghastly-looking medieval dagger or sword coming out of her chest. But I didn't scream, not like the women always do on television. I just stood there, frozen to the spot. I couldn't believe she was actually dead. I wondered at the time, if the whole thing had been staged, like in a play or a film."

Benedict sat up straight again. "In what way?"

She screwed up her eyes. "Everything was so neat. The way she was lying – straight – her hands at her sides, palms upwards. A brown raincoat under her right hand. It was like someone had decided exactly how they wanted her to look when she was found. I can't imagine anyone falling down in such a way."

Benedict scribbled a few notes. "Did you observe anything else that was unusual?"

"Er, only when I went out to the letterbox." She picked up her cigarette packet and opened it.

"Go on."

"It was just after two-thirty, before I'd gone over to the Roydons'. I'd not long got home and was expecting a parcel, but it hadn't arrived.

"Did I mention Aldo was just leaving their property?" She leant closer to Benedict now, her eyes shining. "After closing the letterbox, I looked up and there he was."

"Aldo Sherwin? Are you sure it was him? This is important." He stood up and walked up and down the room to kick-start the circulation in his legs.

Lilac also got up from her chair. She flung open a window at the side of the room and went and stood there while she lit a cigarette, inhaling deeply. "He had his back to me, but his shape and the auburn hair were undeniably his. I called out, but he didn't turn around. He just rushed away, really fast. Maybe he didn't hear me?"

"Which way did he go?"

"To the right."

"And got into his car?"

"No, I don't believe so. It could have been parked further along the street I suppose."

"Can you remember what he was wearing?"

Lilac flicked some ash outside. "Yes, of course: a green-coloured knitted jumper and grey trackpants. I still have the notes I wrote on the day. The police told me not to share what I'd seen at the crime scene with anyone else. So, all I told Aldo and Astrid was that Francine had been stabbed to death."

"So, he can't have been wearing his raincoat?"

"No, he wasn't." Lilac looked wide-eyed at him although, he wasn't sure why.

"So, what were you doing on the morning of the day in question?"

"I was out shopping, and then I went to get my yearly flu vaccination, so I didn't get home until two."

He was intrigued now and wondered how accurate her witness statement was. "Can I see your notes?"

"Sure. You might pick up something the police have missed."

He nodded.

She put her cigarette into an ashtray on a table near the window and scurried away, arriving back with a piece of notepaper covered in neat handwriting. She held her statement out for him to read. It was dated May ten, 2024.

'Today, Friday, May 10th, 2024, at about 2:30 p.m. while looking in my letterbox, I saw Aldo Sherwin rushing away from the Roydons' place. I called out but he didn't acknowledge me and soon disappeared from

sight. Later I went over to the Roydons' to see if Francine could check out my car as the steering was pulling to the right.

I entered their property through the gate in the hedge just after 3 p.m. and noticed, to my left, the feet of a woman sticking out from under one of the olive trees. The toes were pointing upwards and the shoes were shiny and black. I slowly walked over and saw Francine Roydon lying on the ground with a knife sticking out of her chest. It looked like some kind of old dagger. I also saw what I thought was an item of clothing lying on the ground next to her. I looked closer, and saw there was a brown raincoat beneath her right hand. Her eyes were staring straight up into the sky and I knew she was dead.'

Benedict handed the piece of paper back to Lilac. "Thank you so much, Ms Browne. I wonder... do you know who lives in the two-storey house that backs onto the Roydons' property?"

Lilac stubbed out her cigarette. "Call me Lilac, everyone else does. It's the Seyners' – Wayne and Wendy. Lovely old couple. He's been laid up with a broken leg, or so Wendy said when I bumped into her in the supermarket the other day. He's had to go back into hospital to have his fracture re-set."

"I'll need to speak to them. If you think of anything else, can you give me a call?" He held out one of his business cards.

Lilac took it then put her hand up as if to stop Benedict from leaving. "Just a moment, please don't rush off. I wanted to tell you what happened on the evening of the day of the murder. You see I need to get everything off my chest and I can't talk to anyone else about it. But as you're a private investigator, I know you won't repeat what I tell you.

"I was back at home, exhausted after so much questioning by the police, when at around seven p.m., Astrid phoned and asked me to come over to her flat. It's in Fernhill Crescent, a couple of streets away. She said Aldo was already there and they were having a drink or two and wanted me to join them. She said the three of us needed to unwind."

"Was that usual – for the three of you to have a drink together?"

Lilac's eyebrows shot up. "Not really, but we were all in shock. Aldo always tells people he doesn't drink, but that's because of the problem he and Francine had in the past."

"Was he an alcoholic?"

"No, but Aldo started drinking in 2005, after Francine lost the baby. They'd only been married a few months when she had a stillbirth. She was already pregnant when they married. Only seven months old, it was, the poor, wee thing. Aldo was really depressed afterwards; so much so he had to be sent to a psychiatric hospital for three months. They had to do it as by then he used to drink so much he passed out just about every day – all because Francine had lost the baby. Francine was really upset too, naturally, but she handled it better than Aldo. I can't even count the number of times he came over here with a bottle of wine that we'd polish off together. I know I shouldn't have encouraged him, but he said it helped him forget things for a while. Francine didn't need alcohol. She was always the strong one."

"Has Aldo been all right since then?"

Lilac picked up her packet of cigarettes again. "Er, I think so. Now and again he still has a drink but not like in the past."

Benedict found Lilac Browne interesting; primarily because when someone volunteered information he hadn't asked for, his curiosity was piqued. He was now asking himself, why she had chosen to tell him the specific things she had…? Did she have something to hide, or did she want to tell him more?

***

Lilac picked up Scamper and stroked his head as she watched Benedict Aberthorp drive away. "Good boy." The fluffy, grey cat purred with pleasure. "He doesn't have to know everything, my little one, does he?"

Her thoughts returned to the night Astrid had unexpectedly phoned to ask her to come over. She remembered being relieved because after the murder and all the questions the police had asked her, she was downright dejected. Sitting alone in her kitchen afterwards, she had wondered if they suspected it might actually have been *her* who had committed the murder – especially that detective.

When she'd arrived at Astrid's flat, Aldo was drinking himself into oblivion, although Astrid didn't seem to be doing the same, which was unusual, in the circumstances. After Astrid had poured Lilac a large glass of sparkling wine, the reason for her sobriety became evident when, moments later, she covertly signalled Lilac to follow her out into the hallway. She reasoned that Astrid had something to tell her. Lilac had nodded her agreement and quickly drank a few mouthfuls of wine before following. In the hallway, Astrid had given her instructions. Lilac had readily agreed, secretly relieved to be in favour with Astrid again, since she seemed to have turned against her when Cindy appeared on the scene. Cindy who'd left Seagrove when she was still a teenager. Lilac hadn't liked being on the outside, feeling miserable and cheated, and so that night she'd blindly fulfilled Astrid's request, without even thinking about the consequences, because, if the police ever found the coat there, they'd blame her alone for trying to frame Aldo. Besides, it had already been part of her and Astrid's original plan anyway, until smarmy Cindy came along and spoilt everything.

All this she decided to keep to herself. There was no way she was going to tell Benedict Aberthorp what she'd done. It was between her and Astrid and no one else. Yet still, Lilac was consumed by guilt, because to her it was a shameful act; one she'd done in a perfunctory fashion after firstly telling Aldo she was going out to buy potato chips for them all.

***

Lilac let her mind drift back to the day in April when she'd looked through the Roydons' hedge and seen Aldo and the two women seated in the gazebo. The prickly hedge leaves had tickled her face, but she'd hardly noticed, so absorbed was she in what was happening in the Roydons' backyard. One of the women she was well acquainted with, but the second... surely it couldn't be Cindy? It must have been twenty years since she had last seen her, but there was something about her voice that Lilac recognised. She kept looking at the scene, unmoving and silent. *Why are they pricking their fingers, and saying those creepy words?* she wondered.

Less than a month later, Francine Roydon was dead. Lilac had been the one to find her – worse luck – and something she often complained about. Then all those questions the police had asked afterwards, like why had she gone to her neighbour's place that day? On and on the questioning went. Now she had to put up with more probing, by the private investigator Aldo had hired – Benedict Aberthorp. Aberthorp might pretend to be casual with his seemingly laid-back approach, but Lilac saw how his shrewd, intent eyes, followed her every movement, no doubt summing her up in his professional way.

The body of Francine had been a horrible sight. Lilac couldn't forget it and sometimes, when she was trying to relax in the evenings, the picture came back into her mind. Lilac hated the way it was so hard to erase it from her memory. The other part she remembered clearly was when Scamper, the Roydons' cat, had meowed loudly as she'd stood, looking down at Francine's body. Lilac had whirled around, her heart thumping, to see the grey, fluffy animal looking up at her imploringly. "Sorry mate," Lilac had said. "She looks dead."

Chapter 3

Wednesday 29th May

Benedict had already picked up a copy of the murder report before arriving at Gail's beachside bungalow. He sank back into the leather couch. "You know, I'd love to know where the knife came from – the one they found in Francine Roydon's chest. As I already told you, someone had pinned her to the ground with it, for God's sake!"

"I found that so bizarre," Gail said, while making them some coffee. "Must've been a big one."

"According to the police report, it was a German Saxon dagger, circa 1600."

"Hell. Have you seen the coroner's report yet?"

"No, but it's on my to-do list."

He passed Gail his copy of the police report and she spent a couple of minutes reading it. "So, what's bothering you?"

"The raincoat found at the murder scene. In the report

it says it was beneath Francine's right hand. So, if Aldo is telling the truth and he left the house at one-thirty, wearing his raincoat, whose raincoat was left at the scene?"

Gail stood up and stretched. "Exactly. Whose? Perhaps it belonged to his wife?"

"No, he told me her raincoat was black. Anyway, I've got my own theory about the raincoat business," he said. "Think about it like this: if Aldo is telling the truth, the killer was clever. Not only did they pick the day of the month when Aldo always visits Francine, but they also dressed like him and possibly wore a wig."

Gail took a sip of coffee. "Has Aldo seen the raincoat found at the crime scene?"

"No. I suppose when the police asked him if Francine owned a brown raincoat, he surmised there was one at the scene. Of course, Lilac Browne was there first and would have seen everything."

"And this was just after three, so the police report says."

"Yes, but her statement to the police said she was sure Aldo was leaving the property at about two thirty p.m. Now she's petrified that Aldo knows she saw him. It's making her jittery, because Aldo told me he left at one thirty p.m. He's adamant he had to go then because he had a dentist appointment in town at two p.m."

Gail smiled. "Then it's simple: Aldo can't be the killer."

Benedict sighed and stretched his legs out. "But that doesn't explain Lilac's sighting of him. Unless, of course, he came back to the house later, did away with Francine and left again, this time not wearing the coat. I'll need to check out the dentist appointment."

"How'd you like some help with this case? I have plenty of spare time. No more nursing contracts for at least three months," Gail said.

Benedict breathed a sigh of relief. "Great. I could do with someone to check a few things out for me. For example, when exactly was this dentist appointment of Aldo's? And how long was he there? Could you find out? I'm sure he must have a letter, text or email showing at least the exact time of his appointment."

"Absolutely! Besides, he's probably already asked the dental practice to confirm this for the police, if that is his alibi for the time of death."

Benedict wasn't keen on going to the police for this kind of information, and he was hoping that because Gail was a trained nurse, she'd think of a way to get the information they needed. She seemed positive about her new assignment.

He leaned back on the couch again. "I don't know about Lilac. I think there's more to her than we know about. A lot more. And now we must find out what she *hasn't* revealed."

Gail smiled. "So, you're going to re-interview her?"

"I think so, but I want it to seem like a random meeting. Can you come to my office tomorrow and we'll make a plan?"

"Okay."

"There's just one more thing: when I visit Roydons' Antiques and interview the shop manager, Charley Raymond, I suggest we go together." He finished his drink and placed the mug on a coffee table nearby.

"Sure. Does he run it alone?"

"I believe so. I'm told he's just come back after being away for a while."

***

While driving to his home at forty-three Plover Street, Benedict noticed a small blue car parked in the Bartholomews' driveway at number seventy-one. They'd gone to England for six months and were renting out their house for the duration, but until now Benedict hadn't seen a sign of anyone living there.

"Keep an eye on the house will you, Benedict?" Jed Bartholomew had said. Apparently, their next-door neighbour, Mrs Shields, had been asked to do the same.

He was acquainted with Mrs Shields, a pleasant woman who loved to garden and chat to passers-by as she worked.

Once he'd parked in his driveway, he looked back just as the blue car was reversing out onto the street. He couldn't see the driver, but presumed it was a woman when he glimpsed a coloured headscarf. Benedict watched until the car disappeared south, perhaps to the Seagrove shopping centre. The vehicle looked to be a Fiat Bambina.

Then his phone vibrated; it was Aldo Sherwin. "Did Lilac tell you about the man leaving our place on the day of the murder?" he said.

"Er, yes, but she said she didn't know who the man was," Benedict said, carefully.

"She told Astrid and me the same. Perhaps it was one of Francine's business friends?"

"I suppose it could have been." Benedict exhaled relieved Lilac hadn't said anything about the man looking like Aldo's doppelgänger.

"I don't always believe what Lilac says, you know. She's away with the fairies most of the time. Didn't you know not to rely on what she tells you?" Aldo said.

"No, I didn't. So what exactly did she tell you?"

There was silence for a few seconds. "She told us she'd seen a man rushing up the road when she was out checking her letterbox. Later she found Francine lying there and rang the police immediately."

"I was told the same story." *Why are you so worried about this?* Benedict wondered.

"So, what happens now?" Aldo said.

"Don't worry, I'll be in touch soon."

"Thanks."

Once inside, he poured himself a glass of cold lemonade and began going through the small address book he'd found in the Roydons' lounge. It must have belonged to Francine, as he soon came across the name Tegan, with a phone number and address alongside. According to the book, she lived in The Blue Cottage, at Gull Bay – a seaside settlement south of town. The only thing for it was to visit her, but first he needed to make a plan.

Chapter 4

Thursday 30th May

Lilac had always known that her partner, Dominica, had 'the second sight' – clairvoyance – the ability to perceive future events. She'd told Lilac about her gift just a few days after they'd first met; sometimes it was intrusive, and Dominica needed to explain what was happening to her. "I'm telling you because sometimes I see horrific accidents, and even murders."

Lilac remembered Dominica saying, "If anything happens to me, you need to look for the letter I've already written, and read it."

"How will I find the letter?" Lilac had asked.

This was around the year 1990 when life had seemed idyllic and Lilac had tried to laugh it off. "Nothing's going to happen," she had said, although deep down she was convinced that Dominica was trying to tell her something important, and she dreaded what it might be.

"You've got to remember what I've told you," Dominica had insisted. "I won't tell you which piece of furniture I've hidden the letter in, and please don't start looking yet because you won't find it. It's far too early in the day for that."

Now she kept thinking about Dominica's words – those dreadful words. If only Lilac could blot them out, but she couldn't. Wine didn't help; it only made it worse. So now, even though she didn't want to, Lilac summoned up the courage to begin searching for the letter, written all those years ago. What had Dominica predicted? Lilac couldn't bear to think about the night in question when so much had happened. The lie she had told often, about Dominica leaving her for a man was convincing, but there was always the chance that some astute person, like that private investigator, might see right through her story and start to wonder if what she had told them was the truth.

And now she thought she could hear Dominica whispering to her in the night; her voice urgent, compelling, ever more so since Francine's murder. Yet it was never about the letter. It concerned a phone-call Dominica wanted her to make. Lilac didn't want to let her down this time – not ever again.

The first time Dominica had spoken to her, Lilac had

been shocked. It had happened late one night, while Lilac was tossing and turning in bed, trying to get to sleep. Dominica's soft voice had murmured, "Make the phone call, my love, and when the recorded voice says for murder, press three, you must do it." Her voice had been clear and adamant.

When Lilac had asked her what number, she was to dial, Dominica hadn't answered. The following day, Lilac had dialled the Seagrove police station, but there were no options given – just a serious voice asking what her call was about. "Sorry," Lilac had said, "wrong number."

A few days later, Dominica spoke to her again, insisting she make the phone call and that when the recorded voice said, for murder press three, she was to do it. Yet once again, she'd not been forthcoming with the number she wanted Lilac to dial.

Then one day, unexpectedly, Dominica spoke the same message again, but this time, when Lilac asked her what number, she was to dial, Dominica said, "No, not yet. There's one more."

Lilac had been excited and said, "So, press three means three murders?"

Dominica had simply replied, "Three is three."

***

As he sat in his office in Rowan Street, planning what his next move was going to be, Benedict opened his notebook and read aloud his current summation of facts:

Francine Roydon, 36, female of 9 Korimako Street, Seagrove. Murdered Friday May 10, 2024.

Aldo Sherwin, 38, her husband, had lunch with her on the day she died. He lives alone in their beach-house in Seagrove and has done for over a year, since they separated.

On the day of the murder, Aldo claims he arrived for lunch with Francine, just before 12 noon and left at 1:30 p.m. He said he had a dentist appointment at 2 p.m. and had to rush off.

Astrid, the housekeeper, who comes in on Mondays, Wednesdays and Fridays, was also there on the day. She says she left the house shortly after Aldo – probably about 1:35 p.m. – and walked to her flat in Fernhill Crescent, a few streets away.

Lilac Browne, the neighbour, who found the body, said Francine had been stabbed in the chest with a dagger, and a brown raincoat was found beneath her right hand.

***

Benedict picked up the police report and looked at it again. One passage caught his attention:

'The body was located on the ground, partially under one of the two olive trees in the back garden. She was supine, with eyes closed. There was a long-handled dagger protruding from the left side of her chest.'

This account differed significantly from Lilac's statement:

'Francine Roydon's eyes were open and she was staring straight up into the sky.'

He'd need to check this disparity.

While he was placing the report back into its envelope, a text came through, from his neighbour, Jed, telling him not to worry as the blue car he'd seen in their driveway belonged to a woman who was renting their house for a couple of months.

After pouring himself a drink of ginger-beer, Benedict went outside to the back porch, where there was a chair and a wooden table where he often ate his lunch, in the warmer weather. The floor of the porch was high enough for him to gaze at the sea beyond, and he stood, watching the cold-looking white-caps on the grey water in the bay, trying to make sense of what he'd been told. After Lilac claimed she'd seen Aldo leaving the Roydons' property, that day, Benedict could only presume that she'd been mistaken, or someone was lying. Now, as he began to go over what both Aldo and Lilac had said, he realised there was no way of knowing which of them was telling him the truth.

The front doorbell chimed, and he put his glass down on the table before hurrying through the house to answer the door. A courier, who'd parked in his drive and left the van's engine running, was holding out a large, plastic envelope. He gestured for Benedict to sign a handheld digital device with his finger as proof of receipt. Afterwards, Benedict cut across the top of the envelope and pulled out a single sheet of thick paper. It was a summarisation of the coroner's report, and he soon learned the full extent of Francine's injuries:

'A haemorrhage of the brain with a fracture of the occipital font. She also received a puncture to the left heart ventricle with a pointed dagger. The blade had sharp edges and was also used in a sweeping motion to damage the heart before being pushed right through the body, evidenced by an exit wound in the left posterior chest. The wound to the victim's heart was the main cause of death. The definitive time of death was somewhere within a four hours' time-frame.'

He shuddered, finished his drink and went back inside.

In the morning he'd see Tegan, and then afterwards pick up Gail and visit Charley Raymond at Roydons' Antiques.

He'd already phoned the other neighbour, Wendy Seyner, who had informed him that her husband, Wayne, was still in hospital. She assured him she'd let him know when Wayne was discharged.

Benedict suddenly felt invigorated. He had never investigated a murder case before, but he wasn't going to worry about that. From experience, he was well aware that the solving of *any* case meant finding the truth; gathering the strands of evidence like wool left by the sheep on the barbed-wire fences of his father's farm. His mother used to gather it up to use in her art-work. His truth-gathering would also create a picture; one that showed what had really happened on the day of the murder.

Chapter 5

Friday 31st May

As he drove south around the coast, he came to a steep hill and automatically braked for the descent, looking left, out over the sweep of sea, glittering in the sun. Benedict smiled. He loved this part of the coast, and Tegan's cottage was one of only a handful hugging the shoreline below the cliff.

"Can I help you?" Tegan's tone reminded him of the rustle of soft silk, complementing her sophisticated appearance. Although she was slight, the light blouse she was wearing was a loose-fitting style, which did not hide the fact that she was pregnant. Her face was lightly tanned, with dimpled cheeks, and she had almond-shaped eyes.

"Tegan Tresco?"

She nodded, half-smiling.

"Benedict Aberthorp – private investigator. I'm investigating the murder of Francine Roydon." He showed her his identification tag and Tegan glanced at it, a puzzled frown crinkling her otherwise flawless brow.

"I've told the police everything I know. They were satisfied – or so they led me to believe."

"I've been employed by the victim's widower, Aldo Sherwin, to find her killer."

Her face grew solemn all of a sudden. "Oh, you'd better come in then. Would you like a drink?"

"No, thanks."

She led Benedict into a lounge that was sparsely but tastefully furnished. Benedict made himself comfortable on an olive-green two-seater velvet designer couch, while Tegan sat opposite in what was probably a Perugia-armchair – what would surely one day be considered a classic – made in the same colour and material as the sofa.

"When was the last time you saw Francine?" Benedict said, once they'd settled themselves into their seats.

Tegan picked up a tall glass, taking a sip of a lemon-coloured drink and placing the glass down on a small table beside her. "The day before she was murdered. She was here in the afternoon and left about seven in the evening."

"So, when did you find out about her death?"

Her face was deadpan. "When I rang her the following evening. There was a message on the answerphone to phone the housekeeper, which was unusual. I did so, and the bitch told me Francine had been murdered."

Tegan's expression became grim, and she seemed to be barely keeping her emotions in check, as she picked up her glass again, took a sip and cleared her throat.

Benedict gave her time to regain her composure before carrying on with his questions. "Any ideas who might have done this?"

Tegan looked down and seemed to be thinking, then she raised her head. "Oh yes, I do. How do I know? Because Francine had enemies, and there's two who I suspected straight away. She was a strong woman who went after what she wanted, and she didn't really care if anyone got in the way. She either pushed obstacles aside, or rode roughshod over them. I admired her for not allowing others to rule her life."

Benedict sat up straight. "I see. And were there any such *obstacles* leading up to her death?"

"Yes. But if you're thinking her husband was someone she must've hurt badly, I suppose she did, but that wasn't the main reason he took it hard when they split up. She said he would never leave her because he needed her money. He had always known she was dripping in it.

"She also told me her husband had a weird kind of friendship with the housekeeper. Apparently, they spent a lot of time together and Francine was angered by their friendship. She used to argue with her husband about it. When I became re-acquainted with Francine, she was on a downer – there's no two-ways about it. Her marriage wasn't going well at all. But I had no idea they had it in for her."

Benedict wasn't expecting this and found himself liking Tegan; perhaps because of her straight-talking manner. "So, you'd known her in the past?"

"We lived next door to the Roydons when I was growing up, but I didn't see Francine much in those days because I was sent to boarding school. Her parents left half of the family home and business to each sister, even though Irene was already a wealthy woman, having married into money when she was very young. Years later, when I returned to Seagrove again, after Mum and Dad had died, Francine and I ran into each other in town one day. Initially we'd meet now and again for a drink, but I went back south again, because that was where most of my friends were, and it was several years before we were reunited. That only happened after I'd come back to the area and decided to settle here. It was about eighteen months ago that we began having an affair. I'm now six months pregnant with our child. We went through IVF treatment, using a donor egg from Francine. She was so happy because she really craved for us to have a baby. She even made a new will, leaving a large chunk of her money to our son, to be kept in trust until he turns eighteen. As for the house, well, it belongs to me now. Francine was adamant that she and I would be joint owners, but if anything happened to her I would have total ownership. She wanted to make sure we were well provided for, and did this just in case something untoward happened."

Benedict's jaw muscles tensed and his breathing became shallow as he listened to what Tegan was saying. "Like she knew she was in danger?"

Tegan averted her gaze and looked away, past Benedict. "I don't know, but Francine definitely wanted me to live with her in the house in June, so I could settle in before the baby was born in August. Aldo was living in their beach-house, and Francine had already given the housekeeper three months' notice. She wanted to be fair, so gave her plenty of time to find a new position. She really didn't want Astrid around anymore, especially since she found her going through some papers in her room. The truth was that Francine couldn't wait for Astrid Lorning to go."

"Was Astrid upset about losing her job?"

"Oh yes. She didn't take it well at all. But I was relieved she was going too."

***

On his way back to Seagrove, Benedict pondered all the things Tegan had told him and, unless she was lying, Aldo's description of Francine was now less convincing. Benedict was also puzzled as to why Astrid had told him she couldn't wait to leave the Roydons' place. Both Aldo and Astrid insisted they had no animosity towards Francine.

His conversation with Tegan now became the high point of his enquiry, especially when it came to motive. Perhaps Aldo resented what Francine had done? Benedict wasn't so sure about Astrid, but one thing was clear: their safe, secure worlds were in the process of cracking and crumbling around them. With the new will in place, murdering Francine wouldn't change anything for Aldo or Astrid. The unanswered question was whether or not Aldo knew about the new will? If he did know about it, then he might have been angry that the estate would no longer be his. If it had been, then Astrid would be allowed to stay working at the property because he'd be the sole beneficiary.

***

The shop window of Roydons' Antiques was crammed full of antique weaponry, protected by thick metal security bars. Even a ram-raider would have difficulty getting through it. There were short, dangerous-looking daggers and swords, as well as spears and shields. Benedict searched for the same kind of dagger used to kill Francine, but there were none.

He and Gail went straight up to the counter, where a thickset, balding man carefully watched them. He wore glasses and was stationed behind the counter, reading a newspaper.

The man looked up. "Can I help you?" he said.

"We're investigating a murder." Benedict showed his identity card. "And this is my assistant, Gail Hollingford. The murdered woman's name is Francine Roydon whom I believe once owned this shop. Are you, Charley Raymond?"

Charley sucked in his breath. "Yes, I'm an old school friend of Francine's. Been working here for the past eight years. Come out back and we can talk. I'll shut up the shop for a while."

Benedict and Gail waited while Charley put up the 'closed' sign.

"We're looking for antique daggers. Do you have any

German ones, say Saxon, circa 1600?" Benedict said.

Charley hesitated. "They're not all on open display, for obvious reasons. Can I ask the reason for your interest?" His manner seemed a little surly.

"It's all part of our investigation."

Once the 'closed' sign was in the glass door at the entrance to the shop, Charley led them out the back where there was a kitchen area with a faded yellow Formica table and four chairs.

"I don't suppose you know about Francine's sister, Irene? She is certain Aldo is the culprit," Charley said, frowning.

"No. Aldo didn't say. Perhaps he's not aware of it. But we must start from scratch and work things out step by step, in our own way," Benedict said, looking over at Gail who nodded and produced a notebook and pen from her handbag.

Charley took his glasses off and began cleaning them with a grubby-looking cloth. "Irene is sure Aldo was involved," he said, breathing on his glasses and continuing to polish the lenses. "She's never liked him though."

"Do you know why?"

"It goes back a long way – about twenty years in fact. There was a group of us who'd all been friends at high school. After we'd finished school, some of us who couldn't afford to go away anywhere, kept in touch.

Even Francine Roydon was part of our group, even though her parents were wealthy. They didn't mind us going to their place. We'd go there and have barbecues and go swimming, and talk about what to do with our lives. It wasn't easy for some of us to get employment in Seagrove back then. Mind you, Francine didn't need to worry as her future was tied up with her father's shop."

"So, Irene and Aldo were part of the group?"

"Yeah, and Irene didn't like to see Francine hanging around Aldo. She wanted her sister to go out with someone higher up the social ladder. But in the end, she married Aldo anyway." Charley laughed bitterly.

"Aldo's family were poor?"

"No, not really, but Aldo's mother brought him up alone. I don't know where his father was. Single mothers were not always accepted around these parts."

Benedict was familiar with how people regarded single mothers. It was the same just about everywhere. "No, unfortunately they're not. Did you know Tegan is pregnant?" he said, watching Charley's face.

He nearly dropped his glasses. "No, Francine hadn't told me that.

"But she did tell me a teenage girl from Scotland came to see her sometime last year, claiming to be her half-sister, and wanting to get to know her better. Francine, who knew about the girl, told her that her father, who died in 2007, had always maintained he was not her father. She gave the girl her marching orders."

"Was that true?" Benedict said. "Or was Mr Roydon the girl's father?"

"Yes, I believe he was. Andy Roydon took a shine to Cindy Herskington, the girl's mother, but it was all hushed up and when she was still in the early stages of her pregnancy, she went with her father to Scotland where he was emigrating. He and his new girlfriend were buying a sheep farm over there."

"What happened to the girl after Francine turned her away?"

"No one knows. Probably went back to Scotland, to her family over there. It must've been pretty bad for her, coming all this way and getting news like that. Apparently, she'd been told her birth father had died but she hoped to get to know Francine. They were half-sisters, after all."

"Did Francine ever talk about this girl?"

"No, not to me anyway." Charley inspected his glasses and put them back on. "So, what did this dagger look like?"

Benedict pulled out his phone and brought up the photograph to show him.

Charley examined it and scowled. "*Mmm*, interesting. So, this is the German one you mentioned earlier?"

"Yes. Would it have come from this shop?"

Charley scratched his head. "It's not one I've seen here, but we do have one that's similar, except longer. Come and take a look for yourself. One of our buyers used to go to Germany from time-to-time to pick up some valuable items for us."

He led them into a small room off the kitchen area, that was nothing more than an enlarged cupboard. Charley turned on the light and quickly shut the door behind them. Nausea immediately overcame Benedict. He often suffered from claustrophobia, but said nothing, even though the clamminess of sweat prickled all over him. Gail looked at him and raised her eyebrows. He shook his head and she understood that to mean keep quiet.

After taking down a framed picture from the wall, Charley twirled a dial and opened a small, heavy-looking safe. He reached in and drew out a long object wrapped in cloth. He showed them a dagger, very similar to the murder weapon.

"There you are. I'm told this is a rare dagger, and it's not for sale. We were asked to keep it safe for its owner, who has never returned. I don't even know if he's still alive. But until someone comes and can prove they are entitled to it, here it stays. Pick it up," Charley said.

"Take a good look at it." The dagger was heavy and Benedict passed it to Gail, who held it at arm's length and soon passed it back to Charley, who had a strange look in his eyes. "This is a fine dagger. It's sending a surge of power right through me."

Benedict gave Gail a sideways look and said to Charley, "I can see you have a love of antiques." What he didn't say was just how creepy his statement about a 'surge of power' had sounded.

Charley smiled and put the dagger back in the safe, locked it and replaced the framed picture. "Will you both join me in a toast to the memory of Francine?"

"Well..." Benedict looked at Gail, "all right then."

Once they'd come out of the small room and were sitting at the table again, Benedict took a deep breath and his heart began to return to its normal rhythm. Charley poured them each a tiny glass of expensive-looking Portuguese sherry. "To you, Mr Aberthorp, and your assistant, Miss Hollingford, and for the loss of my dear friend, Francine." They raised their glasses, clinked them together and sipped their sherries until their glasses were empty.

Charley poured them another, and Benedict tasted its strong flavour as a sensation of peaceful calm wrapped itself around him, like a warm, comforting blanket. If partaking in an afternoon tipple meant gleaning more information about Francine to help find her killer, he was all for it. "I believe the shop was closed for a while after the murder," Benedict said, sipping his second drink.

Hesitating for a moment, Charley said, "Yes, but I had already gone on holiday the day before, so the shop hadn't been open at all that day either. Francine was quite happy to leave the shop closed until the Monday morning, she told me."

Benedict was pleased to see Gail jotting down this new information.

"I see. May I ask where you were on the day in question?"

"Yes, of course. Down the coast at the Bayside Lodge in Moana."

"I know the place," Benedict said, carefully placing his small glass down on the table.

Charley looked at him with a kindly expression. "I'm glad you're looking out for Aldo. He's not had a happy time of things."

He poured them a third drink, despite Benedict waving it away in protest, and began telling them about his past. They listened; Benedict fascinated and so, it seemed, was Gail, who was now happily half-way through her third glass of sherry.

"I know I haven't lived a perfect life," Charley said.

"But the worst thing was letting my parents down. They'd already both passed away, but I used to think about them all the time when I was inside."

When he was eighteen, Charley had robbed a bank and been jailed for twelve years. After he was released, Francine offered him a job at the shop with accommodation, and he'd been there ever since. Benedict was left wondering about the pieces of the story Charley had left out, like why did he become a crook in the first place?

***

At the same time as they were leaving the shop, a woman hurried past. She had a scarf wrapped around her head that covered half her face as well, concealing her identity. Yet there was something about the way she walked that seemed familiar to Benedict. He was sure it was Lilac Browne, who at that moment had just scooted around the corner. By the time Benedict and Gail got there, she'd gone.

"I'm certain that was Lilac Browne, the Roydons' neighbour," Benedict said.

Although Lilac was aware that Cindy was back in Seagrove, Astrid hadn't told her where she was staying, or why she was there in the first place. In fact, Astrid was evasive about the whole thing. This made Lilac suspicious, especially as Astrid had told her to store Aldo's brown raincoat in her house on the evening of the day of the murder, without anyone else knowing, of course. That was why Astrid had been plying Aldo with wine that day, so he wouldn't notice his coat was missing when he got home.

Lilac's suspicions had been roused ever since the plan she and Astrid had made, and talked about for so long, had been unceremoniously abandoned soon after Cindy's arrival. Lilac's suspicions had been roused even more, when Francine was murdered by someone. Who was her killer?

She remembered the exact details of how she'd gone round to Astrid's flat on the evening of the day it happened, where she'd found Aldo, drinking wine with Astrid. Ah, motherly Astrid. She'd always been there for Aldo, and without her, his marriage to the wayward Francine wouldn't have lasted five minutes, such was her desire for both male and female lovers.

Lilac's excuse for leaving the flat – was to say she was going to the Four Square to get bags of potato chips. She'd had to hurry, and remembered how scared she'd been, especially when she'd used the key, they'd sneakily had cut months before, in readiness for this moment. She'd gone in and out of Aldo's beach-house quickly, then to her own place in Korimako Street where she had hidden the raincoat. After that, she'd bought three bags of chips and headed back, hoping none of Aldo's neighbours had seen her entering or leaving his beach-house.

This had all been part of her and Astrid's plan to frame Aldo. They'd wanted the day to be rainy so they'd be sure Aldo wore his raincoat – the one Astrid had a version of, although not an exact copy. Astrid had become agitated when Lilac had pointed out the discrepancy, but had said it didn't matter because the police wouldn't know it wasn't an exact replica. Since then, however, things had changed. Lilac could only surmise Astrid and Cindy had carried out the plan, instead; Cindy, who'd turned up unexpectedly and cleverly usurped Lilac's place.

Lilac wondered, not for the first time, if Astrid had teamed up with Cindy because of the blood pact she'd seen the three of them make through the hedge that day. However, Lilac tried not to think about it because it only made her even more confused. Surely Aldo, who was part of the blood pact, couldn't have anything to do with the killing of his own wife, even if they were separated?

And now all she wanted to do was find out where Cindy, who in Lilac's eyes was now an enemy, was living. One way to do this, was to follow the private investigator, Benedict Aberthorp. Surely, he'd have found out by now and might even be going to visit Cindy? That was the reason why Lilac, in her small red Mazda, had followed Benedict. She'd seen the investigator drive to a house near the beach, pick up a woman and go on to Roydons' Antiques.

There was no car park near the shop, so Lilac had had to drive around before finally finding one in a side-street, two blocks away. When she was near the shop, she browsed in an adjacent women's lingerie boutique, keeping watch for any sign of the private investigator and his female friend's departure.

Lilac had been browsing for so long that she was just about to buy something when she saw the two of them emerge. Lilac hurried away, so she could get to her car and follow them in case they were heading to Cindy's place. There was a slight snag in Lilac's plans: she was certain the ever-observant Benedict had seen her. This wasn't supposed to happen, but Lilac didn't let this faze her. Her mind was made up and she managed, through sheer luck, to catch up with Benedict and follow his dark blue BMW. Keeping her distance, Lilac became dispirited when the private investigator and his friend drove back to forty-three Plover Street. Both exited the car and entered Benedict's house.

"My surveillance was a waste of time," Lilac said aloud, thumping her hand on the steering wheel before doing a U-turn and heading home. She'd have to try to get the information out of Astrid somehow.

Dominica had told her she *must* locate Cindy Herskington and find out what she'd been up to. "They're going to pin the blame on you, Lilac. I'm telling you now, these women are more cunning than the devil himself."

Was Dominica, right? Lilac suspected so, because she was the scapegoat who'd stolen Aldo's raincoat and hidden it in her own home. This incriminating evidence made Lilac desperate enough to do something about it.

Lilac grabbed the raincoat from its hiding place in her house, and went back out to her car. The raincoat was now tucked under a cushion on the passenger seat beside her, and she'd made the decision to get rid of it. Just how to do so, wasn't yet clear in her mind. Firstly, she had to find out if Astrid had betrayed her. This was vital. The raincoat could still be used, but not in the way she and Astrid had initially planned.

Like a trump card, Lilac planned to use the raincoat to her advantage, especially if what Dominica had told her was true. Were Astrid and Cindy really setting her up for a crime she didn't commit? If the police found Aldo's raincoat in her house; it would look as if she'd taken it to try to frame Aldo for the murder. This of course was true, but Lilac *hadn't* been involved in the murder. She'd unwittingly helped the real killer, whoever that may be. The position she now found herself in, scared her, and also brought out a cunningness in her she didn't know she had. Now she was like a bloodhound, hot on the heels of Cindy Herskington, the woman who'd turned up, from Scotland. She didn't know the reason for her re-appearance and, worst of all, she'd buddied up with Astrid while Lilac herself had been left out of the loop.

***

"It was Lilac Browne, I'm sure of it," Benedict said again, his eyes searching the street where he'd seen her walk away. "It was like she was trying to hide."

"I wonder why?" Gail said. "Something she wants kept hidden?"

"Possibly, and if so, I'd like to find out what that something is. Anyway, let's go home and have some lunch. I'll make us both a sandwich and then we can go back to the office. Oh, and can you check out Charley's alibi – that he was actually at the Bayside Lodge that day?"

"Sure."

When they arrived, Benedict told Gail what Tegan

had said about Astrid being laid off from her housekeeping position at the end of May, and of her close relationship with Aldo. He also filled her in on all other aspects of the case, and left her his notebook so she could peruse the notes he had taken so far. If she was going to help him solve the case, Gail needed to know as much as he did.

"How did you get on with the lead at the dentist?" Benedict said, while they tucked into their lunch.

"All was as Aldo told you," Gail said. "I was discreet about it and the nurse was definite about Aldo's visit, and his punctuality."

"Good work, my friend. So, who was the man Lilac was supposed to have seen at two-thirty, leaving the Roydons' property?"

"Oh, one more thing: the dentist's receptionist also said Aldo left at two-fifteen. It was only a check-up apparently."

"I see, so where does this take us?"

Gail looked as if she was thinking hard. "How do we know the murder happened *after* Aldo and Astrid had left?"

"You're right, we don't. The definitive time of death was somewhere within a four hours' time-frame. The coroner couldn't be more precise."

"Does this mean we're back where we started?"

"I guess so. And would Aldo have had time to get back to the house by two-thirty, which is when Lilac said she saw him?" He picked up his coffee mug.

"He'd have had to get there *before* then, murder Francine and *leave* by two-thirty," Gail said. "A difficult feat for anyone to achieve, don't you think?"

"Yes, so why don't we have another chat to Lilac? I need to ask her again about the man she claims to have seen that day. Perhaps she might recall some detail she forgot to tell us about."

"But before then, why don't I check out Charley's alibi? It seems it was quite convenient for him to be away when his boss was killed, don't you think?"

Benedict smiled. "You sensed he wasn't telling the truth?"

"Just a little. Anyway, I've taken a liking to this business of checking up on people."

"Say no more. I'll leave it in your capable hands."

Chapter 6

Saturday 1st June

Lilac drove her car back to Plover Street the next morning, hoping to catch sight of Benedict Aberthorp again, whom no doubt would be going to his office in his flashy BMW to sort through his clues (at least, that's how Lilac imagined private investigators worked). She was drawn to a stand of cypress trees on the bend in the street. She straightened the steering wheel after turning, so she could park behind them and still keep watch on the street, as well as observe any through-traffic. Soon there was movement in her peripheral vision. Looking in the rear-view mirror, she witnessed a woman getting into a small, blue car a few houses down from Aberthorp's house.

It had to be Cindy. She remembered how she'd looked that day when she'd stared, bug-eyed, through the hedge into the Roydons' back-yard, and seen her with Astrid and Aldo; this tall girl with a strong-looking figure and long, wavy brown hair.

Waiting in her car behind the stand of trees, she watched in silence to see where Cindy was going. Suddenly the blue car whizzed past and Lilac, trying to remain incognito, followed at what she hoped was a safe enough distance to avoid suspicion. There was no other traffic until they were close to the town centre. "Damn," Lilac said, her hands gripping the wheel so tightly that her knuckles were white. "Where the hell did, she go?"

A glimpse of blue to the left, gave her the answer, and she swung, dangerously fast, into the Seagrove bus station's car-park, where Cindy was parking her small car. Lilac parked, just in the row behind, so she could watch what the mysterious Cindy was up to.

***

After Benedict backed out onto the street and steered his car in the direction of his office, he glimpsed a red car disappearing around the curve in Plover Street. It looked like Lilac Browne again. What was she up to? Benedict sighed and decided to discreetly follow her. He had no idea why Lilac seemed to be sneaking around so furtively but he wanted to find out. He was almost certain that he and Gail had seen the same car the day before, when they'd returned home for lunch after visiting

Charley at the antiques shop. If it was her, she seemed to be following the blue Fiat Bambina. most likely the same one Benedict had seen at number seventy-one the other day.

He took a left turn into Darius Avenue and noticed the same blue car had stopped at the traffic lights. Thankfully there was a flatbed truck and a motorbike between them, so most likely the driver didn't know she was being followed. The lights changed and soon the driver turned into the bus station's car-park. He pulled over onto the side of the road, left his car on the street and walked towards the wooden slatted fence that surrounded the car-park. Soon he'd found a suitable gap to peer through and there was Lilac's red Mazda. She was just getting out of it.

Benedict's instinct had been right. He stood, mesmerised as he observed Lilac watching the female driver of the blue car, who was now striding towards the platform where a bus was waiting. A small huddle of people stood there; eyes trained on the number seven bus whose destination sign read: Dotterel Bay Women's Prison. Benedict watched Lilac as she hid behind a van, peering intently as the woman of the blue car boarded the bus. Who was she? And why was Lilac so interested in her?

***

In order to clear his mind and think about his next move, Benedict headed for the seafront; indulging in a long walk before going to the office. The water was so blue today, and although the sky was only a little cloudy, a wind was picking up and the forecasted rain seemed to be threatening its arrival. The tide was high and the waves crashed onto the pebbly beach before being sucked out to sea again; the way they always did there because of the strong undertow. Although it was too dangerous for swimming, Benedict loved its abandoned wildness.

As he trudged along, the sea pounding to his left, Benedict pondered how much of the information he and Gail had gathered so far, actually didn't seem to make any sense. He suspected they were missing something. All the people he'd interviewed so far had said things that puzzled him in some way or another. Okay, Francine had been murdered; of that there was no doubt. Yet everything else he had so far learnt about the case was questionable. For example, Lilac claimed her partner, Dominica, had left her for a man, but had she really? Then there was Astrid who said her husband, Elroy, had been killed in March, 2005. Benedict had asked Gail to investigate the latter further. With any luck they'd be able to verify the truth of Astrid's statement and move on to Dominica's backstory. Had she really suddenly departed to Australia with a new lover?

***

Gail was already at the office when Benedict arrived, jotting down questions she wanted to find the answers to. Benedict had asked her to investigate exactly what had happened to Lilac's female friend? *What was her name again?* she thought, as she flicked through the notebook. *Oh yes, Dominica Frimble.* She tried to picture what Dominica might look like now, but soon gave up. It was a pointless exercise, because in the past, her imaginings had been completely wrong. When she'd finally met the person or seen a photograph of them, they had borne no resemblance to the image she had pictured in her mind.

Benedict had also asked her to search for Elroy's death certificate through the Department of Internal Affairs. Gail was sufficiently computer-savvy to know how to browse for the facts she sought. However, so far, she had failed to find any record of his death. Similarly, she had been unable to locate any evidence suggesting a potential rape victim had been saved by a man who was subsequently stabbed to death.

With no leads to follow on Elroy, Gail turned her attention to Charley's version of events. Was his alibi as watertight as he'd said? She would book a night or two at the Bayside Lodge, Moana to find out. She picked up the phone and dialled the establishment.

"Bayside Lodge. How can I help?" a female voice said.

"Hello there. A friend of mine, Charley Raymond, stayed at the lodge recently and had so many good things to say that I decided to come for a weekend."

"Oh, really? When was your friend here?"

"He arrived on the ninth of May, and stayed for several nights. He told me he had thoroughly enjoyed himself." Gail listened to the rustling of paper, and envisioned the woman rifling through her guest-attendance register.

"We don't usually give out private information about our guests, but... oh yes, I remember now: he was booked to arrive on the ninth but didn't get here until early evening, the following day – tenth – a Friday, it was. And he had a woman with him. Said it was his sister. So, when would you like to come, Mrs...?"

"Oh, sorry, I'll have to phone you back, a customer has just walked into the shop. I'll get right back to you after they've gone."

"Certainly, madam, look forwarding to hearing back from you."

***

Cindy pulled her wine-coloured gabardine trench-coat close around her, and turned up the collar, as she stood shivering at the Seagrove bus station. The weather was changing and the forecast of rain and wind looked likely to transpire. That didn't matter, however, she'd go anyway, if only to see the glimmer of hope on her daughter's face when she walked into the visitors' area.

An agonising sense of guilt dug its claws into Cindy's heart every time she visited Jenniver, irrationally feeling her daughter's situation was somehow her fault. Yet why was she blaming herself for her daughter's descent into meth-taking, followed by a five-years' sentence for selling the drug to feed her own habit?

The number seven bus was at the station with its doors closed; the driver waiting for the exact time to allow the small crowd to board. The journey to the prison was an hour's drive away, and the wait to get on the bus, gave Cindy time to think. She pulled a book from her bag and opened it, to start reading; a way of blotting out the reality she could only just bear – the fact that her darling daughter – her only child – was locked up for five, long years. She wanted to cry, but stopped herself from doing so, as the bus door finally opened and the throng of prison visitors began to jostle each other as they boarded.

As always, Cindy assumed a cheerful expression, so that onlookers would see a happy-go-lucky woman who never let anything get her down. This was the persona she'd determined to show to the world, because if she didn't, the old demons would appear once more and take up residence inside her heart. There was no way she wanted such an experience ever again; it was too terrifying. She had to keep those demons at bay, at all cost. That resolve was all she had left now to keep the thread of sanity strong within her; the thread she could barely hold on to, especially now, after what had happened to her Jenniver. And of course, him… no, she wouldn't think about it. She blotted him out of her mind. It was just her now, and Gregor, who loved Jenniver too. In fact, meeting Gregor Carollan in Scotland was one of the best things she'd experienced since arriving in the strange, cold country. She had to keep remembering that, no matter what.

***

On that Saturday morning, Lilac Browne wasn't the

only person taking an interest in Cindy's movements. Astrid Lorning, was on the number twelve bus on route to the supermarket. She was idly looking out the window at the same scenery she observed every trip, when, as the bus turned into the station, to pick up more passengers, something caught her eye. There was Cindy, boarding the bus to the prison. The bus driver manoeuvred the number twelve into a space just a few metres behind the number seven. Astrid realised this was her best chance of trying to make contact with Cindy who, after being so friendly when she had first arrived from Scotland in April, was now aloof and secretive. This change was annoying Astrid considerably.

She rushed to the front exit door of the bus, dragging her shopping trundler behind her. Her sudden frantic decision to speak to Cindy, and reassure herself that all was well, did not please the driver, who liked departing passengers to exit via the rear door; notably because of others wanting to board. In this case the passenger in question was a large woman, who at that moment was struggling up the steps and also dragging a shopping trundler. Her bulk meant she took up most of the room, but Astrid was determined to exit from the front of the bus regardless of whoever stood in her way.

"Move aside," the corpulent woman snarled. "Go to the back if you want to get off."

"Please step back and let the oncoming passengers board," the bus-driver said, joining in the confrontation, his gruff voice loud and authoritative.

"Shut-up!" Astrid, her hair pulled back into its usual neat bun and her face contorted with rage, continued to shoulder her way past the indignant shopper. Why couldn't people just step aside rather than trying to bar her way? She tasted the old bitterness welling up and briefly hated those terrible moments when she'd been trapped in her marriage to Elroy. He was always putting up barriers too, in his possessive, controlling way.

"Driver, driver," the woman said, her voice a plaintive whine.

By now Astrid had managed to push past the woman and was rushing towards the prison bus, but it was already pulling away. She was too late. Astrid could see Cindy seated next to a window near the front of the bus so she waved and called out to try to get her attention. However, Cindy was looking the other way and appeared completely oblivious to Astrid's frenzied actions.

Cindy had told Astrid what had happened to Jenniver after Francine had denied the family connection. Apparently, the teenager had turned to drugs and started partying with a group of teens she met up with. She was planning to travel around New Zealand, but it never happened – not with the potency of meth in her system. After one mind-blowing dose, she was hooked and then cravings began. Cindy had told her how Jenniver only found peace when she was taking meth but the drug was expensive, so she had started selling it. From that moment there was no turning back.

***

From a distance, Lilac watched Astrid pushing her way down the bus steps and upsetting a huge woman who was trying to board. There was a loud exchange of voices and she trembled at the sight of Astrid's strong stocky frame as she vented her fury at the woman for not getting out of her way. Then, to Lilac's surprise, Astrid ran towards the prison bus and called and waved to someone inside. Lilac could only suppose Astrid was trying to get Cindy's attention, but it was no use. Whether deliberately or not, Cindy was looking in the opposite direction as the bus pulled out slowly and headed in the direction of Dotterel Bay Women's Prison.

As she watched, Astrid looked defeated. With her head bowed, she turned and walked slowly to one of the seats in the bus shelter, dragging her shopping trolley behind her. Lilac now felt an unusual twinge of pity for her and decided to offer her a lift. She walked over to where Astrid was sitting sobbing quietly while searching her pockets for a handkerchief.

"Are you all right, love?" Lilac said, sitting down on the seat next to her.

"Oh, it's you. No, I'm not as a matter of fact. I wanted to speak to Cindy, but she turned away and didn't even acknowledge me. Smarmy bitch."

"Why is she going to the prison? I don't understand why Cindy is here. What on earth did she come back for?"

"You think I know everything, don't you? Well, I don't, so it's no use asking me. You need to get on with your life, Lilac, and stop worrying about what other people are doing."

"I do want to get on with my life, but I have to know the truth, Astrid. You and I made a plan, remember? We spent months talking about it and making sure it would work. I trusted you – until a ghost from the past appeared out of nowhere, and suddenly everything changed. Once bloody Cindy arrived you forgot all about me. It wasn't fair. You betrayed my trust." Lilac turned away, pulling out a handkerchief from her pocket as her tears fell.

"It wasn't my idea, you silly thing. If you must know,

cunning Cindy needed me as I was the housekeeper, and did some snivelling and grovelling. Anyway, she was doing you a favour, believe me. You don't even want to know what happened after Cindy came back. And don't try to make me tell you. But I will tell you one thing – seeing as you're determined to know everything: her daughter, Jenniver, is in the slammer for five years. For selling drugs. A damn shame. Still, her half-sister got what was coming to her."

Lilac's eyes bulged. "Her half-sister? What do you mean, Astrid?"

"So, you don't even know that much?" The look of disdain on Astrid's face was apparent. "What planet have you been living on all these years? Francine, of course, who else? Andy Roydon, Francine's father, managed to get sixteen-year-old Cindy, pregnant all those years ago, and it's caused a lot of trouble ever since. The result was Jenniver."

Lilac sucked in her breath. She could hardly comprehend what Astrid was saying. At first it made no sense to her at all, but then she remembered how Cindy had hung around Andy Roydon all the time – after Francine had stolen Aldo away from her. And Andy had loved the attention. Yet that was so long ago. What did all this have to do with now? When she looked at Astrid, she shuddered inwardly. Astrid had that sinister sneer on her face again. Lilac hated that smile because she didn't understand what it meant. It made her nervous. *What exactly is Astrid keeping from me?* "I understand now, Astrid," she said carefully. "I know Cindy liked Andy a lot and it probably went too far and he was a grown man and she was just a child. But it's all in the past now, isn't it? Anyway, would you like a lift to the supermarket? I'm going there myself."

"Yes, I would like a lift, thank you. And no, it's not all over now. You don't know the half of it, and it's probably just as well you don't. Now come on, before all the specials have gone."

Chapter 7

Sunday 2nd June

Cindy hadn't been idle since re-acquainting herself with her former boyfriend, Aldo, and chatting to the now considerably older housekeeper, Astrid Lorning. Cindy wanted to renew her bond with them both, so that she'd know everything she needed to know in order to set about carrying out her plans; plans driven by a sense of righteousness and justice, and the need she had to make a difference. That was her primary aim because when she'd travelled to Scotland all those years ago when she was pregnant at only sixteen, she'd known she was expendable. She'd left without a fuss, like a meek and mild lamb led to the slaughter, while those left behind carried on as if she had never existed. For Cindy, that had been the hardest pill to swallow; that of being so insignificant that she was almost invisible, on the day she'd boarded the plane with her father and his pretty Scottish girlfriend. Her father had insisted it was for the best that

Cindy went with them.

Now, twenty years later, she had come back. On the long flight over, she'd had plenty of time to consider her plans and now she was all set to execute them, minus the cheerful, kind and understanding persona she had deliberately presented to everyone on her return. It was easy to cast it off, like throwing away an itchy, heavy coat that only caused discomfort.

Rising at five a.m. and having a quick breakfast, she set out, a few minutes after six a.m. in her blue car, heading for Oceanside Drive. She parked at the bottom of the road, where there was a small bushy area. She left the car, and slowly made her way up to number twenty-two on foot to wait for Aldo to leave for his morning walk along the beach. For her plan to work she had had to find out the routines of those who needed to be taught the errors of their ways. After careful surveillance, she was becoming familiar with Aldo's routine and hoped it remained the same today.

Luckily, Mrs Shields, the nosey-neighbour next door to where Cindy was staying, hadn't yet appeared in the garden with a trowel in hand as she usually did, smiling and waving annoyingly every time Cindy stepped outside. At least in Scotland, there were no such people, making note of her every move. Out in the highlands there were only the sheep and heather to gaze upon.

Cindy wanted it all to be over so she could get back to the cold, yet safe, sanctuary of Scotland, where the past wasn't able to permeate every fibre of her being, the way it did here, in this tiny place. She felt claustrophobic with people everywhere, watching her, smiling, wanting to talk and befriend her. It was stifling, and she'd had to pretend far more than she'd planned to. Compassion, good cheer and benevolence were her chosen persona, besides a devil-may-care nonchalance about anything bad that might have befallen her sweet and innocent daughter.

So far it had worked a charm and she'd been able to shrug off all the darts of concern and worry people insisted on firing at her, like a hundred small plasters stuck all over her: "How do you cope?" and "You're so wonderful," wearing thin after the first week. Indeed, they became a sickening irritation.

She stood behind a large pine tree, waiting for Aldo to emerge, as he did each morning, and make his way down the track to the beach. Cindy could smell the pines, and the birds were so loud she almost forgot why she was there. Then she saw him, dressed in his usual blue wind-breaker, yellow beanie hat and trackpants, heading straight for the cliff-side path.

***

At her home at eleven Korimako Street, it was eight a.m. when Lilac leapt out of bed, her purpose for the day already set in her mind. It was her duty to watch Cindy's house, now that she'd found out where she lived. The stand of cypress trees in Plover Street, just on the bend was such a good place to park. It meant her car was hidden from the house where Cindy was staying. And in order for Cindy to get into town, or go just about anywhere, the quickest exit out of Plover Street was past the point where Lilac sat waiting – ready to start her reliable little car and casually, follow at a safe distance. Astrid had generously told her that Cindy's surname was now Carollan, but she wouldn't tell Lilac anything else of note; nothing to break the bond Astrid apparently now had with this woman who was at least thirty years her junior. Lilac thought it all so mysterious and puzzling.

So, what was it about Cindy that gave her so much control and power over Astrid, a woman who wielded a significant amount of power herself? In fact, over the past month, Astrid's authority had begun making Lilac tremble, slopping her porridge as she lifted the spoon to her mouth each morning. Poor little Scamper had had his fair share of porridge lately, as he sat patiently at her feet gazing up as she spooned the hot rolled oats into her mouth with a shaky hand. Lilac pitied Scamper, both his owners having left him, for one reason or another; the death of Francine being one, of course, and Aldo, now living in the beach-house, had cajoled Lilac into taking over Scamper's care. Lilac didn't mind. She loved the fluffy grey cat and found solace in his company and loyalty. Not once had Scamper turned his back on her, like everyone else had.

Now Lilac was in the business of watching Cindy's house, and, when possible, following her wherever she went. She hoped Cindy didn't know the colour of her car, or, worse still, remember what she looked like. Lilac presumed Cindy hadn't seen her since arriving from Scotland, whenever that was. Astrid wouldn't tell her a thing, so now Lilac was going to find out for herself. That was the only way.

***

At eight a.m. Benedict was woken by the insistent tune of *Smooth Wave*, jarring him out of a particularly puzzling dream. Bleary-eyed, he groped for his phone. It was Aldo.

His words came out in an incoherent jumble.

"What is it? What's wrong?" Benedict said.

"Someone's been here, into the beach-house. I know, because the back-door was open and the radio was on. I took an early morning walk on the beach and I never lock the door. I just close it. It's usually very safe here. But when I came back, the door was open and I could hear music and found my radio was on and turned up loudly. And I never turn it on until I get back." His voice was strained and the words came out fast.

"Please, try to calm down. Stay inside and just wait. I'm on my way."

Benedict dressed quickly and raced out, starting his car engine, which gave a roar. Twenty-two Oceanside Drive wasn't far from the small shopping centre he often went to. To get there he had to drive up a steep hill, and soon pulled into the driveway next to Aldo's beach-house. The weatherboard L-shaped exterior was coloured cream and pink, with a view from the clifftop overlooking Seagrove Bay. Benedict parked around the back, where Aldo was waiting to let him in, and hurriedly pushed the back-door shut as soon as they were both inside.

"Thank God you're here," he said, his face pale and his thin, wiry body shaking. He hesitatingly led Benedict into the kitchen and they sat at the table facing each other.

"Has anything like this happened before?" Benedict said.

"No, but it's scary. I don't like being here on my own

now."

Benedict tried to think and had the idea that only Aldo himself could possibly understand who might have a grudge and be trying to frighten him. They must've been watching him, to see he'd gone out for an early walk along the beach. But why had they done it, and were there going to be any more surprises in store for Aldo? Benedict wanted to tell him he had nothing to worry about, but he couldn't guarantee that.

"What's going on? Any ideas?" Benedict watched Aldo get up and take two glasses from a side cupboard. He placed them on the table along with a half full bottle of whisky.

Aldo shook his head and poured out a measure. Benedict looked around the room. His attention was drawn to the servery on which stood a photo of Aldo and Francine on their wedding day, both looking radiantly happy. Their marriage hadn't produced any children. Lilac had told Benedict about the stillbirth Francine had had a few months after she'd married Aldo.

Aldo added ice-cubes from a bowl into one of the glasses and pushed it towards Benedict. He never drank this early in the day, although it seemed to suit the situation. Was Aldo going to join him? He didn't think so, as Aldo had already told him he never touched alcohol, despite what Lilac had said. This was confirmed when

Aldo filled his glass with water and ice-cubes.

"For visitors," Aldo said, placing the cap back on the bottle.

Benedict nodded, savouring his first mouthful, not admitting to Aldo that he never usually drank whisky. He took a long swallow, and as it surged through him, a welcoming calmness seemed to follow. Benedict wanted to tell Aldo to go ahead and drink, knowing he was the one who needed calming.

"Let's think about anyone you know who might have done this." Benedict placed his glass down on the table.

Aldo sighed. "There's something I've always regretted. You see I married Francine just two months after we found out that Cindy was pregnant by Andy Roydon, Francine's father. Cindy was my girlfriend before that. Everyone hoped I'd marry her – but I was in love with Francine by then. When Cindy went away to Scotland, Andy Roydon was relieved, of course. His affair with the young Cindy, just turned sixteen, was supposed to be a secret, but it wasn't."

"And did Andy not try to help her?"

Aldo looked away. "I don't really know, but I was ashamed at the time, because while Francine and I had been having a secret affair, she had also become pregnant. Cindy accused me of betraying our relationship. It was true, Francine and I had both betrayed her because our affair had started before I had broken up with Cindy. But at seven months, Francine delivered a stillborn baby. She was told earlier that its heart had stopped beating, but she couldn't bear to tell me. It was the worst day ever." His facial expression communicated its own story. "Francine changed afterwards. I don't think either of us ever got over it."

"I can relate to your grief," Benedict said. "Because my wife, Bryony died ten years ago, when her heart stopped beating too. She had a heart attack in our garden and that's where I found her. We'd only been married eleven years."

"I'm sorry," Aldo said. "How did you cope?"

"Not very well, I'm afraid. I went to pieces and couldn't even leave the house, which had become my safe haven. Sometimes, even now, I find myself dreading having to go out."

"I believe I know what you mean." Aldo said. "Grief can take away our self-confidence and make us into shadows of our former selves."

"Come on." Benedict got up from the table. "Let's go outside, and see if there's any clues to tell us who's been here."

On one side of the house were several Manuka bushes that made excellent cover for whoever had entered the house, while the section on the other side was empty, apart from some flax bushes bordering Aldo's driveway.

"You'd better stay with a friend until we sort this out. What about Lilac?"

Aldo grimaced. "I think Lilac's had enough drama for a while. Anyway, she's hardly spoken to me lately. I could stay with Astrid, though."

"All right. How about 'phoning her, and I'll go with you to her place."

His facial expression became softer. "Thank you so much. I'll phone her and then pack a few things."

While he was gone, Benedict had an impulse to half-fill his glass again and tossed it back before Aldo re-appeared.

"I'm going to phone Lilac too and let her know where I am, in case someone is looking for me," Aldo said.

After he'd made the call, they secured the beach-house and Benedict followed Aldo in his car as he drove to Astrid's flat.

***

As he drove, Aldo was shaking. Talking about Francine's stillbirth transported him to the trauma all over again, and the old emotions flooded back. Being told afterwards there was no heartbeat had induced feelings of guilt and failure. Afterwards, a black cloud hung constantly over him, accompanied by panic attacks. He had started drinking in an effort to make it all go away. Despite his promises to stop, he was sent away, to a psychiatric hospital for two months. Francine was his only visitor and she only came once. His relationship with her died with the baby, and life as he'd known it changed forever.

And now someone was trying to scare and frame him. But who? Could it be Cindy? He told himself not to be silly, but the truth was that since Cindy's arrival from Scotland, Aldo's guilt and shame had returned. Cindy was constantly cheerful and friendly, which only seemed to exacerbate Aldo's sense of failure – as if Cindy brought with her the power to re-open the wounds in Aldo's heart.

He wrestled with his memories of Cindy. Had she done this to make him suffer? Was she at last getting revenge for his betrayal all those years ago, when he'd married Francine so soon after Cindy's departure for Scotland? He was originally supposed to marry Cindy, but he hadn't because they'd had a break-up, and only Aldo knew about the part he'd played in that. Perhaps it wasn't just *his* secret any longer, and possibly never had been. His mind continued to spiral downward, further and further to where he imagined himself as a crouching figure, clawing at the walls in despair.

Astrid welcomed them into her flat and was soon busying herself making instant coffee for the three of them, while Aldo and Benedict sat in the lounge. Benedict was about to ask Aldo how he was, when Aldo's phone beeped. He looked down at it and his face paled.

"What's wrong?" Benedict asked, looking directly at Aldo in an effort to read his worry lines.

"A text. It says: 'You know what you did and you're going to pay.' I don't know what it means. Pay for what?" He looked helplessly down at his hands, which were holding onto his phone tightly.

"Who is it from?"

"I don't know. What is it I'm supposed to have done?"

Benedict's opinion was that Francine's murder was most likely an act of revenge, but he wasn't going to presume it had anything to do with Cindy. He had to keep an open mind. The text message made it sound as though Aldo was implicated in whatever it was Francine had done, but if so, why hadn't Aldo been killed too? Either way, it looked like Aldo was now going to be made to suffer. The text message was something only Aldo could work out. Did he already know what he'd done, but was too frightened or ashamed to say?

"Can you think of anything you might have done to

cause this?" Benedict said.

"No. Francine yes, but the incident happened last year."

"Tell me about it." Benedict's thoughts were forming now, wondering why Aldo had cleared himself of any blame so quickly. Perhaps to distract from something in his past he didn't want anyone to start prying into?

"As I said before, it's why I ended up finally leaving Francine – the eighteen-year-old, from Scotland, Jenniver, who turned up one day, to become acquainted with her half-sister. She was no doubt expecting a warm welcome."

"And why would that involve you?"

Aldo seemed to be weighing things up. "I'd known Cindy well. There was a group of us who used to go out together. We supported each other after leaving school. Most of us hadn't a clue what to do with our lives. Cindy and I were part of that group."

So, what was Cindy doing on the day of the murder? Benedict asked himself. She was the only suspect left on his list who hadn't accounted for her movements that day.

"Has there been anything else?" he said, looking with a kindly expression at Aldo, who now looked even more haggard than before.

"There was an incident a couple of months ago, but

it wasn't much. It involved our neighbour, Lilac Browne."

Benedict leaned forward. "Go on."

"It must have been the second Friday in February. I arrived for my meeting with Francine, a little earlier than usual, and while walking up the path I heard someone yelling. It was Lilac, standing at our back-door. She said, 'You've done something bad to my car. It won't start straight away like it used to. And the petrol tank's nearly empty. Where did you go in it, Francine? Out to see your floozy was it, while I was under the impression you were fixing it?'

"I'm sure Lilac was drunk and when she saw me, she tried to hide it by being extra friendly. 'Oh, Aldo, it's you. How nice to see you. Francine fixed my car for me. Wasn't it nice of her?' Then she left, returning back to her own place. Francine called out, 'Okay, I'll come over tomorrow and give you some petrol money.'

"It was strange because I'd never seen Lilac drunk before. She liked her wine, but to my knowledge she never drank to excess. And I didn't know Francine was in the habit of fixing her car. While we were having lunch, Francine told me how Lilac liked to knock it back, especially since Dominica had been in touch and told her she wanted the house sold so she could have her share of the money. When I questioned this, Francine gave me a strange look and said, 'Yes, that's what she wants'…"

Benedict put down his cup. "Mmm, I see. Was Astrid there at the time?"

"No, she was away in Germany visiting her mother."

"Yes, I remember you telling me about the incident," Astrid said, appearing beside them. She placed a tray down on the coffee table with a *clunk*. It held three mugs of coffee, together with sugar in a bowl and a jug of milk.

"Did Lilac ever mention it again?" Benedict said.

"No, but next time I came over, there was a 'for sale' sign on her fence. She'd put her house on the market."

Benedict pulled out his notebook. "And how long was it on the market for?"

"Until the day of the murder."

Benedict looked up and glanced at the others. Both held their coffee mugs to their lips, their faces inscrutable. So, Lilac had taken her house off the market on the day of Francine's murder, but why?

***

After Lilac pulled into her lookout point on the bend in Plover Street at eight-thirty, she was twiddling with the radio, trying to tune into the talkback station, when the

93

blue car appeared. She cursed silently. *Damn, it's Cindy, returning home, but where from?* Lilac instinctively blamed herself because she'd missed something important. Cindy never went out this early in the morning.

"The state of the economy is plummeting today," the talkback announcer said. "Does anyone have any solutions to this problem? There are five free lines."

Chapter 8

Monday 3rd June

"Good news," Gail said with a smile, when Benedict entered the office the next day. "It's about Astrid Lorning's story about what happened to her husband."

"Go on."

"No such record of him dying after being stabbed while rescuing a woman from being attacked. Nothing at all."

"Really?"

"Absolutely not. I didn't want to say anything until I was sure, but I'm afraid there's no truth whatsoever in what she told you."

"What was the exact wording, again?"

Gail flipped through Benedict's notebook and read it aloud:

"'It happened in March 2005 when Elroy tried to save a woman who was being attacked by two men. Unfortunately, the attackers turned on him and stabbed him several times'."

Benedict sat down, realising his hunch had been right. Astrid's story had been recited like a line of carefully rehearsed script. "I need to have another talk to her. Thank you, my friend. I suspect we've been fed a multitude of lies and have been running around in circles."

"So what are you going to say to her?"

"I'll say I'm going over everyone's statements to seek clarification."

"Okay. I suppose our next move is to find out where the mysterious Dominica now lives, and who with?"

"Oh yes. I don't like to see you sitting idle during your vacation! I won't even ask you how you're going to find out. I know you'll nail it somehow."

Gail rolled her eyes. "Your trust in me is overwhelming. But I have some more interesting news, this time concerning Charley."

"You're a genius."

"No, not really. All I did was say the right thing."

"Tell me more."

"I rang the Bayside Lodge, in Moana. I told them a friend of mine, Charley Raymond, had stayed there recently and had so many good things to say that I decided to come for a weekend. The receptionist was impressed and asked when my friend had been there. I said May nine and he'd stayed for several days and thoroughly enjoyed himself."

Benedict sat down and opened his laptop. "Do go on."

"Then after a few moments, she said, 'Oh yes, I remember now, he was booked to arrive on the ninth but didn't get here until the following evening – tenth – Friday, it was. And he had a woman with him. Said it was his sister'. I made an excuse then and said I'd phone back."

"Oh my God," Benedict said, a chill going through him. "So where was Charley? That's just blown his alibi to smithereens. The same goes for Cindy. I'd bet my life on it that she was the woman who arrived at the lodge with him."

"I agree, but how come?"

Benedict was speechless for a few moments. "I wonder if I'll find Astrid at home today. Her phone doesn't seem to be working."

When he looked through the office window to the street outside, the rain was sheeting down.

**

Lilac sat in her kitchen watching Scamper who was curled up asleep on the mat. She was sure now of what she had to do: take Aldo's raincoat and hide it in Astrid's flat. The old cow had already told her she'd be out all day. She'd got herself a job, cleaning for a wealthy woman who lived two streets away, and it was such a large house that it took her hours to clean. Plus she had a huge pile of their ironing to do every week. Astrid had been smug about this new position, which she'd found by looking on the supermarket noticeboard. The extra money (paid under the table, Astrid had said with a sly grin) would supplement her unemployment benefit until she was old enough to get the old age pension. Lilac would soon be entitled to this, when she turned sixty-five on June five. "Lucky bugger," Astrid had called Lilac, her mouth turning down at the corners as she did so.

Dominica had ensured that Lilac still had some money if anything happened to her, and Lilac supplemented this by having three part-time jobs helping elderly women in their homes: a ninety-three year-old who needed help with showering, an eighty-one-year-old who needed someone to clean her house, and an eighty-year-old, with signs of early dementia, who she took grocery shopping once a week. This gave her enough to live on. Besides, she liked chatting to these lonely ladies who had very few visitors.

Luckily there was a steady drizzle of rain today, so

Lilac could wear both raincoats – hers on the outside and Aldo's underneath, so no one would notice. If something went wrong and she saw Astrid on the way there, she could just spin her a story that she was coming to see her and had forgotten it was her cleaning day.

She got out Aldo's raincoat and held it up, reading the label aloud and smiling to herself: 'Quelrayn Brinylon. Wash in warm soapy water. Rinse thoroughly in cold water and allow to drip-dry. If the coat needs pressing use only a warm iron. Do not dry-clean.'

Lilac wondered if Aldo might be fretting about his raincoat and wondering where it had gone. Perhaps he already suspected it had been stolen? Had he gone out and bought another one yet? After all, winter was slowly making itself felt, and he'd need it badly. She laughed softly as she put it on. It was long, and this was going to be a problem, because her own was shorter. *Never mind*, she thought. She'd wear a belt and tuck it up so it didn't hang down below the hem of her own raincoat. Lilac's coat was brown too, but a cheap plastic one, not tough and made-to-last like Aldo's. In fact, Lilac's coat was similar to the one Astrid had showed her one day, months ago, when the two of them were planning their nasty deed. Astrid had told Lilac how she'd bought the brown plastic raincoat in Bonn, Germany, when she and

Elroy were over there on one occasion. Astrid was visiting her mother and Elroy was there buying antiques for the shop, he having been Roydons' chief buyer at the time.

When she was ready, Lilac left the house and was soon sitting behind the wheel of her car, reversing out of the driveway. Once on the road, she looked in her rear-view mirror. Scamper was sitting on the wicker chair on the front porch. He liked the soft cushion she'd put on the chair especially for him.

"Bye, Scamper, love," she called as she drove away. He was always there, waiting for her return, and he'd jump down and greet her with his tail in the air when she got out of the car. She loved Scamper so much, and Dominica had approved of him too. Dominica told her she was really glad Scamper had come to live at her place.

"You won't be so lonely," she'd said, and Lilac could tell she was smiling as she said it because of the warmth in her voice; the husky voice she'd always loved.

"Oh, Dominica," she said. "Whatever am I going to do? Life is so hard without you."

***

Astrid lived in a block of flats at number twelve, Fernhill Crescent, a deprived area of Seagrove. Hers was flat three. Even though it was only a short distance away from the affluent residents of Korimako Street, the contrast between the residences was marked. Fernhill Crescent was considered an undesirable place to live and Astrid had often told Lilac about some of the goings on there. Armed police had visited one of the flats last year, and another had been raided by the drug squad who arrived with a sniffer dog. Afterwards two handcuffed men were brought out and roughly pushed into the back of a police car.

Lilac parked in the next street, by the Four-Square store, and walked through the alleyway into Fernhill, using her umbrella to hide her face. It was still drizzling steadily and she was pleased as it meant she wouldn't be so obvious to anyone who happened to be looking out of one of the flat windows. Of course, there was the neighbour opposite who knew who she was, from when she used to visit Astrid more often. Miss Wilson was nosey and didn't miss anything occurring in her line of vision. However, it didn't matter, because Astrid had told Miss Wilson if she ever saw Lilac arriving at her flat, not to worry because she was a good friend. Astrid had also told Miss Wilson that Lilac knew where the spare key was and it was all right if she turned up and let herself in. Such familiarity and trust were a thing of the past now though, when she and Astrid used to be on good terms.

Lilac chuckled to herself as she pulled the spare key from under the rosemary pot and inserted it into the door of flat number three. She deliberately kept her umbrella up to disguise herself until she had the key in her hand and had opened the door. A sudden dizziness overcame her, as she feared Astrid was at home after all. However, all was silent as she quietly let herself in and closed the door gently behind her, making sure not to leave any drips of water from her umbrella that might not dry before 'her ladyship' returned.

Once inside the flat, Lilac quickly took off both coats. She folded Aldo's neatly into a small square, trying to make it as tiny as possible, so she could hide it where Astrid wasn't going to find it any time soon; at least not unless she decided to do a thorough tidy-up and rummage around in the furthest corner of her wardrobe. Lilac was confident Astrid was unlikely to do this, as she'd always known her to be rather untidy at home, leaving things in place for months on end. Lilac told herself not to be so judgemental, remembering that Astrid had spent most of her days since 2005, cleaning and tidying other people's messy homes, so that by the time it came to doing her own, all her energy had been drained away. The number of wine bottles stacked untidily in Astrid's recycling bin, suggested she had been drowning her sorrows. If only Lilac could get Astrid to tell her what had happened on the day of the murder. She was certain Astrid was hiding something.

As for Cindy, well, Lilac had never trusted her; not even at sixteen when Cindy would be at the Roydons' residence, day and night, giggling on the front lawn with the rest of the teenage gang. Then of course there'd been Aldo, whom Lilac knew spent time with Francine, when Cindy wasn't there. She'd seen them kissing once, out near the olive trees, when they thought no one was watching. At the time, Lilac had been trimming her side of the hedge and witnessed things her neighbours were unaware of. She wasn't stupid; she knew what was going on. In fact, she and Astrid used to talk about everything that happened at the Roydons'. The friends were close then and, for want of anything better to talk about at the time, the pair discussed everything together in minute detail.

A sudden twinge of nostalgia for the way things had once been almost overwhelmed Lilac, until she told herself to concentrate on what she was doing.

Dominica had told her often enough not to dwell on things. She'd said, "Get on with your life and forget about the past. The past is over and done with, and nothing can be changed."

***

Gail wished Benedict good luck, watching as he pulled on his coat and left the office just after nine-thirty. Benedict drove his BMW straight to Fernhill Crescent, remembering the day he'd first gone here when Aldo had stayed with Astrid for a while. She was Aldo's 'motherly' friend, it seemed. Although the block of flats where Astrid lived and the surrounding streets were considered by some to be of lower socio-economic status, Benedict recalled that Astrid had at least tried to keep her place tidy. Thinking of exactly how he was going to tackle the subject of what had happened to Elroy in March, 2005, he parked the car and headed for flat number three. It was still raining, and he saw a woman wearing a brown plastic raincoat protected by an umbrella, hurrying towards the alley. *Poor thing, must be off to do her shopping,* he thought. It transpired that Astrid wasn't home, so rather despondently, he decided to return that same evening in the hope of talking to her then.

***

"His death happened in Germany," Astrid said, as they sat in her lounge that same evening. Benedict had returned at seven p.m. and heard the TV going inside when he knocked on the door. She made him a mug of instant coffee and turned the television off.

"Oh, I see." Benedict sipped from the thick, chipped china mug. "It must've been a terrible time for you."

"Course it was. We loved each other so much. We'd gone over there to see Mum, and Elroy, well, he was on the hunt for antiques as usual. He was the buyer for the Roydons' shop see, and it was how we originally met. He was over in Germany, and I was also working there for an antiques dealer. Course my family was originally English – from London – and we moved over to Germany when Dad decided he wanted to live near his folks. They lived in Bonn, so we settled there. Mum was English and Dad was German. I didn't like it there much, so when I met Elroy, it was good, because as soon as we married, we shifted to New Zealand."

"So your connection with the Roydons was through Elroy's job?"

"That's right. As well as being his employer, Mr Roydon was a good mate of Elroy's. It was he who offered me the housekeeping position – after Elroy was killed. I came back home, of course. I needed an income and I'm afraid I didn't have much choice. I was supposed to be ever so grateful to him at the time and I said I was. He was seen by everyone as such a kind man. Even I was of that opinion at the time. But I was so vulnerable during that stage of my life, as I'm sure you'll understand." She took a large swallow of wine and gazed into the room, as if thinking painfully of the past. "Course he died in 2007, did Mr Roydon. His wife, Morag, had gone a few years before. Fell down stairs and broke her neck, poor thing."

Benedict listened while trying to read Astrid's facial expressions and body language; gauging whether or not she was wound up like an alarm clock ready to go off. It would seem not, however. It was like she was telling her story by rote, having told it before in exactly the same way. Yet Benedict hadn't forgotten how adamant Astrid had been when she'd told him about being so glad to be rid of her position at the Roydons'.

He finished his coffee and stood up. "You've been most helpful, Mrs Lorning. Thank you so much."

"No trouble at all. If there's anything else you need to know, just call round. My phone is on the blink right now. How's the investigation going, anyway?"

"It's progressing slowly, but headway is being made."

Astrid smiled ingratiatingly. "Good. People think

they can get away with these horrific crimes, but they can't. No way." She took another large mouthful of wine, put her glass down unsteadily and rose to see Benedict out.

As she opened the door, Benedict hesitated. "Just one more thing, if you don't mind?"

"No, go right ahead." Astrid was hanging onto the door-frame for support, and Benedict could smell the wine on her breath.

"It's about Dominica, Lilac's partner. Did you know her well?"

Astrid seemed to be caught off guard, and her face turned pale, but she quickly recovered herself. "Oh yes, of course I did – through Elroy's dealings with the Roydons. They had various social gatherings and Lilac and Dominica were often invited over."

"Thanks, Mrs Lorning, you've been most helpful. Goodbye."

***

Astrid heaved a sigh of relief when Benedict Aberthorp left. She was well aware of the dreamlike state she'd been in when answering the private investigator's questions. After all, she'd rehearsed everything countless times so that nowadays she re-told the story without hesitation, as if it had really happened that way. Of course some of it *was* true, and that gave her story its authenticity. Now, as she swallowed some more wine, the fuzziness enveloped her and she wondered why Lilac hadn't told her she was dropping by earlier today. Astrid had only found out from Miss Wilson.

True to form, Miss Wilson had been watching through her window the whole time, and as soon as Astrid had arrived home, the old crone had knocked on her door.

"Yes, Miss Wilson?" Astrid had said, expecting some trivial morsel of local gossip.

"You had a visitor today. Oh, yes." Miss Wilson was smiling knowingly as she spoke. "Your friend, Lilac, let herself in." Miss Wilson had a gleeful look on her face. "But she tried to hide behind an umbrella. Couldn't fool me though. It had to be her because you told me she's the only one who knows where your key is."

Astrid was worried. Miss Wilson said she hadn't actually seen Lilac's face because of the umbrella, nor had she seen her leave, having been in her kitchenette making herself a cup of tea at the time.

Now Astrid was going to have to pay Lilac a surprise visit of her own, to find out what she'd been doing, sneaking into her flat. It was imperative she found out.

Of course, she'd known for a while there was a rift in their friendship, but even when they were close, Lilac had a way of not divulging information about herself, she always had, but beneath the façade, Lilac had an enquiring mind like Sherlock Holmes's. What concerned Astrid the most was the fact that she knew her friend would need to know the truth; that one way or another, she would convince herself it was her duty to find out everything. This need to know all was Lilac's weakness. She could just never let sleeping dogs lie.

Chapter 9

Tuesday 4th June

Restraining his frustration, Aldo climbed into his Suzuki Swift and shut the door. The police had been so sure the brown raincoat found beneath Francine's right hand, belonged to him. They had ordered him to come to the police station, to show it to him, watching his face carefully to gauge his reaction. Aldo had been expecting something like this and he stated firmly, in a calm voice, that the raincoat definitely wasn't his. It did not belong to him. He had never seen it before. His raincoat was a vintage Quelrayn Bri-nylon from England – not this thin, cheap, plastic thing, that looked far too big for him. He'd even found a photograph (admittedly taken several years ago) of him wearing his own brown raincoat. He'd had the same one for years. Yet Detective Finnegan, who was interviewing him, was not convinced and continued looking at him with a stony-faced expression.

"Then where is your raincoat, Mr Sherwin? The one

you were wearing on the day you went to have lunch with your wife? On the day she was murdered." The detective chief inspector's facial expression was set as if in a permanent frown, his eyes boring into Aldo's.

At that moment, Aldo had seen himself as a puny earthworm about to be devoured by a hungry blackbird. "I don't know, but I've hired someone to find it. He's going to find it. He won't let me down."

"You can go home now, Mr Sherwin, but you might be called in again for questioning at any time."

Aldo never doubted that someone had taken his raincoat, planting a similar-looking one at the scene after killing Francine. He still didn't know who the murderer was, and didn't want to even think about who it could be. He just wanted to blot it all out and leave it to private investigator Benedict Aberthorp to solve. Aberthorp always gave him a reassuring smile and told him not to worry, but the text message he'd received kept coming into his mind, re-playing itself over and over.

'You know what you did and you're going to pay.'

***

Benedict was in the office with Gail, looking over everything he had gleaned from his conversation with

Astrid the night before. He was just as worried and puzzled as he had been before the visit. He had a strong hunch Astrid Lorning was hiding something. Something had happened to her husband, of that he was certain, but so far there was no record of what the something was.

"You'd better keep trying to find out more about Astrid's past."

"Where do I start?" Gail said, looking up from her laptop.

"Astrid told me her mother lived in Bonn, as did her father. She also lived there before marrying Elroy, and she and Elroy went there again in March, 2005. I didn't ask for an exact date because I didn't want her to get too suspicious of my motives," Benedict said.

"Bonn. Let me see…" Gail tapped the computer keys. "Here we are: 'Bonn is a city on the banks of the Rhine in the German state of North Rhine-Westphalia, with a population of over 300,000. Ludwig Van Beethoven spent his childhood and teenage years in Bonn.' So, sometime in March, 2005, a man called Elroy Lorning was stabbed to death while trying to stop a woman being raped. Right?"

"*Mmm*, I'll leave it to you to confirm, or dispute otherwise. I'm meeting Aldo for lunch at Coffee Mania. Be good, and I'll see you later. We'll discuss everything over a glass of wine."

"It's a date. Good luck."

***

When Benedict walked into the café, Aldo was sitting in a corner, a half-eaten egg omelette on a plate in front of him.

"Hi, how's things?"

"I've had a hell of a morning," Aldo said, looking almost tearful. "The police wanted me to come to the station to look at the brown raincoat they found beneath Francine's right hand. They were suspicious before when I said I couldn't find my coat. But this one was *nothing* like mine. As I still have no idea where it is, I told them I'd hired someone to find it for me. The detective looked surprised when I said that. He obviously hoped they were going to catch me out."

"Look, I'm doing some groundwork around what people have told me so far, and I want to make sure I'm getting an accurate story from everyone."

Aldo looked at Benedict, wide-eyed. "Which people are you referring to? Not me I hope!"

"I'm starting with Astrid Lorning, then Lilac Browne and I hope also, Cindy Carollan. I believe her daughter, Jenniver, is in the women's prison, which seems to be the main reason Cindy's come over here. Can you tell me anything more about her?"

Aldo didn't reply immediately, as if weighing everything up. "I don't know a lot about it, not a lot at all. But…"

"Her address?"

"*Um*, I was told she's renting a house in Plover Street. She's also driving around in a small blue rental car – a Fiat Bambina, I think it's called but she always gets the bus to the prison. She goes about three times a week to see Jenniver. Apart from that she mostly keeps to herself."

"It must be hard on her."

"Yes, hard, but Cindy doesn't let things get her down. We used to be good friends, but I don't see a lot of her now. I think she prefers to keep to herself most of the time."

"Can you tell me about March, 2005, when Astrid and Elroy went to Germany to see her mother? I presume her father had already passed away."

Aldo hesitated.

"Is something wrong?" Benedict said.

"No, no, it's just that in March, 2005, I was away in the psychiatric hospital."

"I'm sorry to have to ask you about such a painful time. Would you mind telling me when you came home to Seagrove again?"

"Not until the end of May. By then, Astrid had returned from Germany and started her new role as our housekeeper. I liked Astrid being there in the house. She was a bit like a mother to me."

"Did Astrid ever talk to you about the death of Elroy?"

"Not really. I remember seeing her crying sometimes, but mostly she stayed silent on the matter. I could relate to that need for privacy as Francine and I were grieving the loss of our baby at that time too. I admit, I was secretly pleased that Elroy wasn't around anymore to beat her up – like he used to. It was obvious to everyone that this is what happened."

Benedict nodded in what he hoped was a sympathetic manner, while hiding his surprise at this latest revelation.

Aldo finished his omelette and put down his fork. "In some ways it was strange," he said. "Because before I went away to the hospital, Mr Roydon and Elroy spent a lot of time together at the house. Astrid was usually there too and we often used to chat. I don't remember her ever saying she was going to see her mother. Her father had died the previous year. Perhaps her mother hadn't been well? I know she's since passed away."

***

Lilac looked up from her washing basket and, to her horror, she saw the stout figure of Astrid walking down her driveway. It was too late for her to pretend she wasn't at home. She'd been caught in the act of unpegging her laundry from the clothesline, and now she stopped as Astrid strode purposefully towards her. Her visitor dispensed of any preamble, and said, "Miss Wilson watched you going into my flat, yesterday." Her dark, sharp stare, was fixed as she spoke.

Lilac's hands shook and she nearly dropped the basketful of clothes. At the same time, Scamper scuttled behind her legs, yowling in a strange way. He always ran from Astrid and behaved abnormally when she was around.

"I was just paying you a friendly visit," Lilac said, trying not to stammer and reveal her anxiety.

"I don't believe you. Why not come for a 'friendly visit' when I am actually at home, like any normal person would? Come on now, tell me the truth, Lilac Browne – for once in your miserable life."

This last sentence threw Lilac into a state of panic. "What? I'm not a liar. Anyway, your phone wasn't working, remember, so I couldn't call in advance. And what about the things *you're* not telling *me*? Or have you forgotten that you and I made a plan, long before Cindy

Herskington came back onto the scene? You were going to start vacuuming the upstairs rooms earlier than normal while I rang the doorbell. Then, when you said she had a visitor, Francine would come rushing down, not noticing the vacuum cleaner cord pulled tight across the top step. We'd worked it all out, remember?"

Astrid's shoulders slumped and she sighed loudly. "Her name's Cindy Carollan now. She's married and you know why she came over here – to visit her daughter in prison. Now I've nothing more to say about her. But let's face it, Lilac, you would never have been able to do what we talked about anyway. It's just not in your nature, despite what happened on that day nineteen years ago. You've got no guts, Lilac. Don't try to deny it."

Lilac put her washing basket down on the driveway and began to sob. She didn't know how to protect herself against Astrid's stinging words. Astrid was a bully who had become more so since Cindy had returned from Scotland; ingratiating herself with both Astrid and Aldo until she'd won their trust.

"Stop snivelling and let's go inside for a cuppa. Come on."

Meekly, Lilac picked up the washing basket and followed her inside. Astrid filled the kettle and plugged it in, the way she used to when they were best friends.

"I went to your place to get my book back, if you must know," Lilac said. How fortuitous it had been to see her book there. She'd grabbed it on her way out in the hope it might stop Astrid from guessing the real reason for her visit.

"Which one was it? I could've still been reading it."

"A crime book with a blue cover." Lilac had found it in a second-hand book sale, and lent it to Astrid when she'd finished reading it. "I wanted to read it again," she said. When she'd spied it on Astrid's bookshelf on top of the usual untidy pile, it had been covered in dust so she was certain Astrid wasn't currently reading it.

"A creepy story, if I recall," said Astrid, slurping her tea noisily and smiling grimly. "You know what, Lilac... I have to tell you this, because he might come round here and start poking his nose into your business as well."

"Who? What about?"

"The private investigator, Benedict Aberthorp, visited me last night. Wanted to know about Elroy, how he died and where it happened. I told him in Germany, of course, in Bonn, where Mum lived. He was getting nosey, I can tell you. But I told him the same old story."

"Oh, Astrid, I suppose he's going to start asking me about Dominica as well."

"Of course, he is. What are you going to tell him?"

"I've already told him Dominica left me for a man and now lives in Australia, so he knows about it."

"But where exactly does Dominica live? And what will you say then? Because he will ask, you know. He'll want an address. Now use your brains and think. All right?"

"I have it all worked out so there's no need to worry. Anyway, why is he prying into our pasts? It doesn't make sense. Aldo employed him to find out who killed Francine."

"Yes, but they're always looking for motives. They want to know everything about everyone."

"Of course. Oh God, this is all making me sick. I can't take much more of this, I really can't!"

"Don't be silly now, he's just doing his job. Anyway, can I be privy to what you have all worked out?"

Lilac silently fought the queasy feeling gathering in the pit of her stomach. Astrid always had a way of making her confess, even when she was determined not to say a word. "I'm still thinking about it, if you must know. Did you tell the P.I. the date Elroy met his untimely end?"

"No, because he didn't ask. Now let's just forget all about it for now, shall we? I hate thinking about those kind of things anyway. It's like dredging the ocean and finding muck at the bottom."

Lilac finished her tea, hoping Astrid would soon go away and leave her in peace. She could see Astrid was more troubled now than ever before, but she dare not try to ask any more questions concerning that day. She picked up her cup and headed for the kitchen.

"Lilac, I want you to take me over to where Cindy's staying. Not when she's home, of course. She's made it clear she doesn't want to talk to me right now, she's gone quiet but I want to drop something off in her letterbox, and as it's a long way from here, well, I'd hoped you might do me a favour. Only if you don't mind? I believe she's staying in Plover Street."

She hesitated before replying, but as always, Lilac felt compelled to do Astrid's bidding. "Do you mean take you there on a day when she's visiting the prison?"

"Yes, dear. She goes there on a Monday, Wednesday and Friday, if my observations at the bus station are accurate. And sometimes on a Saturday too."

"You mean you've been watching her?"

"Not exactly, but whenever I get the bus it stops at the station to make pick-ups just as the Number Seven is getting ready to pull out for the prison. I've seen her boarding on those days, or else she's sitting on the bus already, in her horrible trench-coat with the collar pulled up. You'd think she was a spy or something!"

"All right, but let's not argue anymore, okay? I want

to be friends again – like we used to be. However, there is something I have to ask you."

Astrid looked at her, a frown forming on her forehead. "What is it now?"

Lilac plucked up the courage to ask: "The blood pact that you, Cindy and Aldo made. I was watching you through the hedge."

Astrid screwed up her nose and sighed loudly. "You can be so dramatic at times, Lilac, you really can. It was just some silly thing Cindy wanted to do. I don't know why."

Despite her casual reply, Lilac could sense Astrid's underlying tension. She was trying to seem relaxed, but didn't quite manage it. Her eyes, which looked warily at Lilac as she spoke, betrayed her.

Lilac sought to return to the easy camaraderie that had been developing between them. "All right, you don't have to tell me what went on between you, Cindy and Aldo. It's your business and yours alone. Okay?"

"Nothing went on. And thank you for agreeing to take me. What about this Thursday afternoon, about one o'clock?" She spoke the last sentence quickly as if she'd had it all worked out before she came. She wanted an instant answer.

Against her better judgement, Lilac agreed. "I'll pick you up at twelve forty-five p.m."

"Thanks love." Astrid gave her a honey-sweet smile and headed for the door.

Chapter 10

Wednesday 5th June

"I have some news about Lilac's partner, Dominica," Gail said with a triumphant smile.

Gail was sitting in the office in Rowan Street with Benedict who was eager to hear what she'd found out. "Go on," he said, picking up a biscuit and dunking it in the foamy flat-white Gail had made him.

"I told the librarian I was working with you and that we had been employed to find a missing person. Could she tell me, in confidence, whether Dominica Frimble still had an account at the library? First of all, she said that information was confidential, but as Dominica had been missing for so long, she agreed to look up her account to see if it was still open. It was, she told me, because there were two books still outstanding. One was borrowed on March seven and one on March ten, 2005. That was all she could tell me, she said, very quietly, and asked if I could be discreet about what she had said, or she could be in trouble."

"But how can that help us?"

Gail sighed. "She also said that their protocol was to send the account-holder a letter, requesting the books to be returned. But she couldn't tell me if this had been done for Dominica. So, I thought we could ask Lilac if the library had done this."

"Which brings me to my next assignment, dear assistant: visiting Lilac Browne again. I'll ask about the letter then. You make a superb coffee, by the way." Benedict drained his cup and stood up. "How about we go to Coffee Mania for lunch?"

"OK," Gail said."

"Meet you at there at twelve-thirty?"

"Absolutely."

***

Ten minutes later, Benedict pulled up outside Lilac's home, where he found her busy carting bags of groceries from her car to the house. She stopped and placed two of the bags on the driveway.

"Oh, Mr Aberthorp. What a surprise."

"Hi. I hoped you might have a few minutes to spare? I need to go over some points relating to our initial interview.

"Here, let me help you with those." Benedict picked one up.

Lilac hesitated, then picked up the remaining bag and began walking slowly towards her backdoor. "Thanks, they are rather heavy."

Benedict said, "I know this is a sensitive topic, but I need to ask you about your former partner, Dominica. You say she left you many years ago, after meeting someone else, and now lives in Australia?"

"Yes, Mr Aberthorp, sadly, she did. Just over nineteen years ago. I miss her a lot. Always have."

"And you say it was a sudden departure?" Benedict put a bag of groceries down on the kitchen countertop.

"Oh, yes, it was. It took me by surprise, it really did. I never expected it."

"Just for the record, do you by any chance have her current address? You see, I might need to ask her some background questions in order to further our enquiry into Mrs Roydon's death."

"But Dominica's been gone nearly twenty years, Mr Aberthorp. How could she possibly know anything about what happened to Francine just last month?"

"It might seem a long shot," Benedict said, "but sometimes the past has a bearing on the present, in unexpected ways."

Lilac's face puckered as if she was in pain. "If you

say so." She hurried away into the dining room, where Benedict was able to see her sideways on, through the doorway, opening a drawer and rummaging around in it. "Here it is. I have it here." She came back with an envelope in her hand, and pulled out a piece of thin paper. "It says here her address is ninety-nine Killian Crescent, near Coogee Beach in Sydney. She sent me this letter in 2006, asking if I could apologise to the library for some books she'd taken with her, but they'd somehow got lost in transit. She asked me to look for the books, just in case she'd left them here, but I couldn't find them, they weren't here."

"Can I see the letter, please?"

"Course you can." She passed it over.

"Did Dominica ever write to you again?"

"Yes, just the one letter, but I found it so upsetting, I burnt it. I think I hated her then, but I just had to accept everything in the end. She wasn't coming back, no matter how much I wanted her to."

Benedict could see Lilac fighting back tears. "When exactly did she leave?"

Lilac hurriedly lit a cigarette and stood by the open kitchen door that led out onto the porch. "In March, 2005. I remember the day so clearly." She started to sob then, but Benedict continued undeterred.

"Was it during the time Astrid and Elroy Lorning

were away in Germany?"

Lilac dabbed at her eyes with a large handkerchief. "Yes, Mr Aberthorp, it was." Then she took a deep drag on her cigarette and blew smoke out the kitchen door.

"What day in March did she go? Can you remember?"

Lilac took another drag. "It was a Friday, the fourth I think. Oh God it was terrible."

"I'm so sorry to have upset you, bringing up the past like this, but it's an important part of my investigation." Benedict made a few notes and wrote down Dominica's supposed address: ninety-nine Killian Crescent, Coogee Beach, Sydney, Australia.

"I'll be all right," Lilac said, wiping her eyes and stubbing out her cigarette in a glass ashtray. "Any time you want to know anything, Mr Aberthorp, anything at all, I'm only too willing to oblige."

Benedict passed his card over. "If you remember something else, please call me – anytime. I'm available twenty-four-seven. Are you sure you'll be all right?"

"Yep, don't worry, I always cry when I'm reminded of Dominica." She was about to take the card from Benedict's hand but then stopped.

"You've already given me one of your cards," she said, unsmiling.

Benedict wondered how much was left unsaid in tense encounters such as this.

***

Aldo sat on a low seat on his back porch watching the sea and thinking about the first time he'd met Francine Roydon. How fun-loving she'd been. By this time, he already had a girlfriend – Cindy Herskington – a girl he had liked all through school. Cindy had told Aldo one day, how she couldn't wait to have a 'proper' relationship with him. When Aldo asked her what she meant, she'd rolled her eyes.

"Oh, you know. On my birthday, February thirteenth – when I'll be sixteen," she'd said.

Aldo understood her meaning but had no intention of fulfilling Cindy's wishes, because by then Francine was the girl he really wanted to be with.

As time went on, Aldo mulled over how to tell Cindy he wanted to break up with her, but how was he going to do it? Finally, he thought of a way, and even though it was mean and sneaky, it worked.

Afterwards, however, Aldo noticed how quiet and withdrawn Cindy became. Her sixteenth birthday came and went and they all continued to meet at the Roydons' house. Then something inappropriate happened, he began to notice. Mr Roydon (or Andy as he liked to be called) began spending a lot of time talking to Cindy. He asked himself why? Mr Roydon was at least forty and far too old for Cindy. It was like he was cradle-snatching.

A few weeks before Francine's birthday, when she was discussing what kind of party she wanted, Aldo told Francine he'd always liked her and now that he and Cindy were no longer together, he asked her if she would go out with him. She didn't give him an answer.

Two weeks before Francine's sixteenth birthday, Aldo was at the Roydons' house, where a group of them were planning her special day. Aldo grabbed her in the hallway of her home and kissed her. He held onto her tightly and whispered, "I've fallen in love with you."

Francine was flattered by his attentions, but she was also frightened. "You have a girlfriend already," she'd said, trying to pull away.

"No, we've broken up," Aldo said, "I've told you that already." Yet he was still worried about Cindy, the way he had hurt her by what he'd done.

Aldo was confused and didn't know what to think, or how to handle Francine. She wouldn't leave him alone after that, flirting and joking with him whenever no one was there. Finally, on the evening of her birthday, July twenty-three, while her party was in full swing, a storm broke out. This forced a few of them to stay the night at the Roydons'. Aldo was allocated a bed in a spare-room. In the middle of the night, Francine came in and got into bed with him. There was no going back after that, and from then on, he and Francine often spent the night together. Aldo always found a way to push Cindy out of his mind. It was like Francine had cast a spell on him and he was unable to resist, basking in the loving attention she showered on him.

Towards the end of September that same year, Francine whispered a secret to Aldo, in the middle of the night, while they were lying in bed. The pair were trying to be quiet as she suspected her father was aware of what was going on between them. Francine told him that Cindy was pregnant, and she asked him if he was the father. Aldo remembered how shocked he'd been, and told Francine that he and Cindy hadn't had that kind of relationship. Upon hearing the news, Aldo kept thinking about Andy Roydon, Francine's father, and how he'd often seen him talking to Cindy. On one occasion, he'd even seen Andy put his hand on Cindy's thigh.

***

At exactly twelve-thirty, Benedict pushed open the café

door. Gail gave him a wry smile, which he hoped meant she had some interesting information to tell him.

"I've seen a letter from Dominica to Lilac," Benedict said, plonking himself down opposite her.

"Okay. So, what do you think?"

"Nothing at all at this moment in time. Oh my goodness, this has got to be the strangest case."

"So how was your talk with Lilac?"

"*Mmm*, I don't really know. On the surface I'd say all is well with her, but I sensed tension too. She even said at one point that it was silly wanting Dominica's address because she'd been gone for nearly twenty years and couldn't possibly know anything about Francine's murder. When I pointed out that sometimes, in unexpected ways, the past can have a bearing on the present, she just said, 'If you say so,' and fetched the letter. I gave her one of my cards as I was leaving and she reminded me I'd already given her one. Her look gave me the impression that one day she would tell me something important."

"You have had a productive morning," Gail said.

"Didn't the librarian tell you she borrowed the books on March seven and March ten, 2005?"

"Yes, why?"

Benedict riffled through his notebook. "Aha! Those dates don't fit with something Lilac has just told me when I asked her what day Dominica left, she said, 'I remember the day clearly – it was a Friday, the fourth'."

Gail smiled slyly. "So, if Dominica left on the fourth, how could she have borrowed two books from the library on the seventh and tenth?"

"Exactly. Or was it Lilac that borrowed them, using Dominica's library card?"

"*Mmm*, but if so, why didn't she return them? I think we've got something there. And if we can keep digging up more of the stuff, it might turn into something bigger."

***

Aldo had always suspected there'd been some dramatic happenings while he was away in the psychiatric hospital, nineteen years ago. He thought this because when he came home again, he didn't see as much of Lilac as he had done previously. Francine had told him the story, of Dominica's departure; of her having met a man and gone with him to live in Australia. Francine said it was best not to mention anything about Dominica to Lilac, as she was struggling to come to terms with what had happened and had become withdrawn and very sad.

Aldo had liked Dominica as she laughed a lot and always had something nice to say. She was an intelligent woman who ran her own business, although Aldo was never exactly sure what that business was. He recalled how Dominica had come to see him before he left for the hospital and told him not to worry. She and Lilac would be thinking of him every day and wishing him well, and when he came home, they'd take him out for the day – to the cinema or to a café for lunch.

Those events were a dim and faraway memory now, Aldo reflected wistfully. So much had changed and now he was alone too, just like Astrid and Lilac. It seemed fate had brought them bad luck. Lilac seemed preoccupied these days, and Aldo had heard her talking to herself on more than one occasion. Perhaps that's just what happened to anybody who was on their own too much? At least Lilac had Scamper now, to keep her company. Aldo had asked her if she'd like to adopt the cat, when he left to stay at the beach-house. It was obvious she'd always loved having him around, and was so keen to have him at her place permanently that she agreed straight-away.

Aldo often wondered, even now, what had really happened while he was away at the hospital. Back then, there was a stigma attached to suffering from mental health issues. He supposed Astrid had once loved Elroy, but at seventeen, Aldo recalled seeing bruises on Astrid's face, despite her attempting to cover them with makeup. Astrid and Elroy visited Mr Roydon often, to discuss the buying of antiques. Aldo, Cindy and other friends of Francine's were also at the house on many occasions.

As for Lilac and Dominica, they always seemed so happy together in those days, that it was hard for him to believe Dominica could have been so heartless; leaving so unexpectedly, and falling in love with a man. Where did she even meet this mystery man? Perhaps during one of her business dealings at her office, in central Seagrove.

Aldo had his own struggles to contend with, and didn't have time to question the lives of others. He spent most of his energy trying to get himself back to relative happiness. He so hated being depressed all the time. At first, Francine had been supportive and kind, but Aldo feared their relationship would never be the same again. It was like everything had become tarnished and permanently dull, having lost the lustrous sheen of their initial passionate romance.

And now she was dead who was responsible? Aldo experienced guilt at being so light and free again, as if a heavy weight had been lifted off his shoulders. He didn't have to keep proving himself anymore, or pretending to be bright and cheerful when he wasn't. However, there were still questions awaiting answers and his world was now revolving like an out-of-control spinning-top, wobbling, one way and then the other. In a way, he felt a sense of freedom and yet the sticky threads of suspicion were all over him. The police were fixated on his raincoat, and no amount of denial on his part could persuade them he was telling the truth. Now, for the sake of his sanity, he had to go back over the day in question – hour by hour, minute by minute – to try to remember who he'd seen, at what time and where.

He looked at the notebook open on the table in front of him, wherein he'd listed all the names: Francine, Lilac, Astrid, Cindy and Scamper. He was about to scratch out *Scamper,* but stopped himself from doing so. The cat loved company and whenever he'd seen or looked for Scamper, there would be a person somewhere nearby. So, although he knew a cat couldn't commit a murder, Scamper could still provide a vital clue. He re-ordered his thoughts, and began again, starting from the time he'd arrived to have lunch with Francine. Who had he seen? What time? Where? Was there something he'd missed? And why wasn't Benedict Aberthorp trying to find Francine's killer? Aldo didn't like the way Benedict was delving into the past, asking questions about things that took place twenty years ago. What did any of this have to do with now? Then the words from the text message came back to him again: 'You know what you did and you're going to pay.'

Aldo shuddered inwardly and queasiness enveloped him. Surely it couldn't have anything to do with what he'd done? Not after all this time. The old feeling of guilt was rising within him, like a seed sprouting ultra-fast in the Tropics. Cheerful, fun-loving Cindy didn't appear to care about anything – laughing her way through every problem. Yet how could this be true when he remembered a time when Cindy wasn't like that at all. Aldo began to wonder if Cindy really had been hurt by his betrayal after all. Perhaps she'd pretended she didn't care, like now, when she told them about Jenniver going to prison. Cindy had said she wasn't worried: it was nothing to get upset about, because Jenniver would soon be released to get on with her life again; back in Scotland. Jenniver's boyfriend's family were wealthy and he'd be waiting for her. In fact he would even have helped get her treatment for her drug addiction if he had known about it. This was why, Cindy said, she couldn't be bothered wasting her time worrying about her daughter. She was all right, she had insisted.

Aldo picked up his other notebook – the small green one with the worn leather cover, the one he kept hidden from everyone and had done since 2003, when the three of them had made the first blood-pact. He read through one of its pages again, shut it and locked it back inside the top drawer of his desk. He'd kept the key round his neck ever since moving into the beach-house.

Chapter 11

Thursday 6th June

The bus rumbled along the highway, taking its mix of passengers to the prison. Cindy, breaking from her usual routine, was visiting the prison on a Thursday, knowing she wouldn't be going there on Jenniver's birthday in a few days' time. As she looked out the window, she glimpsed a glittering band of deep, teal blue sea as they sped past. The sun's rays shimmered on the water, moving in an ever-changing pattern. The trip took an hour, and Cindy usually read a book, but not today. Instead, as it got closer to Jenniver's nineteenth birthday, Cindy remembered June eleven, when her daughter was born, in the strange, beautiful, yet often cold country of Scotland. By then, she'd only lived in Scotland for eight months, sharing a home with her father and his girlfriend. She'd decided on a home-birth, and the midwife had arrived only minutes after her waters broke. It was after the birth of Jenniver that Cindy found herself learning how to hate; not her new-born daughter, but the man she'd left behind. She tried to shut out his memory now, as he had been then – handsome, charming, yet insincere.

After the party, on February thirteen, at the Roydons' house, when everyone had gone to bed, Andy Roydon came into her room. The pair had secretly arranged this assignation and Andy had fulfilled her wish; something she had held onto until she turned sixteen. Only it wasn't Aldo, as had been her desire, because Francine had stolen him away from her. As the weeks went by, Andy spent countless nights upstairs with her in his room, and she fell deeply in love. He had given her a key and she secretly stole back to the house after everyone else was in bed. She remembered how scary, yet exciting these secret liaisons had been. Talk of the future was never discussed; not until Cindy fell pregnant. The baby was due in June of the following year.

The bus rattled along the country road, carrying friends and relatives of the women who were locked up, away from society. They passed rows of pine trees, and cars zoomed past in the opposite direction. Sitting across the aisle from Cindy was a woman with a black felt hat pulled down over her forehead. She wore glasses and was talking to an elderly man with white hair.

"When is she getting parole?" the woman asked. Cindy couldn't hear the elderly man's reply.

A faint sound of country and western music came from the driver's radio while Cindy studied her reflection in the window beside her: long, wavy brown hair, hanging loosely, and her oval, pale countenance, set with a stony look marring her fine features. Where had her inner peace gone to? Someone behind her started laughing raucously, and Cindy wished it was her laughing in such a relaxed way, instead of the forced way she'd been doing lately, in order to stave off the pitying looks.

After Jenniver was born, Cindy became involved with a church in a nearby Highlands village near her father's sheep farm. There, she learnt about forgiveness, and how to release herself from shame, guilt, disgust, betrayal, hatred and self-loathing. As time passed, she found herself slowly change; becoming more peaceful and accepting of the past. Sometimes she was even joyful, especially as she watched her beautiful daughter, growing into a strong and healthy young woman. Cindy had also met a man in the village, Gregor Carollan, and they'd married in 2008 when Jenniver was three years old.

Yet now, as the bus bumped and heaved its way to the prison, Cindy was so engrossed in her own tangled thinking, she hardly noticed the view outside the window: meadows sprinkled with sheep, herds of cows, contentedly munching grass, rows of poplar trees, leaning in the wind, and the train tracks following the road. Her mind was full of the recent past and had been, ever since she came back to her home country – returning for more than one reason. She had a purpose now and it had grown, like a canker inside her, throbbing with desire, oozing with intent, urging her on and so freeing her spirit from all the constraints in which she'd allowed herself to be bound since entrusting her soul to the care of the church.

Now she'd opted for a different path – some would call it 'going over to the dark side' but Cindy told herself she was only doing what was right. She was freeing herself from the need to forgive, something she'd found impossible to do.

The bus was rounding the last bend now, and everyone was automatically gathering their bags, putting on their coats and wrapping scarves round their necks. As if wanting to punish the prisoners even more than incarceration, this desolate part of the country, was nearly always cold, and windy. The sombreness of the place was further reinforced to the visitors when heavy rain began to fall, just as the bus pulled up outside the prison gates.

They stepped out onto ground already soggy with mud and now covered in fast-growing puddles.

***

Lilac and Astrid crouched inside Lilac's car, just behind the belt of cypress trees in Plover Street. Cindy had left some time ago and they had estimated she would be arriving at the prison about now. This fact reassured Lilac and Astrid that they wouldn't be seen by Cindy. However, the private investigator living just a little further down Plover Street was becoming problematic, principally the fact that because his garage had a roll-a-door, hiding his car within, there was no way of knowing whether he'd already left for his office. However, luckily for them, Benedict had just that moment driven past in his BMW. Lilac hoped he hadn't seen them though as it wasn't easy hiding a red car.

"Okay, now we're here, I'm going to take the plunge and put my little 'gift' in her letterbox," Astrid said.

The letterbox stood at the end of a concrete path, near the footpath.

"Keep an eye out while I'm gone, and if you see anyone coming, come pick me up. Okay?"

"Yes, I understand. But be careful," Lilac dutifully said.

Astrid wore a curly blonde wig, with a fedora hat pulled down low over it, together with dark glasses and a long, black waterproof coat. She'd reassured Lilac they were prescription dark glasses, so she'd be able to see clearly in order to place the 'gift' at number seventy-one. "Let's hope there's no nosey Miss Wilson-type neighbour who sees all the goings on, eh, Lilac?"

Lilac pretended to laugh, but was actually seething at the memory of the nosey old witch telling Astrid she'd seen her going into the flat. It was just lucky Lilac had spotted the book she'd lent Astrid and taken it with her to use as an excuse for her unannounced visit.

She grimaced as she watched Astrid stroll confidently down the street. Astrid had camouflaged her identity well, but looked out of place on the quiet suburban street. This was not the innocuous figure she had hoped to display to anyone who might be twitching their curtains. The mysterious delivery was tucked into one of the deep pockets of the coat. Lilac had known better than to ask what was in the small package, only having caught a glimpse of a square object wrapped in brown paper.

The plan was that Astrid was to place the package in Cindy's letterbox, by the footpath, and keep walking – all the way around the block, so that she arrived back at the same spot ten minutes later. Lilac was to pause for a few minutes and then move the car elsewhere and come back and pick her up, rather than wait, as that would look suspicious.

Lilac soon set off and drove round the streets until the time was up and turned back to Plover Street. There was Astrid, in the distance, so she turned off the engine and waited.

She returned with a crafty smile on her face. Lilac asked no questions; instead, starting the engine and driving off. Astrid began to laugh hysterically.

"Why are you laughing? What is it you left in Cindy's letterbox?"

"She's going to have a meltdown when she gets back, I can tell you! Want to come in for a coffee?"

"Okay." Lilac pulled up outside the block of flats where Astrid lived, wondering if she was going to tell her what the parcel contained. She thought it unlikely, however.

When they were inside the tiny flat, Lilac looked around her. Nothing had changed, as far as she could see. Astrid hadn't tidied anything or cleaned and Lilac was relieved. The raincoat would still be nicely hidden far back in the right-hand corner of the wardrobe, where two pairs of mouldy, smelly old shoes had been thrown on top.

Astrid wasn't putting the kettle on for coffee, as

she'd implied. Instead, she opened the fridge and pulled out an expensive-looking bottle of sparkling wine.

"I think we need to celebrate, old friend," she said, getting down two crystal wine glasses and rinsing them with hot water.

"Oh, yes please," Lilac said, hiding her shock at being called 'old friend'. There was something about that parcel that now seemed to have miraculously wiped clean the mustiness surrounding their old friendship – a friendship that had grown more out of need, over the years, than anything else – both of them having once shared a hard time that had later turned into a secret of monumental proportions. "So what are we celebrating? Is it something to do with the parcel?"

"Oh, yes, the parcel. Cindy needs her comeuppance. She's just a bit too smart for her own good." Astrid was drying the glasses hurriedly with a tea towel.

Once they were sitting down at the small foldaway table in a corner of Astrid's dim kitchen, Astrid unscrewed the wine bottle and poured them both a large glass. They clinked them together carefully and took their first sip. Lilac liked the taste because it was sweet although she inhaled the bubbles, making her sneeze.

"What have I been an accessory to, I'd like to know?" Lilac watched as Astrid raised the glass to her lips and began drinking quickly.

Astrid didn't answer, instead getting up to open a kitchen cupboard and withdrawing a large packet of salt and vinegar chips.

"Let's have these with our wine," she said, a crooked smile on her face. Lilac noticed, how Astrid was getting more lines on her once smooth countenance.

"What has Cindy done to annoy you?" Lilac said, already feeling more confident after imbibing the refreshingly cold wine. Astrid just stared vacantly ahead and said nothing so Lilac tried a different tack. "Hey, remember when we used to celebrate our birthdays together, not so long ago? I used to find a certain comfort in your company then."

Astrid seemed lost in her own reveries, taking mouthfuls of wine and chomping on chips, as if Lilac wasn't there.

"You used to come over, usually after Francine and Aldo had gone out, and tell me about the latest humiliation she had inflicted on you – like having to pick up her panties and filthy tee-shirts and jeans where she deliberately dropped them, knowing you wouldn't say anything, let alone leave them there. You'd tell me how all her washing was expected to be done, dried and ironed on the same day otherwise she would get angry with you."

"I don't care about those things now. I'd sooner forget it all," Astrid said, her facial expression blank and her cheeks slightly flushed.

"I used to pity you then, but we were both in the same boat – under Francine's thumb. Only after the old man died, of course, because Francine couldn't have got away with it if he had still been there. Old Andy liked you a lot, you know."

Astrid remained silent, and Lilac didn't say how she'd often wondered if Andy Roydon had used Astrid as a fill-in for conjugal 'favours' after the death of his wife. Lilac had never voiced her suspicions and Astrid had never confided in her, either way. Such subjects were taboo between them.

Trying to drink slowly, Lilac observed Astrid's behaviour, wondering if her rapidly increasing inebriation would bring forth some hint of what she'd left in Cindy's letterbox. The chips were being consumed at the same rate as the sparkling wine. Lilac, taking a quick peek at the alcohol content on the label of the bottle, noticed with surprise it was thirteen percent. She'd have to be careful she didn't get too drunk herself, especially with Astrid continually topping her glass up.

"Listen... I'm kind of glad you're here, as a matter of fact," Astrid finally said, "because I wanted to ask you something."

"Go ahead, I'm listening." Lilac forgot to be cautious and took a large mouthful of wine, followed by some more chips.

"Well, you know how Francine and Cindy used to flirt around Aldo, all those years ago, when they were both mere children?"

"Oh yes, both girls were after Aldo."

"And didn't he know it. Andy warned Francine to behave herself, but of course, Francine wanted it all – she always did – and she got it most of the time. Her father used to tell her off, but mostly Andy would turn a blind eye. He was too busy with his business anyway, to keep an eye on what went on at home."

"After Morag died, he went to pieces," Lilac said knowingly. "He used to drink whisky straight out of the bottle and hide it in one of his desk drawers." Her expression was triumphant.

"Was that before I was taken on as their housekeeper?" Astrid said, frowning.

"Yes. Morag died in 2003, the same year Aldo and Cindy and all the other young teenagers started coming over to the house. They were all still at school then of course."

"Right... so it wasn't until 2005 that other things started to happen then?" Astrid seemed to have become enlivened now, as if she was re-living everything from the past.

"Exactly – when the girls turned sixteen. I helped out a bit in their house after Morag died – cooking, and cleaning etc. so I wasn't blind to what was going on."

Astrid got up unsteadily, wobbled over to the fridge and extracted another bottle of sparkling wine. "Let's have another, I need it. Well anyway, as I was saying, I wanted to ask you something."

As Astrid struggled to open the second bottle, Lilac was also getting drunk and began to care less. In fact, she liked being inebriated, as it felt as though all her worries were being taken away, gradually releasing her from their relentless grip. She wondered if Astrid had forgotten what she was going to ask her.

***

Benedict was sitting at his office desk, researching the German city of Bonn, when Gail said,

"So, what is it about the past that's got your interest?" She was pouring coffee from a large plunger on the bench, which she'd brought in from her own kitchen.

Benedict closed the tab he was looking at and swivelled around to face her. "I know it might sound strange, but I think there are secrets from the Roydons' past that somehow impact on the present case. As for their neighbour, Lilac Browne, this is definitely true. I'm hoping she will be the weak link; the one, in fact, who tells me what those secrets are."

"Lilac? What makes you so sure?"

"Probably pressure. Some people can take it, others can't. And Lilac, well, I suspect she's been sitting on something for years that she hasn't told a single soul about. I'm counting on this fact. I know she has one of my cards. Perhaps she wants to tell someone and I've given her the opportunity to tell me."

"So, what's next on the agenda?"

"We need to pay another visit to Roydons' Antiques. I'm still puzzled by the dagger used to despatch our murder victim. Where did it come from? Someone *must* know."

***

By the time Cindy arrived home, she was exhausted – both physically and emotionally. The long ride in the bus there and back, the pouring rain, and the way Jenniver had looked – all had taken their toll on Cindy's already fragile state. She was barely managing to keep herself going. It wasn't easy pretending to be the kind of person she wasn't; this persona of fun-loving, devil-may-care jollity wearing thinner by the day.

If she heard, "I don't know how you cope," or "You're so kind and yet look at what you have to deal with yourself," once more, she'd scream. The truth was, she wasn't coping or dealing with anything anymore; not after seeing the way Jenniver looked today – gaunt and hollow-eyed, her skin thin with a bluish sheen, probably from lack of sunlight. Cindy hoped her daughter wasn't ill.

"I'm worried about you, Mum," Jenniver had said, as soon as Cindy sat down. She had wanted to protest that she was fine, as she could see her daughter was the one who needed the concern, not her. Cindy had quickly asked her daughter the usual questions: is the food they give you okay? What do you do all day? You're not being bullied, are you? In return, she'd got the usual replies. Jenniver was good at evasion and Cindy suspected she'd learnt it from her mother over the years. Children always noticed when their parents weren't at their best, however hard they tried to camouflage it. And now she wondered why she'd even bothered to outwardly pretend to be someone else yet internally she was the same. What good had it done her? She briefly considered what life could have been like had she been totally honest all the time, showing her true self to those closest to her.

When she saw bruising around Jenniver's left eye,

she became even more afraid for her daughter. "You'd tell me if anyone was bullying you, wouldn't you, love?" Jenniver hadn't replied and that made Cindy worry even more. The abused were often too afraid to speak up for fear of retaliation.

"I'm glad you came over, Mum," Jenniver had said. "I love you."

Cindy was relieved, knowing then it was all going to be all right between them. "I love you too, darling. Don't ever forget that."

On the way back to Seagrove, Cindy sat next to a woman who'd said her name was Zoe. Zoe began crying softly but Cindy barely had the strength to offer her words of comfort. Her heart had shrivelled up, like a dried mushroom in her chest. However, despite this, she'd tried to offer the other woman some glimmer of hope to hold on to, after hearing how her oldest daughter was in prison for the third time and was now serving a seven-years' stretch.

Cindy parked her car in the driveway, letting out a sigh of relief. She got out, locked the car and looked in the letterbox before going inside. Her eyes widened in anticipation and surprise when she saw a package there. She eagerly took it out. Perhaps Gregor had sent her something from Scotland? However, there weren't any stamps on the package, and the address on the brown paper wrapping was written in an unfamiliar hand. She frowned and looked up and down the street, but there was no one about. Apart from a dog barking further along, the whole street was quiet. Usually, Mrs Shields, was out in the garden, tending to her flowers, but as it was now just after five in the evening, she would have long finished her outdoor tasks.

Although she was curious about what was inside the package, Cindy rushed inside and went straight to the fridge and pulled out a half-full bottle of white wine. She poured some into a glass and drank most of it in one go, before even taking off her coat and shoes. She eased her feet into a pair of fluffy pink scuffs she'd bought for wearing around the house.

Finally, she sat down with her now half-empty glass of wine. She took another big gulp and then picked up the package again. She looked at it, then shook it, holding it up against her ear for any sign of a clue, but nothing. Then Cindy went into the kitchen to fetch a knife from the draw and began to slit open the thick masking-tape.

Chapter 12

Friday 7th June

Early the next morning, Lilac woke up on Astrid's couch. She peered at her wristwatch with half-closed eyes: 7:12 a.m. She was still in her clothes and had a musty-smelling duvet covering her. There was a thick, fuzziness in her head and her mouth was dry. She remembered the night before as if it were something she'd dreamt about, weeks ago. She pushed herself upright. Everything was quiet, except for the snoring coming from Astrid's bedroom. Lilac quietly eased herself to her feet, folding the duvet neatly and placing it on the end of the couch. Her head throbbed as she walked to the kitchen, where she surveyed the mess on the table: two empty sparkling wine bottles, two wine glasses, and two empty chip packets.

She tip-toed stealthily towards Astrid's bedroom and peeked in. Astrid was lying on her back, with her mouth open, gently snoring. Lilac winced at the sight and quietly made her way to the front door. She left, got into her car and started the engine. She wondered if Miss Wilson was already at her window, witnessing her departure. It wasn't until she was nearly home that Lilac remembered what Astrid had told her. It was during their last glass of sparkling wine when by then Astrid's voice was slurred and her dark eyes were bleary-looking behind her spectacles. Despite being hampered by the alcohol, Lilac could still hear the words clearly and see the crooked, mad smile on Astrid's face: "Oh yes," she'd said, taking great pleasure in confessing to Lilac. "She'll be worried sick when she sees what I've left her. If only I could be there to see the look on her face when she sees the earring."

***

Once home again, and holding Scamper in her arms, Lilac wondered when Dominica would speak to her again. Her voice was becoming more and more insistent now. Lilac was guilt-ridden after helping Astrid. Why had she helped her? She knew the answer to that question: because she'd always helped Astrid and somewhere deep inside her, there was a compulsion to do so. Astrid had no one else, but despite this, Dominica had told her not to.

"Don't trust her, Lilac, she's up to no good. She can't be trusted. She's trouble with bells on."

And Lilac would try to answer her dear friend, "But you know why, Dominica. You know what happened and I can't free myself of it. It's tormenting me, day and night."

The important thing was that she and Astrid had once made a plan together to get rid of their tormentor – the one who had been threatening them both since 2007, after Andy Roydon had died. She'd been doing it for seventeen long years and Lilac had had enough. Lilac's house needed painting and repairing, but she never had enough money to do it because every so often, two hundred dollars had to be paid to Francine.

Lilac resented having to use the money Dominica had left her, as well as working three part-time jobs just to be able to give Francine the money whenever she decided she wanted it. Francine, in return, would fix her car whenever it needed it; something she liked to remind Lilac of in a patronising manner. Yet Francine would only repair the car when she wanted to. This meant that sometimes Lilac would have to wait for several weeks before Francine deigned to do the work. Then Francine would claim that her helping Lilac in this way was compensation for the money she demanded from her and made it equal. However, Lilac was no fool. She knew that Francine was making lots of money from this arrangement and doing just as she wanted, like she'd always done, right back to 2004, when she stole Aldo from Cindy.

Then everything changed when Cindy arrived back on the scene, in early April, 2024. Initially, Lilac hadn't known of Cindy's return; not until that day in mid to late April, when she'd seen her through the hedge. Aldo had told Lilac the year before how Jenniver had confronted Francine about being her half-sister.

Aldo had left soon after that, to live in the beachhouse, which was their holiday home, telling Lilac he never once entertained the idea of going back. Despite leaving the marital home, Aldo and Lilac had kept in touch – they'd been friends once upon a time but now, their friendship was hanging in the balance. Lilac didn't know who to trust anymore, and Dominica's warnings were crowding her mind more and more.

"Take care, Lilac. Be careful. Watch out."

When Astrid had told her about the contents of the package, Lilac remembered Dominica's warning: Astrid couldn't be trusted. Yet it seemed her old friend held everything in her hands and was in control, just as she'd always been. Ah, the cunning, knowing Astrid; the abused wife, but holding the trump card all the same.

Both Lilac and Dominica had known what Astrid endured, year after year at the hands of Elroy, but Astrid chose to shut all it out, believing she was the cause of all the abuse – the hitting, thumping, bruising and cutting – being thrown around and yet surviving. Astrid had come to serve her abuser like an idol worshipper because she told herself *she* was to blame. She, who considered herself to be so unworthy, began to live up to her own beliefs. This was how she coped. Until the day... something happened...

Lilac and Dominica researched Battered Woman Syndrome and discovered that one of the side effects for the victim was feeling as though they had no control. Once she had regained her freedom, she made up for this former lack of control in a big way. It had taken some time for her to realise that she now had the freedom to do what she wanted, but in the nineteen years since Elroy had been taken from her, Astrid had put into practice what taking back control really meant.

"What does the earring mean?" Lilac asked Dominica. "I have to talk about this to someone, I really do. I'm going mad without you. That's why you've got to help me, otherwise I might end up telling someone what really happened. You do understand, don't you? My love, the only one I've ever loved. Please."

Chapter 13

Saturday 8th June

The morning sun beamed through the kitchen window of Aldo's beach-house. It was his day off from the café and he sat quietly, listening to the muted sound of the waves, a blank notebook in front of him. Then he picked up his pen and tried to write down exactly what had happened on the day of the murder. Of course, he'd done all this before for his police statement and re-told it to Benedict Aberthorp, but now, in the peace of his own home, he wanted to think about it again, without anyone sitting and waiting, or with their eyes boring into him as his agitated mind scrambled to put everything in order.

He recalled Benedict's words: "What was the weather like that day, Aldo?"

First thing that morning it had been raining. It was dark outside and it had looked cold. He'd got up and pulled back the bedroom curtain, where the sea – a steely grey colour, was covered in white caps. The wind was getting stronger and seagulls swooped and dove in the distance.

On the day of his lunch with Francine, when Aldo was ready to leave home, he had put on his brown raincoat. It was about 11:40 a.m. He remembered the time because he had wanted to arrive early and spend time talking to Astrid, who would be in the kitchen making lunch. Francine was usually in her office and never came out until midday, even when Aldo was visiting. Her routine meant he could always count on some private time with Astrid, who'd been like a mother to him ever since he was seventeen and had just married Francine who was expecting his baby.

Aldo tried to visualise the house and whether there had been anything different that day as he walked from his car around to the back-door, which was always open. He'd called out Astrid's name as he came through to the kitchen, knowing she'd be standing at the bench, buttering the bread and selecting the sandwich fillings.

Sitting still and trying to conjure up the picture in his mind, Aldo gently willed himself to 'be back there' once again. Suddenly, he remembered how Astrid hadn't answered him straight-away and he'd had to call out again: "Astrid, it's me, Aldo."

"Won't be a minute, love," Astrid had eventually answered, and Aldo had taken off his raincoat and shook it out before going into the kitchen. He'd walked around a bit, looking at the way everything was, noting how it was mostly unchanged since he'd left the year before. Then Scamper had come in and run up to him, meowing and purring loudly while rubbing his body against Aldo's legs. He'd stooped down to pat him and told him how much he missed him.

"Now I remember," Aldo said aloud, "there was something on the floor." He recalled reaching down to pick it up, just as Astrid came into the kitchen. It was an earring in the shape of a sun. The sun had a bluish tinge, and a face, surrounded by seven rays coloured green and edged with gold.

Then Astrid was beside him. "Oh, you found my old earring. I wondered where it was" She had reached out her plump hand and Aldo had placed the earring on her palm, whereupon Astrid's fingers had closed around it tightly, swiftly slipping it into her apron pocket. "Nice to see you, love," Astrid had said, and embraced Aldo warmly as she always did.

He'd hung his raincoat on a hook in the kitchen, and later taken it down to put back on when he left.

Aldo opened his eyes and began to write. He didn't know why, but until now he'd completely forgotten the earring. Of course, it meant nothing to anyone, so it didn't matter; it was only an earring. The only strange thing about it, Aldo thought now, was the fact that he didn't usually see her wearing earrings so he was surprised it was hers.

When Aldo closed his eyes again, enjoying the heat of the hot sun streaming through the window, a vague recollection came back to him. He'd seen a similar earring before as a teenager. It had been one of a pair. They were unusual because one earring was in the shape of the sun and the other a crescent moon – Cloisonné earrings. They belonged to Cindy, but he didn't know who had given them to her. Aldo had admired them, and hoped they hadn't been a gift from Andy Roydon. He hated the idea of Andy Roydon sleeping with Cindy. At forty, he was old enough to be her father.

Aldo had wanted to warn Cindy. After all, she was so young. Her mother had died of leukaemia, and because her father was always going away on business, Cindy was often left alone in the house. When her father met and fell in love with a Scottish woman, the couple moved to the Highlands of Scotland in November, 2004 in order to fulfil her longing to own a sheep farm. Cindy went with them – reluctantly, as it turned out.

Aldo was well aware why things had not turned out well for Cindy, but he didn't want to dwell on the past. Yet even as he tried not to, the memories pushed themselves to the front of his mind, so that now, even though the sun was coming through the window, he felt cold all over. What was Cindy's earring doing on the kitchen floor of the Roydons' house, twenty years after she'd left? And, more importantly, it had been seen on the very day Francine was found dead.

He laughed to himself. "Don't be silly," he said aloud. "Anyone could have the same earrings." It was too much of a coincidence for him to be convinced, however, especially given the fact that Cindy was back and had been at the Roydons' house in April *this* year. Himself, Astrid and Cindy, had sat out on the lawn and talked for two hours while Francine was out. Cindy hadn't gone there to see Francine, and most likely didn't even want her to know she'd been there, but it was highly likely that Francine would find out Cindy had been in her home.

After a few minutes, Aldo picked up his pen again and began to scribble in his notebook, the one Benedict had told him to keep so he could jot things down – anything at all, even if it seemed trivial or insignificant. Aldo was now doing as he'd been told. When he'd finished writing, he sighed and got up to make himself a cup of coffee.

While drinking it, he kept asking himself why he'd written this down. After all, it was only an earring, but if it did belong to Cindy, then it linked her to the house on the day Francine was murdered. He had learnt to trust his gut instinct, and if he didn't write it down, the thought would still keep coming back. He asked himself why had he not remembered this incident at the time he was giving a statement to the police? And then again when Benedict questioned him? He was second-guessing himself now. Perhaps he had known all along but had decided not to say anything? Like the time when he was seventeen and had done something dishonest. He hadn't told anyone then either – not a single soul.

***

"I've had a phone-call from Wendy Seyner," Benedict told Gail, who gave him a quizzical frown. "You know, they live in the house that backs onto the Roydons' property. Haven't I told you?"

"No, I don't think so."

"Anyway, I was told by Wendy that Wayne Seyner, her husband, had been laid up with a broken leg and had to go back into hospital to have the fracture re-set. That's why she's phoned me: he's back home now, so we can go round there to interview them."

"Great. When are we going?"

"Now, my friend, and who knows what they might have to say."

The Seyners lived in Mayflower Street, which ran parallel to Korimako Street. Their front yard was separated from the Roydons' plot, by a corrugated iron fence. The fence wasn't tall enough to completely block out everything, as the Seyners' house was two-storey, but did give each neighbour sufficient privacy. If standing in the back yard of each property, in order to see over the fence would necessitate standing beside it on tip-toes, or climbing a ladder or a tree. A few houses down from the Seyners' was an alley-way connecting Mayflower Street with the upmarket Korimako Street properties, much to the disdain of several Korimako Street snobs. They considered themselves to be a superior social class to the residents of Mayflower Street.

"Here it is," Benedict said, as he parked outside number thirteen – a grey, roughcast house with a picket fence displaying off-white, peeling paint.

"Come on in, dearies," Wendy Seyner said with a beaming smile, ushering them in through the kitchen to the lounge room. Wayne was sitting back in a recliner chair, with his newly-plastered leg on display. The couple looked to be in their early-to-mid-eighties.

"Here's Wayne, just home from hospital yesterday, weren't you, dear?"

"Oh, yes, freshly out yesterday!" he said. "And about time too. They didn't set the fracture straight the first time and so it had to be done again."

"I believe your accident occurred on the same day your neighbour was murdered," Benedict said, pleased to find them to be jovial characters who didn't seem to mind being interviewed.

"Right. I had to prune the orange tree, see. Ms Roydon had asked me twice already to do something about it. You'll see it if you go around the back. Anyway, I got out my pruning saw and ladder and set it all up. Then I started work." He paused and looked over at Wendy. "She's heard it all before a few times, haven't you, love?"

"Sure, I have, but not these folks. So you tell them exactly what you told me."

"I don't like to say anything out of place…" He looked questioningly at Benedict.

"It's all right, Mr Seyner. Anything you tell us is confidential."

"Well then, I was up the ladder, like I said, pruning the branches of the orange tree when I witnessed something funny.

"They've got a *big* property." He gave Benedict a meaningful look. "You've seen it, Mr Aberthorp?"

"Yes, I have. Do go on, Mr Seyner."

"Look, I'll be honest with you: I wanted to have a closer look into their back-yard, otherwise I probably would've left the pruning to a later date, and that particular part of their yard couldn't be seen properly from our upstairs window. The night before, I saw a light coming through the hedge, right by our downstairs bedroom window, and it was driving me mad. I could hear voices too – the hedge is a bit thin here, you see – but not what they were actually saying.

"Anyway, when I climbed up that ladder next day, I realised why there had been a light shining through our hedge the night before. There must've been someone staying in the gottage overnight, in the Roydons' backyard. The light wouldn't have been visible from the Roydons' main property, however, because the gottage is too far back, right next to the hedge by our place."

Benedict nodded empathetically. "Go on, Mr Seyner, what funny thing did you see?"

"Not really funny, just odd if you ask me. It was by the gazebo – something long, like a thick carpet or mat rolled up on the ground. I was leaning over at the time, trying to reach a branch that was hanging right into their yard. Well, the rolled-up thing looked weird. I got to the branch and was half-way through sawing it when I bloody fell off the ladder! There was a woman with blonde hair running across the lawn just before that happened. Only Wendy tells me I was knocked out, so I could've imagined seeing her. I lost my memory for a while, didn't I, love?"

"Yes, sweetie, so you probably were mistaken. The housekeeper's got dark hair, hasn't she? I saw her quite often, when I looked out of our upstairs window, in the yard, hanging out the washing. She's been there for years, but I think I've only spoken to her twice. I don't ever recall seeing a woman with blonde hair though, unless she's had it bleached."

"Maybe I was seeing things at the time, although it might have been the housekeeper, Wendy was just referring to. She walks through the alley to reach her flat, because she only works part-time for Ms Roydon since Mr Roydon went to live in the beach-house. People tell me things down at the club, you know," Wayne said, giving Benedict a wink. "I've seen her walking through the alley to her place, going backwards and forwards to work. She's got a place in them block of flats. Me mate, Dave, lives there and he spends all his time watching everyone out the window. Nothing else to do, he reckons. Apparently, they're all doing it; spend their days like caged animals, watching to see who's out there. He told me he sees her coming and going through the alley, to the Four Square in Mayflower Street, and probably further afield, to the Roydons'. But *her* hair is black and she has it in a bun and wears gold-rimmed glasses. Scary-looking if you ask me."

"Now, now, love, you don't know what she's like. Appearances can be deceiving. The times I spoke to her she was pleasant enough. Didn't say much, but she wasn't rude or anything."

"Yes, but you are friends with everyone, aren't you, love?"

"I like to be neighbourly."

"So, did you happen to see the rolled-up carpet too, Mrs Seyner?" Benedict said.

"No, I didn't even look over there. I had to call an ambulance and get this man to hospital quickly. He looked terrible. I was terrified he was dead. Couldn't get no response or nothing."

"Take more than that to kill me. Can't kill weeds you know!"

"Oh, I almost forgot to ask: were you living here in 2005?" Benedict directed his question at Wendy.

"Yes. Why do you ask?"

"I know it's a long shot, but do you recall anything happening in the neighbourhood that year? Someone moving house, for example?"

Wendy and Wayne looked at each other and smiled. "I'm afraid I'll have to get out my old diary to be able to tell you that, Mr Aberthorp. Our memories aren't what they used to be. Can I call you back when I've found something?"

***

From her flat on Fernhill Crescent, Astrid walked along the connecting alleyway, emerging out into Mayflower Street. There, Astrid observed Benedict's BMW pulling up outside the Seyners'. She stood rooted to the spot in fright. What was the private investigator doing there? She carried on, into the supermarket, where she stopped to look out the window, her eyes, like beacons, trained on his car. From her vantage point she saw Benedict and his sidekick – the blonde fancy-lady who seemed to accompany him everywhere. They were entering the Seyners' house. *What the hell do they want with them?* she thought.

And then Astrid remembered. "Silly old me," she said softly to herself, as she picked up a plastic basket at the door to the supermarket and started strolling slowly up one of the aisles. She'd seen the old bugger, Wayne, on the day in question, up a ladder pruning that orange tree. Then he'd disappeared from view. She supposed he'd fallen off the ladder because a short time later there were voices talking loudly over the back fence. She'd picked up enough words to know the silly old coot was being taken away in an ambulance. *Serve him right for not taking the proper precautions,* she thought uncharitably. Suddenly, a knot of anxiety began forming in her stomach. "So... what exactly had he seen?" she said absently to herself, as she searched the shelves. "Oh well, there's nothing I can do about that now."

She pushed the anxious thoughts away and picked out two bottles of sparkling wine, four packets of chips and a bag of salted peanuts, before going to the vegetable aisle. "First things first," she said softly, humming a tuneless ditty as she walked. Then she stopped. The old coot must have seen something while he was up on his ladder, and was probably now telling that private investigator all about it right now. She tried to remember what time she'd seen him that day, but couldn't.

Astrid missed her friend, Lilac. The other night had been like old times – sitting, chatting and drinking together. She enjoyed that comradeship more than anything else these days, so made up her mind to invite Lilac to drink with her again. She still hadn't managed to sort out her non-working phone, but she didn't need it anyway. In fact, she was thinking of just throwing it away and not bother replacing it. Lilac only lived a couple of streets away so she could just walk to her house whenever she wanted a chat.

As she walked up and down the aisles, looking for special offers and wondering what to have for tea later on, she began thinking about 2006 – New Year's Eve, to be exact.

Before she became the Roydons' housekeeper and Elroy was their head buyer, she and her husband had spent many evenings in the company of Andy and Morag Roydon. Mr Roydon had always liked them to call him Andy, but things changed after Elroy died. When she was appointed the Roydons' housekeeper her status changed too, and soon after she started her employment, Andy told her that it might be best all round if she addressed him as Mr Roydon.

To celebrate New Year's Eve, Francine, Aldo and Mr Roydon had stayed up late to welcome in 2007. Astrid had served the family all evening, making them coffee, bringing in alcohol, and placing bowls of chips and cocktail sausages down in front of them. It had been a jovial night; Mr Roydon downing numerous shots of whisky over ice – ice that Astrid had been asked to bring in every now and then, post-haste. Finally, they'd all gone to bed and she remembered how relieved she'd been. Mr Roydon had been ogling her all night, especially when she'd had to bend over and place dishes on the small table beside his armchair.

Astrid stopped in front of the toothpaste stand as she vividly recalled how she'd just put the light out in her small bedroom on the ground floor, when someone had turned the handle slowly and opened the door. "*Shhh,*" a man's voice had said. And suddenly there he was – standing beside her bed, looking down at her and telling her to move over. Astrid had been shocked but hadn't protested. There was too much at stake.

After that first time he'd visit repeatedly, waiting until the others were asleep before making his descent down the stairs and into her room. He would appear at random times and that made their affair all the more exciting and somehow dangerous, which added to the thrill. Of course, the next day, she had to go back to being their lowly housekeeper and glorified maid, which was humiliating for her. After he died of a heart attack later that year, her shame grew a thousand-fold as Francine began treating her like her personal slave. She told her she'd always known what Astrid and her father had been up to and despised her for it. Now, Astrid must do whatever Francine said or she threatened her with the loss of her job and home, on top of revealing the other secret that no one ever talked about. Astrid gave in to her demands out of sheer terror, but not before reminding Francine that she had also been involved in the 2005 secret. Francine had simply smirked and walked away.

***

Instead of going straight home, Astrid went to Lilac's house. She needed the comfort of chatting to her old friend; the only one left now with whom she could share her memories and past trepidations.

"Oh, it's you, Astrid. What a surprise." Lilac had been enjoying her own company and was reluctant to invite Astrid in. "Why are you here? Is there something going on?"

Astrid walked past Lilac and stood in the kitchen. "The P.I. Has he been doing any more questioning? Or probing into your younger days?"

"Oh God, he's a real digger, he is. Seems to think something happened back then that has a bearing on now, for goodness's sake!"

"Why on earth would he think that?"

Lilac sucked in her breath, her chest tight all of a sudden. "I have no idea. How could I possibly know what he's thinking?"

"Did he ask you for an address? You know what I mean?"

"Yes, and I gave it to him."

"You what?"

"It's all right. Don't worry, Astrid. You and I are the only ones left now."

"No, we're not. There's Aldo."

"He was away at the time, and even when he got

back, he was sick for ages; lying around, trying to get his head sorted."

"What about Cindy?"

Lilac looked hard at Astrid, not understanding what she meant. "You betrayed my trust, Astrid. We had a plan. Remember?"

"Look, aren't you going to at least offer me a seat? Can't we have a wee tipple together? Have you eaten yet?"

Lilac decided it was better to at least pretend to be friends again with Astrid. This seemed to her to be a way she could at least cope with Astrid continually turning up out of the blue. "Yes, I have, but I'd love some of that macaroni cheese you make some time. I really like the way you do it."

"Then come round tomorrow night and I'll make us some."

Lilac forced a smile and took a deep breath. "I'd love to. Want a hot drink and a toasted sandwich before you go?"

***

Later that night, Benedict's phone rang as he was putting away his supper dishes.

"Benedict Aberthorp."

"Wendy Seyner here. I've looked in one of our photo albums and discovered that Wayne and I went to Australia in 2005. We took a tour in the Northern Territory in February and arrived back the second week in March. Neither of us have ever forgotten that trip."

"Thanks for getting back to me, Mrs Seyner. So, when you arrived back did you notice anything different in the neighbourhood?"

"It's funny you should mention that, Mr Aberthorp. You see Wayne and I have been discussing this and racking our brains to recall what it was that struck us as unusual when we got back."

"Yes?"

"I don't remember the exact date, but I know that the Trescos, who lived next to the Roydons in Korimako Street, had moved out because there was a 'sold' sticker on a sign outside their house."

"Did anyone say why they had moved or where they'd gone?"

"No, because we weren't really close to anyone in Korimako Street. We only realised they'd sold their house when we took a walk that way a couple of days after arriving back from Australia. Wayne and I always walked around the streets in the early evening, to help us keep in shape."

"Well, thank you so much for getting back to me,

Mrs Seyner. You've been most helpful."

"Glad to be of assistance."

Chapter 14

Sunday 9th June

The rain had stopped and the cloud-streaked sky seemed to stretch to infinity as Benedict walked along the wide footpath by Seagrove's waterfront. There was a small group of women who laughed as they took a dip in the shallows; the strong current meant it was too dangerous to venture further than that. Benedict removed his sandals and stepped down onto the warm, smooth pebbles which covered the beach. The feel of them beneath his feet brought with it a perfect kind of joy at simply being alive. A group of seagulls stayed in situ as he passed; unafraid of this middle-aged man, sharing their space. Knowing that the beach dropped away suddenly further out, he tentatively ventured a few steps only, into the sea. He rolled his cotton trousers up to his knees and went to the water's edge, where the sea surged, frothy and white over his toes, then further up his calves and even right up to his knees, wetting his trousers. Benedict didn't care about the dampness of his trouser legs. A faint breeze stirred his senses and reminded him that there were still so many pieces of the puzzle he didn't understand.

How was he going to work out what all the pieces of the puzzle meant? What was he going to say to Aldo when they next met? He was paying Benedict to find his wife's killer and expected answers. Whatever conclusions Benedict drew would be the truth, because for him, truth was of the utmost importance.

Later, as Benedict walked back to his car, his phone rang.

"It's me, Aldo, I've got something I need to tell you. Can you come to my beach-house?"

"Sure. Are you alright?"

"Yes. Can you come round now?"

"I'm on my way." Benedict was excited, as well as a little alarmed, at Aldo's tone. Perhaps Aldo had come to some sort of decision about something and finally wanted to get it off his chest?

***

When Benedict arrived at the beach-house, Aldo's pale face looked drawn, and there were dark circles under his eyes. He was holding a glass half-full of wine, and Benedict remembered again the first day he'd met him when Aldo had told him he didn't drink.

"I have a confession to make," Aldo said now, as if reading Benedict's mind. "I like alcohol and drink it often, even though I know it's not good for me. But I don't over-indulge anymore."

"It's not my place to judge. So, what were you going to tell me?"

"There are a hundred things, but first I need to tell you the truth: I was responsible for me and Cindy's breakup. I'm ashamed of myself now, but at the time I was desperate. So, twenty years ago, I used Francine's cell-phone to text Cindy and make out that Francine was telling Cindy that I was also having a relationship with Francine and didn't want Cindy around anymore. The message did enough damage for Cindy to turn away from me. Before anyone could find out the truth, Cindy was leaving for Scotland and I'd asked Francine to marry me. Once Francine became pregnant, her father insisted I marry his daughter, otherwise Francine's allowance would be cut off. But I wanted to marry her anyway. We were in love."

"And now, with Cindy's return, what you did has come back to haunt you?"

"Yes, and that's why I blame myself for what happened when Jenniver came to the house to tell Francine she was her half-sister. Francine's turning her away like that was the last straw for me. Although I knew in my heart that it wasn't really my fault that she had an affair with Andy Roydon, and I had no way of knowing that Jenniver would one day claim kin with my wife and she'd turn her away. Nevertheless, it was then that I decided to move out. Our marriage was one of pretence by then anyway, and had been for years. She'd been having affairs ever since her dad died; maybe even before, for all I know." He picked up his glass again and took a swig.

Benedict stood up and went to the window. "So, I guess what you're saying is that you think it was Cindy who sent you that text?"

"Yes, although she's never said anything to imply as much. To be honest I hardly ever see her now. There *was* that business here though when someone broke into the beach-house. I'm sure it was her."

"Have there been any other incidents since you returned home from Astrid's?"

"I'm afraid so, and I'm sorry I didn't tell you. I regretted what I'd done years ago, and was too ashamed to admit it to you. I came home one day to find that someone had shifted a potted-plant on the deck."

"Any more incidences?"

He seemed reluctant to tell Benedict at first, but then began talking. "Yes. The next time I was convinced it was definitely Cindy. The word *guilty* had been spelt out in pebbles on my deck. I nearly phoned you, but there was nothing anyone could do, so I decided to tough it out."

"*Mmm,* I'd rather you had let me know, then Gail and I could have set something up to prove who'd done it, should they attempt anything like it again. It's always good to have proof."

"You mean like a hidden camera or something?"

"Possibly. Did you keep in touch with Cindy after she went overseas?"

"No. I didn't even try to contact her – not after what I'd done and the hurt feelings I caused. Andy Roydon never contacted her either, according to Francine. He even denied he was the father of her child."

"It would appear as though she has made a good life for herself in Scotland, with her husband. Perhaps you don't need to worry."

"But what about Francine's murder? Did Cindy have something to do with it? She might have hated the way Francine rejected Jenniver, who is now in prison as a result."

Benedict didn't tell Aldo that Cindy was his prime

suspect, although he had three other names written down too. He chose to conceal the fact that Aldo was among them. "You don't really think she could be capable of such a thing?"

"Well, she does have a motive – more than one. And there's something else: when we did meet up – with Astrid too, Cindy seemed distant and unfriendly at first – but later she was overly friendly and cheerful. I don't think she even wanted to see me initially – but she did eventually. I got the impression she was hiding her true feelings about me as she suddenly became overly friendly and cheerful in my company. Then I started to feel guilty again for what I'd done all those years ago."

"Was this meeting before Francine was killed?"

"Yes, soon after Cindy arrived. It was near the beginning of April, not long after Jenniver went to prison." Aldo drank the last of his wine and stood up. "Would you like a glass?"

Benedict wanted Aldo to trust him, so he agreed. "Sure, I'll have one."

A few moments later, Aldo passed Benedict a large, glass of white wine that he'd poured from a carafe in the fridge. Benedict took a sip of the cool, semi-sweet liquid.

"You could say I have a motive too, if you want to know the truth," Aldo said.

"Really?" Benedict said.

"Our house, for one thing. She's left it to Tegan Tresco. She left me the beach-house and enough money to comfortably keep me going for life, but the house was left to Tegan. The rest of her money – a large amount – is for her and Tegan's child, to be kept in trust until the child turns eighteen. The house will go into Tegan's name, if it isn't already. Only the beach-house is mine. Francine hadn't told me about all this, by the way, but she had told me she'd met a woman she was in love with and they were planning on having a baby together. I think it's due in August. I don't care about the house, anyway; it holds nothing but sad memories for me. This place is different though, I nearly always stayed here alone because Francine didn't like being so close to the sea. She once told me she hated the sound of it. I don't know why."

They sipped their wine in silence. If Aldo was being truthful, most of the facts he'd told Benedict would only have been made known to him *after* Francine's death; all except the part about Tegan. Aldo had known she had a lover of that name, but didn't know then it was the same Tegan who, as a child, had once lived next door to the Roydons.

Benedict finished his wine and said, "Have you been writing anything in your notebook?"

"Nothing of any importance, although there was something trivial I remembered. I did as you said and wrote it down."

Benedict's suspicion was aroused. "Well, you know how it is," he said, leaning forward, "even a tiny morsel may be important. Do you mind telling me about it?"

"It was the same day as Francine's murder. I was in the kitchen, just before lunch, when I noticed on the floor a Cloisonné earring in the shape of the sun's face. It was a design I recognised as Cindy used to have a pair just like it – a sun for one earlobe, a moon for the other. They were attractive. I'd bent down to pat Scamper, you see, and the earring was tucked under the cupboard. I picked it up. Then Astrid came in and said it was hers so I gave it to her. She was pleased I'd found it and slipped it into her apron pocket."

"So, it belonged to Astrid, then?"

"I don't think so. I've known her for a long time and I've never seen her wear earrings."

***

Cindy was putting on her trench-coat in preparation for another visit to the prison. She picked up the small box that had been left in her letterbox. It contained an earring, shaped like the sun; a Cloisonné earring just like one of the pair she'd been secretly given by Andy Roydon for her sixteenth birthday. She'd always loved the earrings but the one someone had left in her letterbox, made her tremble. She found it hard to breathe. Where was the other one?

She'd taken them off and slipped them in her pocket on the day of the murder. Somehow, they must've fallen out of her pocket. She realised she'd lost them because the following day she'd searched everywhere, desperately trying to find them. It would seem she had been careless and now someone had found the earring. She reasoned it had to be Astrid, because she worked there. Lilac visited from time-to-time, as had Aldo before Francine's death, but he wouldn't be going there now so it couldn't have been him. Unless he'd found them on that day, when he came for lunch? If only she could remember.

As Cindy walked to the garage, Mrs Shields was in the neighbouring garden, bending over her marigolds. "Oh, Mrs Carollan, I meant to tell you: yesterday a woman put something in your letterbox as she passed by. You were out at the time. Not the postman. The woman had blonde hair, and wore a hat. Do you know her, dear?"

Cindy stopped in her tracks. She didn't know a woman with blonde hair; not in Seagrove anyway.

"Thank you, Mrs Shields. Yes, I did get the parcel. I noticed it didn't have a stamp on it."

"She was wearing a long black coat, dear. A stout woman, with dark glasses."

"Thanks so much for telling me, Mrs Shields. I really do appreciate it. Well, I must be going, I have an appointment."

Mrs Shields smiled before watching Cindy getting into her car and driving off. The automatic garage door came down with a low rumble as the car sped away. Mrs Shields frowned as she bent down and began plucking dead leaves from around the flowers.

***

Lilac was sitting in her car, watching as Cindy drove past. It was not a usual prison-visiting day for Cindy and yet there she was. After waiting a few minutes, Lilac drove to the bus station. Was Cindy breaking with routine by going to the prison two days in a row?

As she drove into the car-park, Lilac looked over towards the prison bus. Its passengers were just starting to board, and Cindy was among them. Lilac stared hard and then blinked, as her eyes started to water. She wondered if the parcel Astrid had left in Cindy's letterbox had affected her badly enough for her to now have to rush off to tell her daughter all about it.

Once Cindy had climbed aboard and found her seat, Lilac lowered the car windows and lit a cigarette. She didn't like smoking and driving at the same time, so waited a couple of minutes to enjoy the cigarette. Lilac then stubbed it out in her car's ashtray, started the engine and drove off. She was going to Astrid's place for tea that night and couldn't wait to see her face when she told her of this unexpected happening. Lilac laughed softly as she pulled out of the car-park and headed home.

She didn't notice the BMW pulling out just after her, Benedict Aberthorp at the wheel. Benedict was aware of Lilac's comings and goings in Plover Street, and was interested to note Lilac's reaction when Cindy had broken her normal routine. Benedict, too, was interested, not just in Cindy's behaviour, but also in Lilac's. Gail had told him about the stout, blonde, Fedora-hatted, black-coated woman with dark-glasses she'd seen getting into a red car yesterday. By chance, Gail had been at Benedict's house picking up some notes he'd requested, when she had glanced out of the lounge window and seen Lilac driving away with a passenger in disguise.

***

While walking up the path towards Astrid's flat, Lilac couldn't help but notice Miss Wilson's curtain falling back into place. The movement was so slight, she was sure Miss Nosey Neighbour had no idea Lilac had even seen it. Lilac's only reaction was the sucking in of her breath as she knocked on Astrid's door. She imagined Miss Wilson's probing eyes, boring holes in her back, and could imagine the old prune picking up her knitting to resume the *click-clack* of her needles.

It was nearly five thirty p.m. Astrid took a while to answer the door before swinging it wide and beaming as Lilac entered. "Sorry, I was just grating some cheese for our tea."

"It's okay, no rush."

"I suppose Miss Wilson is still on guard duty?" Astrid smirked.

"Yes. Her curtain moved as I came to the door."

"She's in good form then. At least I don't get burgled – not with her around, anyway! Let's have a drink before tea, shall we?"

"Yes, let's," Lilac said, taking off her coat and hanging it behind the door.

"Come on then, love. Come into the lounge this time. All I have to do now is cook the pasta, but that can wait. Or are you hungry?"

Lilac was, but didn't say as much. "No, I can wait, it's all right."

"Good, then let's get started."

"*Mmm*, nice," Lilac said, after taking her first sip. "Same as last time." She watched as Astrid took a long swig, the way she always did. Astrid liked to get drunk quickly.

"You know, I've been thinking about what you said." Astrid took another swallow and Lilac saw Astrid's wine glass was nearly empty already. "You know, about me and Cindy – the way she got all friendly with Aldo and me when she first arrived back. It wasn't supposed to happen the way it did, you know. How was I to know she was going to turn up out of the blue? She was always strange, darting about the place, never telling anyone what she was up to."

"It's all right, I don't even want to know about it," Lilac said, a little nervous now as Astrid launched forth on a subject that always seemed to get both of them feeling anxious.

"No, it's not all right, Lilac. I'm not happy about Cindy, coming along like she did and interfering in our lives again. She had no right. And now she's avoiding me like the plague." Astrid filled her glass again and stared straight ahead as if she was thinking hard. Lilac sensed she was stewing on something and pretty soon she'd want to talk about it.

"It's Aldo I feel sorry for now," Astrid finally said. "What with Tegan getting the house left to her and a large swag of money put aside for the child when it turns eighteen."

"Oh dear, I didn't know." Lilac finished her first glass and Astrid leaned over to immediately re-fill it.

"Aldo does have the beach-house though and he loves it there, always has, poor man. Mind you, he did something pretty bad way back, and now… well, he's not had a lot going for him ever since, if you ask me," Astrid said, nonchalantly.

Lilac had no idea as to what Astrid was referring, and found herself not really caring anymore. A fuzzy haze had begun to penetrate her brain, and she remembered the wine's thirteen percent alcohol content. She needed its strength right now, and drinking on an empty stomach was accelerating her rate of inebriation. Astrid was still talking, as if to herself.

"First Francine lost her baby, and then she was carrying on with various men *and* women. Finally, it was Tegan who must be about six months pregnant by now, by all accounts. I know a lot more than Aldo does, I can tell you. She came to the house often enough, did Tegan. And my job was to make them lunch, wasn't it? I never said a word to Aldo about Tegan getting pregnant. I figured he was better off not knowing."

"If it wasn't for you, Aldo wouldn't have stayed with Francine as long as he did," Lilac said. "You were like a mother to him. At least he's made his own life now – up there on the hill overlooking the bay, and working part-time at the café. I think he's going to be okay," Lilac said, a dreamy look on her face. She was a true romantic at heart.

Lilac didn't like to remind Astrid of the fact that originally, they had planned to frame Aldo for Francine's murder. With the numbing effects of the wine, none of that mattered now. She looked over at Astrid, who was slurping down the last drops of her second glass of wine. Her eyes had a glassy look and her spectacles were slipping down her nose.

"How could we have been so callous? Which brings me to a change of plan, Lilac – the reason why I wanted you to come over tonight." Astrid's face had become stern now, bordering on severe.

Lilac nearly choked. What on earth was Astrid getting at? "Change of plan? You mean our *original* plan?"

"Well, we won't go into the details right now, but yes, of course I do. I'm referring to the raincoat. I want you to bring Aldo's raincoat here and we're going to find a way to hide it in Cindy's house. I think Cindy is the one who deserves to be blamed now."

Lilac's body went cold all over and she could hardly breathe. She remembered Aldo's brown raincoat, sitting in the back of Astrid's wardrobe in the dust, surrounded by ancient, smelly old shoes. How was she going to get it back again? Her mind was spinning. "The raincoat. Yes, all right, I'll bring it round next time I come." Lilac tried to keep her voice normal, but it seemed to be coming out in a scratchy, high-pitched tone.

"You hadn't forgotten about it, had you?" Astrid was looking closely at her now, scrutinising her face with her dark, alcohol-filmed eyes.

Lilac laughed. "No, of course not. How could I forget?"

"Okay. Anyway, I'll be doing my housework job tomorrow – and the ironing, of course but you could bring it round later tomorrow. Say about four-thirty? In the meantime, why don't we have our macaroni cheese and we can talk about how we're going to get into Cindy's place to plant it there for Benedict to find. I need your help with this, so don't let me down. And don't tell anyone about it. All right?" Astrid was standing now, her two hands flat on the table, leaning towards Lilac as she spoke.

Lilac squeezed her hands together under the table.

"Of course I won't. I know how to keep things to myself."

***

When she finally drove home and parked her car in the driveway, Lilac was trembling and struggling to regulate her breathing. Scamper ran to greet her and she scooped him up, stroking his fluffy fur. "Poor Scamper, your mummy's in a whole lot of trouble now. Oh, yes, she is. And she has to think of something fast. You'll help me, won't you, puss-cat? I know you will."

As she lay in bed, Dominica's words were like a torrent of hailstones, raining down into her tired mind: "Look what you've done now. I told you not to trust her. Go there tomorrow, get the coat. She won't know. Don't let her take over your life. I've been warning you, now I mean it. Be careful, watch out."

Lilac pictured Miss Wilson, sitting near her window, watching everything. If only the old woman would go out. She wondered how she could lure Miss Wilson out of her flat, so she could sneak into Astrid's unobserved to get the coat. She grabbed the telephone directory and began going through the Wilsons' listed in Seagrove. There weren't many entrants – not many residents still had a landline – but Lilac was gambling on the fact that Miss Wilson did.

Chapter 15

Monday 10th June

"C'mon, let's see what Charley has to say about Elroy. He must know something about him. Even though he was long gone before Charley started working at the shop, if Charley was a regular visitor to the Roydons' in his teens, he might've met Elroy at their house at some stage," Benedict said.

"Yeah, I reckon he might. It's worth a try." Gail folded down the lid of her laptop and reached for her jacket.

They found a parking space just along the street and entered the shop, Benedict going in first. Charley's thickset frame leaned on the counter and his bald head was shiny as he pored over an old-looking brass table lamp before him. A middle-aged woman was standing nearby, waiting expectantly.

The private investigator and his assistant busied themselves by walking around the shop, browsing. After a while the woman left and they approached the counter.

"Hello again. Have you got anywhere yet? With the case I mean?" Charley said.

"Things are moving along. Actually, that's why we're here. You see, we've been doing a little background research into the Roydon family and their close friends to see if there's any connection between past and present."

"Really? So you think something in Francine's past could've caused someone to want her dead?" Charley ran a hand over his face and Benedict noticed he had a thick growth of stubble.

"It's always a possibility. Do you have time for a chat?"

"Yes, of course I do. Come out the back. The shop bell will ring if anyone comes in."

They followed him as before and were soon sitting at the same faded yellow table. Gail had her pen and notebook ready and Benedict had a headful of questions.

"So, how can I help you?" Charley said, taking off his glasses and inspecting them carefully for specs of dust.

"It's about Elroy Lorning," Benedict said, noting Charley's slight intake of breath at the mention of the name. "Did you ever meet him at the Roydons' when you were a teenager?"

Charley picked up a soft-looking cloth from the table and began to polish his glasses slowly and carefully before answering. "Yes, of course. I met Elroy on several occasions. He and his wife were regular visitors at the Roydons'. I'd see them when I'd go there to hang out with Francine, Aldo and a few other school friends."

"Can you tell us anything about him? What sort of a person he was? We're just trying to form a picture of his personality and what he was like, you see."

Charley paused for a while, breathing on the lenses of his glasses, and polishing them again, as if he was thinking hard. Then he said, "I might as well tell you what I was told about him. It could help you; I don't know." He put the glasses back on and began. "I was told he used to lay into his wife – like, all the time. Apparently, she was used to it so didn't even try to do anything about it. I remember noticing she wore a lot of makeup. Then later, after he'd gone, she started working for the Roydons as a housekeeper. When I got out of prison, I used to see her there at the house all the time. She'd changed a lot by then, of course."

"*Mmm*, so you were in prison when Elroy died. Did you ever hear what happened to him?"

Charley took a deep breath. "Speculation was all. The story was that he and Astrid had gone over to Germany to see her mother and it's where Elroy was attacked and killed. Francine told us about it. She also told me something else."

"She did?" Benedict's interest was piqued, wondering if he and Gail were finally going to find out what had really happened to Elroy. "It would be a great help if you could tell us what that was." He watched Charley's face, which now looked as if he was relieved to be finally speaking the truth.

"Francine told me I wasn't to say anything to anyone, but I will tell you this much: the Lorning's never even went to Germany in 2005. I often wonder why they'd said they had."

"Did you ever find out why? Did Francine say?"

Charley suddenly became guarded, as if he'd already said too much. "Look, I'm sorry, but I can't tell you any more about it. I didn't like Elroy. None of us did. He was a weasel of a man, who tried to act tough. I think he hated women, full stop."

"All right. Thanks for being so candid." Benedict paused for a while in the hope Charley might say more. "It all helps to paint a picture for us and hopefully a trail to lead us back to what happened last month."

"I don't understand how," he said. "But there's one other thing you might find helpful."

"Yes?" Benedict looked over at Gail who was leaning on the table, her pen poised over her notebook.

"Well, sometimes – so Francine said – Elroy used to keep a few of the antiques he bought overseas for himself; those he really liked. And she reckoned Elroy had some nice antique daggers and swords. He kept them in their house, locked away somewhere. As far as I know, Astrid still has them. Francine knew about them and was going to ask Astrid if she wanted to sell any of them to the shop. I don't know if she ever got round to it though."

"At her flat in Fernhill Crescent?"

Charley laughed. "Yeah, I guess so. They used to have a nice house in town, but it was sold when his missus moved into the Roydons' place. She hadn't a hope of paying the mortgage on her own. Nice woman, but she certainly had to work hard. I pitied her, to tell you the truth. I mean, she'd been like a friend to the Roydons, but by 2016, she had been reduced to their glorified servant. She referred to Andy Roydon as Mr Roydon. It was like she'd morphed into a Victorian housemaid."

"Life can be cruel sometimes." Benedict handed him one of his cards. "Just in case you think of anything else."

"Of course. I spend a lot of my time alone here now.

Even Irene, Francine's sister, keeps her distance. Don't ask me why, but then she's always been a bit of a hermit. She owns the place now but leaves it all to me to run, and just phones once a week for a catch-up."

As they were driving back to the office, Benedict turned to Gail. "Can you do a background check on Charley? You know, criminal history, girlfriends, ex-wives, that sort of thing. I mean, he seems genuine, but he's being cagey about something."

"Definitely. I'll get onto it straight-away. Oh, and I meant to tell you – I haven't been able to find a death certificate for an Elroy Lorning anywhere in Europe or New Zealand. It seems like our Elroy has disappeared off the face of the earth."

Benedict listened with interest, but without surprise, especially after what Charley had just told them. Astrid and Elroy Lorning hadn't even been in Germany then. It was all a lie. So, what really had happened between March and May, 2005 – the time period during which Aldo was receiving treatment at the psychiatric hospital? What had happened to the two people who vanished from Aldo's life – Elroy Lorning and Dominica Frimble? Benedict added the Trescos, to the list as well as it was around the same time, they'd put their house on the market and moved away.

***

Cindy woke up, panicking and wanting to scream – like a primal scream. She'd decided to confront Astrid Lorning. It was time they had a talk; something she'd never wanted to do, ever again. Yet she was sure now that Astrid must have the other earring and Cindy wanted it back. In fact, Cindy was going to insist Astrid hand it over. Astrid would have to obey, especially when Cindy threatened to expose the secrets of Astrid's past. She'd been trying Astrid's phone all morning, but it was never answered, so she'd go round to her flat instead.

She hadn't been to the Fernhill Crescent flats before, and upon arrival, intensely disliked the area. She conceded that many of the residents may be church-goers, just like she'd become after going to Scotland. Yet not anymore. Cindy told herself she was finished with religion altogether. She regarded it now as a placatory tool to keep downtrodden and vulnerable people from fighting back and getting what was justly theirs, and from the life over which they had no control at all. Cindy, for all her good upbringing and cosseting, had found out she too fell into the category of those who needed to be comforted by the words of the Bible, as a way of keeping the pain away. However, now she knew that the internal pain and feeling of emptiness would never leave her.

"'Forgive us our trespasses'," she murmured to herself, as she drove her Fiat Bambina into Fernhill Crescent, "'as we forgive those who trespass against us'." She found a parking space right outside the flats and switched off the engine. "'And lead us not into temptation'." She looked through the front windscreen of the car and sought out flat number three.

An elderly woman, using a walker, was struggling to get as far as the letterbox. She shuffled along, head bent as she headed for the row of boxes to the far right of where Cindy's car was parked, partially hidden by a box-hedge.

Cindy locked her car and made her way up to Astrid's flat. She was about to knock on the door when Lilac Browne came silently out, her eyes widening at the sight of the unexpected visitor.

"She's not home," Lilac stammered, while quietly locking the door to the flat and placing the key back under the rosemary pot. Then she began edging her way past Cindy, obviously in a hurry to get away.

"What are you doing here, Lilac?" Cindy said, deliberately blocking Lilac's escape route. Lilac stood cowering like a cornered mouse being eyed up by a hungry cat. Cindy's eyes were staring at Lilac, her face as pale and puffy as raw pizza dough.

"I'm a friend of Astrid's, as you well know." Lilac scanned the area out by the footpath, where she'd enticed Miss Wilson to go, by 'phoning her with a fake message from the 'Post Office' about a parcel left in her letterbox.

"You look so guilty," Cindy said. "Anyway, when will Astrid be back? I want to see her about something."

"L-later on, after f-four," Lilac stammered. "So, what are you wanting her for?"

"I've a question for her, that's all"

"Well, I've got to go." Lilac said, before finally getting past Cindy and strolling casually through the alleyway next to the flats. She'd left her car outside the Four-Square in Mayflower Street in order to keep it out of sight of the prying eyes in the flats. There were bound to be more Miss Wilson-types with eyes fixed on the view beyond their windows.

Cindy turned to see the old woman from earlier with her head bent low, slowly shuffling her way back from the row of letterboxes. She went back to her car, got in and started the engine, just as Miss Wilson looked up and stopped for a minute to observe the Bambina backing out and driving away. Miss Wilson continued on her way, shuffling slowly back to her flat with a scowl on her face.

***

"The way Elroy treated you was wrong," Lilac said, as she raised the glass, half-filled with sparkling wine, to her lips. She'd been glad when Astrid had pulled the bottle out of the fridge, knowing she was always easier to handle when she'd had a couple of glasses to soften her hard edges.

"I don't think so," Astrid said. "I was a hopeless case way back then, as I'm sure everyone was well aware of."

"No," Lilac said. "You were under the mistaken *impression* that you were worthless and a hopeless case, but the rest of us knew differently."

"My doctor quizzed me every time I went to see him. My blood pressure was sky high and he wanted to know why."

"Did he ever ask you why you had headaches all the time?"

"I never told him a thing. I had to protect Elroy. He was so vulnerable."

"*You* were the vulnerable one," Lilac said, yet knowing her words were not being listened to. She could hardly bear to listen to the loyal way Astrid spoke about Elroy.

"And then the stupid doctor wanted me to go on medication for my anxiety, but I said no, I was all right. Anyway, that's enough about all that. Miss Wilson said there was a small blue car pulling out from here today, while I was slaving over a hot iron. I've never known a family with so much laundry!"

"It could've been anyone." Lilac tried to steer Astrid away from thinking the visitor was Cindy.

"Look, let's forget about the past and concentrate on how we're going to get the raincoat into Cindy's house."

"Yes, I think framing Cindy is the right thing to do. I'm so glad we're friends again. I missed you, dearie. You do believe me, don't you?" Astrid looked on the brink of tears.

Lilac was glad she'd steered Astrid in a different direction, as she didn't want her thinking it might have been her who visited. "You've never said anything like this before."

"Well, I couldn't, could I? Not after what happened on the day. I dreaded you'd never forgive me."

"But I was the same! I dreaded you'd never forgive *me*. So does this mean, at last, that you and I can call it quits?"

Astrid poured herself another glass of wine. "I think we should, I really do. You know why, don't you?"

Lilac frowned; she hadn't a clue. "No, why?"

"You're so dim sometimes," Astrid said, taking a big

swig of her drink. "Because of Cindy, of course. She's the one who caused the split in our friendship, after all."

"Let's drink to us," Lilac said, raising her glass and clinking it against Astrid's. "You and I are friends forever, old girl."

"Too right."

All of a sudden, everything in Lilac's world was just as it should be. She wanted to go home now though, to Scamper, who would be waiting patiently for her return. "Poor old sod," she said.

"Who?" Astrid looked askance at Lilac. "Who's a poor old sod?"

"Scamper – my little grey bundle of joy. I love him, and he'll be wanting his tea."

"I'm going to confront Cindy and show her the handkerchief she left in my bedroom," Astrid said.

Lilac nearly choked on her wine. She said nothing; just looked at Astrid, knowing she lost her own handkerchief just a few hours before, and wasn't likely to admit where she dropped it.

Astrid held up a tiny pink square, neatly folded. "She must have dropped it when she got into my flat. Crafty vixen. But how did she get in?"

Lilac swallowed with difficulty, as if she had a huge lump of scone stuck in her throat. "Yes indeed, how?"

"I don't know, do I, but she must have – the slimy

worm. Oh, yes, this must be to do with the earring. Do you think so?" Astrid looked at Lilac with a stern expression, her gold-rimmed glasses glinting in the kitchen light.

Lilac inwardly shrank from Astrid's stare and decided to play dumb. "How would I know? I'm not a mind-reader, am I?"

"No, but think for once, why don't you? I have to spell everything out to you, Lilac Browne, I really do."

"I have to be going soon," Lilac said, deciding to feign ignorance about the motives for Cindy's visit. After all, hadn't she read somewhere how ignorance is bliss? Lilac couldn't think straight anymore. She told herself it was on account of the wine. Although feeling befuddled by the alcohol, she knew that she just needed to convince Astrid she was in the dark. This, she knew, was the safest path to tread. Dominica had warned her, again and again:

"Admit nothing, Lilac, love. Play dumb. Then she can't get her claws into you. Watch out. Be careful. Pretend you're ignorant."

Chapter 16

Tuesday 11th June

Aldo was sure now that Cindy had come back with a score to settle, and Jenniver's imprisonment had brought everything to a head. Aldo no longer quite believed Cindy's cheerful, devil-may-care persona. It seemed to him that she was only *pretending* to have changed; she wanted everyone to think that she wasn't capable of harming anyone. She had told them that she was a devout Christian, and said to Aldo how she'd finally found peace in her heart – peace *and* forgiveness. Yet deep down, Aldo suspected otherwise. Nor had he forgotten the blood pact – something Cindy had insisted they all do again, like a renewal – and they'd passively agreed, not wanting to anger her. The blood pact had been re-enacted in the gazebo, following the consumption of a quantity of alcohol. Aldo hadn't wanted to do it, but saw no alternative other than to agree.

He remembered the day of the 'renewal' well – both

occasions in fact; the first being back in 2003. Aldo was surprised Cindy even wanted to think about doing it again, because such a ritual was at odds with the Christian faith. That caused him to be confused about Cindy at first. She hadn't totally fooled Aldo, who had always had doubts about this supposed act of bonding, right from the start. He'd been sixteen and Cindy was only fifteen when the first blood pact was made. Astrid of course, was much older. They'd only known her as Mrs Lorning then, a frequent visitor to the Roydons' house with her ghastly husband, Elroy.

Twenty years later, in April, 2024, not long after Cindy's return, she insisted they all renew the vow to maintain their silence about the day Morag (or Mrs Roydon, as they had to call her) had tumbled down the stairs, broken her neck and died. Cindy had rushed down, saying she wanted to help Mrs Roydon, but Aldo remembered looking down to the bottom of the stairs and seeing Cindy removing a greenstone pendant from the deceased's neck. That's when he became aware that Astrid was also silently watching. This meant all three of them – according to Cindy – could be implicated in the incident, so they quietly pledged never to say what had really happened, although neither Aldo nor Astrid actually saw Cindy push her. Morag Roydon was an unpopular woman, with many openly hating her, resenting her wealth and the way she abused the power that came with that. Yet despite her many adversaries, Cindy still insisted that she, Aldo and Astrid could be the ones in the frame for her death.

Verbally pledging their secrecy wasn't enough reassurance for Cindy so she had insisted they make a blood pact, which she said would last for the rest of their lives. The three of them all consented. Poor Astrid, who was regularly being attacked by her abusive husband, was biddable to almost anyone at that stage.

It came back to him how, just a few weeks ago, he'd looked at Cindy, sitting across from him in the gazebo, and seen an emotion reflected in her eyes. It had seemed to him like a hardened resolve, full of smouldering menace. Cindy was also wearing the greenstone pendant that day, that she told them had once belonged to her mother. That was why she'd hated Morag Roydon, around whose neck it had once been attached. Cindy had told them a jumbled story about how her father must have given it to Morag, in the year after Cindy's mother had died and she reckoned her dad and Morag must've had a secret affair.

When Cindy noticed Aldo watching her, she had smiled and laughed, so maybe he had only imagined the sinister look in the first place? Yet that didn't explain her attitude now. The initial camaraderie was gone and now Cindy held herself aloof from both him and Astrid. He wanted to go to her place to ask her if she was all right. He felt uneasy, as if he'd done something wrong, which of course he had, but that was such a long time ago. Surely it had all been forgotten about by now? Yet he couldn't forget the text: 'You know what you did and you're going to pay.' And then the fact the radio had been turned on that day when he'd returned to the beach-house. Aldo trembled and moistened his dry lips with his tongue. Cindy was capable of anything – at least she had been at fifteen when she'd not shown a single ounce of remorse at the death of Morag Roydon.

***

The following morning, Lilac was parked in her usual spot behind the stand of cypress trees in Plover Street, when Cindy's car came into view. It was a prison visiting day, but as Cindy had gone there two days in a row, Lilac didn't think she'd go back today. Surely there was a limit to how many times she could suffer the long bus trip and the gloomy, morbid atmosphere of the women's lock-up? Lilac had only ever driven past the grim place and always looked with dread at the sombre concrete walls, with its curls of razor wire along the thick brick facade.

However, Lilac decided to follow her to see where she was heading. She did a U-turn and sped up so she didn't lose sight of the car. Keeping pace was fortunate, because Cindy turned left, instead of taking the usual right turning to the bus station. The excitement surged through her body as Lilac realised her hunch had been correct. If her target wasn't visiting the prison today, where was she going? Lilac turned on the car radio in time to hear the announcer:

"There are four free lines, call and let's talk about the worsening of our economy and the high rate of suburban burglaries, especially in the seaside town of Seagrove."

"What a laugh," she said. "There has been a stolen raincoat and a single earring. Now, where is Cindy going? I have to find out and, when I do, I might even phone Benedict Aberthorp and pretend I'm trying to help him. What do you think, Dominica?"

"Yes, yes, you have to pretend all the time. It's the only way to become an innocent bystander. You live a double life and no one will ever find out the truth because they will see how pure and innocent you are, my little treasure."

Lilac imagined herself as pure and innocent as she continued to follow the little car. She wanted to find out Cindy's movements, because, as Astrid kept saying:

"Cindy's up to no good. She's fooled us into thinking

she's fun-loving and cares about others. But I, for one, can see right through into her core. And it's not a nice place to see. So you must act for both of us and track her movements, Lilac. Then we can put the brown raincoat in her house and sit back and await what happens next."

Lilac didn't object to Astrid's firm commands. Despite the many times Dominica had warned her to keep away from Astrid, there was still a bond between them and she couldn't break it. However, she only pretended to do Astrid's bidding and had reassured Dominica of this fact many times; just as she pretended to help Benedict Aberthorp. It was the only way, because, as Dominica had reminded her often enough, Lilac was unable to say no to these dominant figures in her life.

Lilac was brought back to the present moment when, to her astonishment, she realised Cindy was heading for Roydons' Antiques. She'd parked her blue car a little way down the street and Lilac stopped too, out of sight, but where she could clearly see Cindy. The well-dressed woman strode with confidence as she walked boldly towards the shop.

"But why?" Lilac said aloud. "There's only Charley there." And then she gasped as she remembered that Charley Raymond used to visit the Roydons all the time, with the rest of the teenagers. And now she remembered something else: at some stage after he'd left school,

Charley for a while had stayed in the Roydons' accommodation behind the garage. They used to call it a gottage – part-garage, part-cottage. Perhaps there was a connection between him and Cindy?

She decided to stay in her car and wait for Cindy to come out, but as half an hour turned into an hour without any sign of her, Lilac began to wonder what they were doing in there. Astrid said she had to have everything spelled out to her, but this time she thought she might well know what was going on. She got out of her car and locked it before walking up the street to the antiques' shop. She glanced quickly at the closed door as she passed by, with an 'out to lunch' sign on display there. "Bloody hell," she said to herself. "Now I suppose I'll have to go home."

***

Gail and Benedict leant over the office desk, studying the list in front of them. Gail had sorted each suspect in the order of who she thought was the most likely killer.

"Let's start with our client, Aldo," Benedict said, amazed at just how much raw data they'd now managed to accumulate on each of the suspects.

"What? You haven't put him at number one on the suspect list, have you?" Gail chuckled while drumming her fingers on the desk; a habit Benedict found annoying in its frequency.

"No, of course not, but you have to admit he has an interesting back story. He was at the house on the day in question so he had the means to do it. And probably the motive too."

Gail stopped drumming her fingers. "Yes, of course, providing he could get his hands on the dagger. But also, he would have needed help to move the body."

"*Mmm*, only if she wasn't killed in the backyard where the body was found... anyway, let's begin at the beginning: it all began when, fairly late in the day, on Monday, May twenty-seven, Aldo came to see me in my office. On that first visit I made a note about him telling me he didn't drink alcohol."

"But you had one anyway?" Gail said, smiling.

"No! The point is, he'd lied to me. You see, Lilac filled me in on what had happened on the evening of the day Francine was killed; that she went to Astrid's flat and found Aldo already there. According to her, Aldo was drunk by then."

"But why lie about it? Drinking alcohol is no big deal. Is it?"

"Not to us, no, but then Lilac told me how Aldo began relying on alcohol after Francine had the stillborn baby. It turned out that drinking *is* a big deal to Aldo, and when I went to his beach-house the other day, he was drinking a glass of wine and admitted he liked to have alcohol now and then, but it seems he has to be careful not to fall back into his past ways of overindulging."

"Right, so that has been explained. Is he in the clear now?"

"Let's see." Benedict scanned the piece of paper. "What about this raincoat of his? He said the police are fixated on it, and he's worried, because it hasn't turned up yet."

"Simple: If they consider the killer was Aldo, then he left his raincoat at the scene of the crime, or if they don't suspect him, someone different stole it and planted it there to frame him."

"Promising, but Aldo swears it's not his. He says it's too big and made of a cheap plastic, instead of Bri-nylon like his."

"But still, it was obviously enough for the police to suspect he killed her."

"Lilac said something, though, that I still haven't worked out: she said Aldo was rushing away from the house around or shortly after two-thirty that day. Yet we both know Aldo turned up for his dental appointment around two."

"True, but don't forget the receptionist told me Aldo

was out the door at two fifteen p.m. It was only a check-up," Gail said, shrugging her shoulders.

"Okay, so he had time to drive back to the house and leave again at two thirty p.m. but did he have time to kill Francine, drag her out and lay her under an olive tree and rush off again? If it was Aldo, he'd hardly have left his raincoat there."

"So, if he did go back there, why?"

"Exactly. And why didn't he mention the fact that Astrid's employment was ending at the end of May? Astrid did – when I first interviewed her."

"*Mmm…*"

"Also, both Aldo and Astrid wanted me to think they were on good terms with Francine. Yet I find that hard to believe of either of them. Francine had already given Astrid notice, and Francine's new girlfriend was pregnant, which must have been hard for Aldo to accept, if he'd been told about the pregnancy that is."

"Then there's the text Aldo was sent when he was with me: 'You know what you did and you're going to pay.' Who sent him the text and why?"

"Didn't he tell you he was the one who broke up his and Cindy's relationship in 2004?"

"Yes." Benedict remembered the way Aldo had looked when he told him about it – gaunt, haunted, guilty, and unsure of himself. "And someone went into his house that day and turned on the radio. It really freaked him out. On another occasion he told me he'd come home to find a pot plant on his deck had been moved, and then the word 'guilty' had been spelt out in pebbles on his deck in a separate incident."

Benedict recalled the time Aldo had called him over. He had been in shock, wondering who had entered his house. "He hasn't spoken of any of these instances since. There's something else he told me the other day too. I gave Aldo a notebook, and a pen, just as I do with all my clients. It's so if they remember anything, no matter how trivial, they can write it down and then tell me later. It works well, I've found."

"Good thinking."

"Thanks. Well, when I was at Aldo's, he'd written something in his notebook. He said it was nothing important, but when he told me about it, I wasn't so sure."

"What was it?"

"On the day of the murder, Aldo, as you know, went round as usual to have lunch with Francine. While he was in the kitchen, waiting to chat to Astrid while she prepared lunch, he bent down to stroke the cat and found an earring tucked under the cupboard. When he was looking at it, Astrid came in and reached for it, saying it was hers."

"So it belonged to Astrid?"

"No, apparently not, according to Aldo. He said he's never seen Astrid wear earrings. It was a Cloisonné earring in the design of a sun with a face on it. Aldo said Cindy used to have a pair just like it – the other half being that of a crescent moon. Astrid then quickly slipped it into her apron pocket."

"So where is the crescent-moon earring?"

"Presumably with Astrid. We could pay her another visit?"

***

Today was Jenniver's nineteenth birthday but Cindy had already told her yesterday she wouldn't be visiting. She'd wished her a happy birthday although she knew it wasn't going to be a happy one for Jenniver. How could it be? It almost broke Cindy's heart to see her daughter in such a dark and dingy place; her once shiny hair now dull and lank, her beautiful face turned sallow.

She no longer trusted Astrid and had never really liked her. Yet when she first came back, she'd tried to befriend her as well as Aldo, practising her new persona as the happy, carefree person, transformed by the church. She'd considered such pretence would make her more likeable to them, and her plan had worked. Astrid, in particular, had seemed persuaded by this new version of Cindy and had taken her aside one day to confide how in 2004 she'd seen Aldo with Francine's phone, while they were all picnicking on the beach. Astrid had simply been present to help with the food. Cindy had once suspected Aldo might have been behind their breakup, especially when he and Francine had married so soon afterwards, but then her instincts told her it would've been Francine's idea and Aldo had just obeyed like the weak person he became when he was with her.

She remembered how Astrid Lorning was always wearing lots of makeup. When she was only sixteen, Aldo had once told Cindy, that Mrs Lorning was like a punch bag for her husband. Aldo described the abuse as Mr Lorning kicking, beating and throwing his wife around. Yet Astrid was always smiling and cheerful when Cindy visited the Roydons'; so much so that Cindy had always wondered if Aldo had told her the truth, despite the fact he was adamant he had.

Cindy had first learned how to deceive others from Mrs Lorning's example, who covered up her internal pain and her external bruises. Mrs Lorning had learnt how to stop her pain from spilling over like a flooded sink, which proved she was an expert at pretence. She looked like a happy and cheerful woman and it was this persona Cindy had tried to emulate. Astrid had been through so much yet had come out the other side, her horrible, skinny husband stabbed to death in Germany, or so it was said. Yet the more Cindy pondered this, the more she could see how opportune his death had been for Astrid. She now wore hardly any makeup; only covering the signs of ageing rather than the evidence of her abuse that Astrid had found so shameful.

Cindy put on her most provocative clothing and applied makeup, to highlight her best features. She then drove into town. She and Charley had decided it was too risky to meet during the day, so they only met at night, in his tiny flat above the shop. However, today, she would surprise him and walk straight in, just before lunch, to show him how daring she could be. Silly old Charley; he'd always been besotted with her, right from their school days. Back then, she'd strung him along for a while, until he started getting ideas about their future. Besides, she and Aldo were only waiting for her sixteenth birthday and then things would get better. Charley just had to find someone else. Only despite all her planning, it hadn't worked out that way.

She still remembered the hurt look on Charley's face when she told him she didn't want to see him anymore. After that he rebelled and ended up robbing a bank for which he'd received a twelve years' prison sentence. Cindy hadn't had time to care about his situation, because she had had her own pain to deal with: being dumped by Aldo, going to a strange country and knowing she was pregnant and would become a single mother. Andy Roydon had seduced her with his charm, after her breakup with Aldo. He had helped her to feel as though she mattered to someone again.

It was now, twenty years later, and when she'd first visited Charley again, he had been delighted to see her. Her interest in him bolstered his ego. Cindy seduced him with her flattery, and two nights later, in his upstairs flat, their affair began. She smiled to herself, because her plan had succeeded. When Charley had taken off his shirt, there were tattoos covering his upper arms and chest, which filled her with desire. These were prison tattoos normally hidden from view. Charley had to keep his arms covered in the shop so the customers wouldn't see them, for if they did, they may be offended and that could affect sales, or so Francine told him. Charley had obeyed. Yet Cindy couldn't take her eyes off them. On his chest was a clock with the words 'time waits for no man.' The clock's hands were set at ten past eleven. He also had the words 'hell' and 'bent' inked onto the backs of his fingers – 'hell' on the fingers of his right hand and 'bent' his left. Francine had said these on his fingers were okay, and he'd told her as much, laughing at the comment, as he and Cindy made love. Sometimes he'd close his fists and put his hands together so she could read the words in full – hell-bent – and he'd pick up a whisky bottle, taking a large, long gulp. He made their affair exciting, because he was uninhibited, and even a bit rough at times. He also told her he was infertile so not to worry about getting pregnant.

"Hi," she said in a low voice, hoping there was no one else in the shop.

Charley looked up from his paper as she stood before him. "What the hell?" he said, his eyes looking beyond her to the door. "Hey, is something wrong, baby?"

"No, I just wanted to see you. I miss you and I'm lonely. There's a private investigator and some old cronies hanging around all the time. Not to mention my nosey neighbour who is always out in the garden, watching my comings and goings. It's driving me crazy, Charley. I needed to see you." She wiped at her tears with her fingers.

"Hey, don't get upset, baby. Come out the back. I'll put up the 'out to lunch' sign and we'll go upstairs. C'mon, baby, don't you worry now. It's all been sorted, just don't get upset. All right?"

Cindy went to the back room while Charley put the sign up and pulled the blind down. Then he was at her side, taking her hand as they climbed the stairs up to his flat. He closed the Venetian blinds and began to take her clothes off. Quickly he took off each of her garments and flung them on a stool in the corner, before ripping his own clothes off. Then they began, in silence, their routine on his freshly-made bed. Cindy liked how he was a passionate person and didn't hold back.

His tattooed fingers lightly stroked her back and the roughness of his bristly face scraped against hers. Even in his lovemaking he was methodical and this always calmed her down until she forgot everything else and just gave herself to his intensity, trying not to think about the time when he'd been hurt. As a teenager, she had pushed him away and he'd gone crazy, ending up in prison.

"The P.I. was round here yesterday," he said, his lips brushing over hers. "He wanted to know about Elroy – the way he died."

"*Mmm*." Cindy was too preoccupied to reply as Charley's warm lips, worked their way down, from her lips to her neck and then further still.

"But I was in the slammer then, and you were in Scotland, weren't you, baby?"

"Yes, darling." She could hardly breathe now, as he gently stroked her forehead and kissed her lips.

"But Francine used to visit me," Charley whispered. "Once a week, she came. And you know what, baby?"

"No, tell me." Cindy felt like she was turning to butter as his lips searched her neck and mouth.

"She used to tell me about some bad things that went on at the house. Really bad."

"Why are you telling me about this?"

"Because, baby, it's why everything happened."

"What do you mean?" Cindy suddenly didn't like what Charley was saying.

"Astrid, what else? Why do you think she helped you?"

"I don't know."

Charley was stroking her face now, and looking deep into her eyes. "Because Francine knew what happened to Elroy. Maybe getting rid of Francine meant no one could tell what really went down that day."

Cindy tensed. "I don't want to know all this."

"But you do," Charley said. "Because it's behind everything."

"Why?"

"You weren't here, baby. But I was. She had too much power."

"Who?"

"Francine, of course."

"What?"

"She had a hold over the two ladies concerned."

"Which ladies?"

"Astrid and Lilac, of course."

"What?"

Charley put his fingers over her lips and said, "*Shhh…*" They both stopped talking. He didn't care anymore. All he wanted was the present moment, with the woman he'd always loved. Now she was his, and he once again, felt like a complete person, just as he had before.

***

Gail and Benedict were just finishing their lunch, before setting out for Astrid Lorning's flat, when Benedict's phone beeped. He began reading the text message.

Gail's eyebrows shot up in a questioning way as she saw the look on his face.

"Over an hour ago, Cindy went into Roydons' Antiques. Charley put up the 'out to lunch' sign. Well, thank you, Lilac. Thank you for letting me know."

***

By five p.m. Lilac was sitting in Dominica's craftwork den, sipping a glass of wine and staring at the dolls' house. The tiny pieces of furniture for the bedrooms and the study were still sitting on the shelf above. She often took them out to dust them but would put each one back in the exact same place, because she wanted the carefully constructed craftworks to stay just where Dominica had left them. Besides, Lilac didn't think she had the right to change anything around in any way.

"This is the only place I'm at peace," she said. "I hope you know that, Dominica."

Once a day, usually in the evening or sometimes late in the afternoon, she'd enter the room carrying a bottle of wine and a crystal wine glass and shut the door behind her. Whenever she had a cigarette, she'd open the window and blow the smoke outside. Sometimes it wafted back in and then Lilac would turn on the fan to blow it back out again. She loved this room and didn't want the specialness to ever leave it.

"The time has come to find your letter, my love. Now is the right time, I know you're telling me to."

Dominica said she'd leave the letter hidden inside an ordinary item of furniture. Lilac had already gone through all the furniture in the house and hadn't found it. There'd been crumbs and a coin and a teaspoon down the side of one of the armchairs, and down the back of the sofa was a tiny book on how to glue dolls' house furniture together – but no letter.

She took a sip of her drink and stared at the same dolls' house she'd been looking at since 2005, and decided it was time to do something different. She opened the front door of the tiny structure, leant down and peered inside. There was a hall in which Dominica had placed a miniscule table with a phone on top. Then, by lifting part of the roof, Lilac admired the lounge, already furnished, with a handmade piano. Dominica had spent hours making a lovely home for the beautiful dolls to live in.

She laughed softly and poured herself another drink. "Is this the place? Is it here you want me to look?"

There was a doll with plaited hair sitting on a stool in front of the piano and Lilac carefully picked her up so she could lift the lid on the stool and look inside. From her own childhood experience of learning the piano, she'd always get her sheet music from inside the piano stool's compartment.

Sure enough, there were tiny pieces of paper with musical notes printed on them in a fine pen. "You thought of everything," she said, admiring the handiwork.

Dominica had been clever and did everything so well, but there was nothing else there beyond the music notes for Lilac to read. She replaced the lid of the piano stool and put the doll back in place, with its hands resting once again on the piano keys.

"Play, my little one, play," she said, as if she was a child again, imagining the keys of the piano ringing out

Beethoven's *Moonlight Sonata*, a tune she herself had had to master.

She sat down, trying to recall the exact words Dominica had said so long ago. It was nearly thirty years, and in all that time, Lilac hadn't really wanted to remember what she'd said. Now she asked herself why.

"You're missing me too much," Dominica had since told her, on more than one occasion. "You're not thinking straight, girl."

And she had agreed with everything Dominica had said, and continued to say. So why now, after all this time? Why was the letter so important? She realised it was because her tormentor was dead and gone, lying in her grave. Now Lilac had more money and could at last relax; something she hadn't been able to do – to truly rest, day or night – for the last nineteen years. Neither could Astrid. Poor Astrid… Lilac found herself wondering if there had ever been a time in Astrid's life, when she hadn't been controlled and mastered by someone.

However, now, the old fool was making up for it in a big way. Astrid had grabbed her power and was holding onto it tightly. She relished it and had laid to waste the spectre of her miserable past – not that Astrid would think of herself in this way, and Lilac could never voice her personal opinion of Astrid. To her, Astrid was like a powerful car with faulty steering: she simply didn't know what to do with her freedom. She didn't even know anymore, how to make the most of her life, and she probably never would. She'd paid a high price for that freedom, a terrible price, with the agony of being pushed down with one hand while the other pulled her up from the ashes of her past.

Lilac drained her glass of wine, placed it on the table next to the dolls' house, and picked up a miniature bed from the shelf. It was time to complete the furnishing of the house. *Time to make things tidy*, she said to herself; to tie all the loose ends together and point herself in another direction. She had to give herself a push, reminding herself every day now that she was out of the quagmire. There was no one else to help her do this. Dominica would always be there to prompt her to take action and to stop being immersed in self-pity, but Lilac was the only one who could take control of her life.

***

On her way home from Charley's flat, just before five p.m. Cindy passed the Holy Angels Church and experienced a twinge deep in her heart. The words of the Lord's Prayer came back to her: 'Forgive us our trespasses as we forgive those who trespass against us.' It was too late for that now, and as she steered the car into her driveway, her neighbour looked up from her garden, as usual, and smiled, one hand holding a trowel.

"Hello, Mrs Shields," Cindy said, mustering a false smile while the familiar tune of her phone sounded. She parked in the garage and answered the call.

It was Gregor, her husband. "I'm arriving in Seagrove tomorrow and will be at your place by six p.m. I wanted to surprise you, darling."

"Oh, Gregor," she said, barely able to disguise her panic.

"See you soon, honey-bunch." His voice sounded so close and full of happiness.

"Yes, sweetie." Her heart was thumping in her chest and she felt as though she was falling into a bottomless abyss. What made it worse was the knowledge that she didn't love Gregor and wondered if she ever really had.

Now she was in love with someone else – Charley Raymond. He was a rough, tough-nut, but gentle too, loving and tender towards her. Besides, he was unscrupulous and she liked that in a man. He'd already told her how much he liked that quality in her as well. Yet as soon as he'd said that, she wanted to tell him how wrong he was. She wasn't actually like that at all, although for a time she pretended to be. It was just the old rage, oozing out again, after so much apparent spiritual healing had taken place.

"Oh my God," she said to herself, as she unlocked the back door and went inside. "What have I done? What am I going to do now?"

Once inside she headed for the fridge and grabbed a bottle of wine, taking a swig while still standing by the fridge. She immediately experienced relief. Then after sitting down on the couch, she took an even bigger glug, put the bottle down on the coffee table and picked up the earring depicting the blue sun with the green rays. If only she had the crescent moon to go with it.

Placing the earring down, Cindy reflected on all that had happened since her return: how she'd contacted Charley and they'd started seeing each other. She could hardly believe how good it was to be with him. He was so passionate, it brought out a different side to her character. He'd been using the word love a lot lately. Cindy always baulked at that because a long time ago, someone else had said the same and she'd made the mistake of believing him.

She drank from the wine bottle again, still enveloped in Charley's love, even though Gregor was arriving tomorrow. His unexpected phone-call had sent her reeling. Why had he decided to come all that way, when she was going home soon? However, the truth was she didn't want to return to Scotland. This was where she belonged now, and coming back had convinced her that this was her home. Plans of revenge on Aldo had dissipated and it was like she didn't care about that anymore. She'd mistakenly built up a picture of him and Francine as a happy, loving couple, which obviously wasn't the case. They were living apart and had been for a while, and Francine had a pregnant mistress. Cindy smiled grimly at the thought, but it served Aldo right!

Charley's love had transformed her from within, despite the fact that her beautiful daughter was behind bars. Even then, if Jenniver hadn't been imprisoned, Cindy would never have come back and met up with Charley again. The man she had once rejected in favour of the charming and handsome Aldo Sherwin. She could see now what a fool she'd been.

Soon she lay down on the couch, the earring still in her hand and fell into a deep sleep. Sometime later, a loud crash woke her with a fright and she didn't know what time it was. She listened intently and became aware there was someone inside her house. Sitting up stiffly, her whole body rigid with anticipation, she tried to work out where the intruder was and what they were doing. She had nothing valuable to steal.

Groggily, she tried to focus and kept listening, her heartbeat like a drum as it pounded in her ears.

***

"I don't want to do it. I can't do it," Lilac whispered hoarsely.

"Yes you can. You've got to," Astrid insisted. "You're slimmer than me and more nimble-footed. Now go on."

"But how am I going to get up high enough to get in?"

The conversation had taken place inside Lilac's car that was hidden behind the trees in Plover Street while they plotted the break-in.

As Lilac tiptoed around, with the brown raincoat tucked securely under her jacket, she could see only one window open in Cindy's house. Having dragged a wooden box silently across the lawn to the toilet window, she now stood looking up at the slender gap it afforded her. Lilac's heart felt like it was skipping several beats as she squeezed her hand inside the opening and undid the latch. Luckily it was a push-open design, but so narrow, she doubted her body would even fit through. Nevertheless, she carried on, spurred on by an unreasonable fear of disobeying Astrid, who had ordered her to do the deed. Lilac couldn't bring herself to say no, or at least protest forcefully.

It was Astrid's sly, crooked, smile that had sealed Lilac's fate. Her expression was something new to Astrid, and as far as Lilac could remember, had only started appearing since the demise of Francine Roydon. Seeing it there on Astrid's face had somehow caused Lilac's words of protest to become stuck in her throat.

As Lilac wriggled her way in through the toilet window, she briefly recalled how Astrid had invited her over:

"Come over to my flat and we can discuss our plan to take the brown raincoat to Cindy's house and plant it there for Benedict Aberthorp to find."

Whereas Astrid had become strong without Elroy – even if she didn't realise it – Lilac had become weak without Dominica, and Astrid was taking advantage of that fact.

She was in the house now, having squeezed herself through the gap like sausage meat coming out of a sausage-maker. Gingerly Lilac had stepped onto the toilet rim and, holding onto a nearby towel rail, lowered herself to the floor, as silently as a cat, walking on tip-toe across the floor.

"We can't do it during the day," Astrid had said, business-like and brusque. "No, because of her stupid neighbour who's obsessed with her front garden. She's there all day, every day."

Astrid, smiling, had tapped her fingers on the table at her flat, drunk down another glass of sparkling wine and looked vacant as she silently planned out what to do. Lilac had hurriedly also had another glass of wine to steady her nerves, fearing what Astrid was planning and not wanting any part in it.

Now, Lilac approached the hallway, and decided to take a left turn. From what she and Astrid had discerned by a reconnaissance of the houses in the street, Lilac concluded that the bedrooms would be at the back of Cindy's property. She quietly walked, hardly daring to breathe. When she came to a partially open door, she undid one button of her jacket and pulled out the raincoat. Astrid had said to leave it either under a bed or in a wardrobe. Such instruction may have been easy for her to issue but it wasn't easy to comply with in a dark house. Luckily some light from a street lamp was shining just enough for Lilac to make out that the room she was looking into had a single, empty bed in it.

She pressed the button on the tiny torch she'd taken from the glovebox of her car a short time ago. Cupping her hand around the light to minimise its glare, the outline of an empty bed reflected in the beam. Nearby was a cupboard that she supposed was the wardrobe. Gently she turned the handle, the raincoat under one arm, and pulled the door open. Something large fell out of the wardrobe, hit her on the side of the head and crashed to the floor.

Lilac suppressed a scream, touched the side of her head and shone the torch down to see a medium-sized suitcase. She put the torch down, flipped the catches and lifted the lid. The suitcase had a few clothes inside, so she shoved the brown raincoat on top of them, closed it, picked up the torch, and ran as fast as she could, back to the bathroom. She stepped up on the toilet, angling herself to once more squeeze through the window. The position made it more difficult this time and she was desperate now, knowing Cindy could be awake and searching the house.

She managed to squeeze her way out without detection, falling to the ground, after missing the box completely. There was a horrible ache in her right wrist, which was now underneath her body, but there was no time to inspect it or even think about the pain. Lilac dragged herself up and was running, panting and sobbing, as she raced down the path at the side of the house. She opened the gate and ran down the street until she reached her car, which would take them safely away. It was a pity Astrid had never learned to drive.

"Are you all right?" Astrid said, noticing Lilac's sobs. "Did you do it? Did you?"

"Yes, it's my bloody wrist. I think it's broken. Come on, we've got to go."

Lilac did a U-turn and they drove away. She looked

in the rear-view mirror and saw that the internal lights at seventy-one Plover Street were on. She drove fast, back to Astrid's flat, barely able to steer the car, as the intense pain in her wrist threatened to overwhelm her.

"Come inside, I'll give you some whisky," Astrid said and Lilac didn't argue. She was shaking now and when she looked down at her clothes, the front was covered in dirt.

"That was ghastly," she managed to say, flopping down on Astrid's lumpy couch. "I don't know how we got away with it."

"Here, drink this." Astrid held out a glass half-filled with whisky that Lilac took with her left hand. Then Astrid draped a woollen shawl around Lilac's shoulders.

The whisky was strong and Lilac drank it down. Her right wrist was swelling by the moment, but somehow, she became aware that it had all been worth it when she saw how Astrid looked worried and was stood there pathetically helpless. The confidence Astrid had displayed lately seemed to have evaporated now. Inside, Lilac laughed at their idiocy while savouring the strength that lay in their combined secret. They were the only two left who'd been there on the evening of March four, 2005. Yet that didn't stop others from still being suspicious, and were even now trying to find out what had happened that day, Benedict Aberthorp for one.

Chapter 17

Wednesday 12th June

Benedict watched as Gail scrolled through the pages on her laptop. They were just finishing their morning coffees in the office before setting out to Astrid Lorning's flat in search of the crescent-moon earring, Aldo had described. Astrid couldn't be contacted by phone, but in some ways, it would be better to arrive without warning. If she had something to hide, Benedict didn't want her to have the chance to conceal the evidence.

By nine thirty a.m. they were standing outside Astrid's flat. Benedict knocked firmly on the faded green front door; a brown plastic number three screwed onto it. The whole place seemed unusually quiet – no barking dogs or cats lurking nearby or a single person in sight.

After a few minutes, the door slowly opened, and Astrid's bleary-eyed face looked out. "What is it?" she said, holding her dressing gown closed at the top.

"Can we come in, Mrs Lorning? There's a couple of things you might be able to help us with."

Astrid frowned, but stepped aside. "Come on then, but I've told you everything I know. Why are you so early?"

"Sorry, we couldn't phone you first." Benedict looked around the room as they entered and got the impression Astrid hadn't been up for long; the smell of coffee permeating the room and there, on the small kitchen table, alongside a piece of burnt toast, a mugful of coffee waiting to be drunk.

"This is Gail Hollingford, my assistant. Please, carry on with your breakfast."

"Do take a seat on the couch," Astrid said, picking up her toast and mug and moving to the small lounge, where she sat in an armchair facing them. "So, what's this all about, Mr Aberthorp?"

"As you know, we're still making enquiries into the death of Francine Roydon. Of course, there are a few loose ends that need tying up but, all in all, it shouldn't be too long before the case is closed."

Astrid's eyes seemed to widen at Benedict's words. "Is that so?"

"Yes, but these things take time. Sometimes our enquiries may seem totally irrelevant to others, but we still have to close off all possibilities."

"What do you mean, *all possibilities*? In what way can I help you?"

"It's about a set of earrings, Mrs Lorning – in the shape of a sun and a crescent-moon. Have you ever owned such a set?"

Astrid almost dropped the mug she had just picked up. "Yes, I did have, at one time."

"So you don't have them anymore?"

She finished chewing and took a sip from her mug, stalling for time. "I have one of the pair – the crescent moon, but the other's gone missing."

"Can we see the remaining earring, please?"

Astrid hesitated. "What on earth for? Oh, I suppose so, but I don't see what my earring has to do with anything."

"Thank you so much."

While she was out of the room Benedict scanned the walls, noting the ancient wallpaper and tired-looking furniture. It must have been difficult for Astrid, he surmised, having no luxuries in her flat.

"Here, look at this," Astrid said in a cheerful tone, smiling crookedly. "You won't see anything made as good as this these days."

Benedict took the earring from her, admiring its beauty and noting the large eye, nose and mouth on the inner curve of the crescent-moon. It was coloured a deep blue and inlaid with golden metal of some kind.

"It's beautiful," Benedict said, handing it to Gail. "So, you don't know what happened to the other one?"

"No, I have no idea," Astrid said, with a fixed solemn stare. "I would tell you if I knew, but unfortunately, I don't."

Benedict detected the anxiety in her voice, and that confirmed what he already knew. She could be calling his bluff, of course, but he was sure she wanted to know how much she could safely disclose about the earrings without digging herself into an even deeper hole in which she currently stood. Astrid continued her desperate quest for information while Benedict kept her guessing.

"Let's just say, we're following a certain line of enquiry, Mrs Lorning. But you don't need to trouble yourself with the details. It's probably just a false lead, like so many little bits of information we have unearthed. Still, it is our job to follow them all up, as they say."

"As *you* say." Astrid's facial expression had darkened in anger and frustration. Benedict wasn't giving her any clues as to why he wanted to know about the earrings. Her defensive reaction only served to reinforce his certainty that the sun earring Aldo had found on the Roydons' kitchen floor was indeed significant. A slight raising of the eyebrows by Gail suggested she was in agreement.

"Thank you for your time," he said, getting up from the couch and noting Astrid's discomfort at their early departure.

"Why did you really come here?" she said, scowling now.

"Just a routine enquiry."

"Ha, you expect me to believe that?"

"Don't worry, we'll let you know as soon as we have more information."

"I don't know anything, so how can I tell you more?"

Her last statement gave Benedict the impression she was making a pretence of wanting to help them but didn't know how. "That's all right. We don't expect you to lie just for the sake of wanting to help, you know." He tried to sound kind.

Astrid smiled. "You know I want to help, Benedict, I really do. If you need me to ask my friends any delicate questions, you have only to say. They might confide in me, rather than you, if you know what I'm saying."

"Yes, I believe I do, and thank you." By placating Astrid, Benedict's plan was for Astrid to unintentionally give something away.

"Goodbye then, Benedict," she said, smiling sweetly and going to the door to open it. "And Miss Hollingford. I'll do what I can to find out more. After all, there must be some clues around somewhere, mustn't there?"

"Yes, and thank you, Mrs Lorning. You've been most cooperative."

Astrid kept smiling and now looked more relaxed, obviously believing she'd fooled them into thinking she was genuinely trying to help. Benedict had no intention of trusting this woman in any way, shape or form.

Once outside in the car, he turned to Gail. "The earring Aldo said he'd found, was of the sun. And he said Astrid had quickly taken possession of it."

"So where is the sun earring now, the one Astrid *claims* is missing?" Gail scribbled in her notebook as Benedict started the car. They drove away, knowing Astrid Lorning was hiding something, but what, and why?

***

After she had arrived home, Lilac had swallowed two 'painkillers' and put ice on her wrist, then fashioned a rudimentary sling to keep it in place, hoping to stop the aching. When daylight came, she'd driven herself to the hospital's emergency department.

Now she was sitting in Dominica's den with her sprained wrist in a bandage and sling. The hospital nurse had told her to take the prescribed pain relief and keep her arm elevated until the swelling had subsided.

Lilac was frightened now, because Cindy might have seen her running up the street to her car. Even if not, she would probably recognise her car if asked to identify it. However, the absence of the police at her door gave her hope that she hadn't been seen by anyone.

Dominica's voice had been shrill as soon as Lilac had dropped Astrid off at her flat and driven the rest of the way home, her arm throbbing. "Keep away from Astrid. She's nothing but trouble. I warned you, my love."

Now Lilac was intent on one thing only – finding that letter; the letter Dominica had written to her, years ago, to be read only if something happened to Dominica while Lilac was still alive. Maddeningly, Dominica had not disclosed the location of the letter. Surely, she could have made things easier by just telling her where she'd hidden it? It would seem that Lilac's journey of discovery was something Dominica considered a road Lilac had to travel all by herself.

"I can't be there, my little one, so you must learn to be strong."

Lilac took from this, that the finding of the letter and its contents were somehow going to change her for the better. She'd gone through a couple of Dominica's old diaries to see if she could find a clue, as to its whereabouts but found nothing.

There were still many tiny pieces of furniture yet to be installed in the dolls' house and Lilac began by picking up a bed and examining it all over. She even went to the extent of lifting up the sheets and blankets Dominica had made, to make sure the letter hadn't been folded into a tiny square and somehow tucked inside.

The sheets, pillow, pillowcases, blankets, quilts and bed-covers had all been cut out and hand sewn by Dominica's skilful fingers. It wasn't until Lilac really examined them, as she was now doing, that she came to see just how beautiful each item was and how much delicate work had gone into the making of them.

One bed had a tiny baby doll in it, dressed in pyjamas. It lay on its side, with eyes closed, beneath a thick woolly blanket. After Lilac had carefully taken the doll out and inspected the bed inside, outside and underneath, there was no letter to be found so she replaced everything in exactly the same position and inserted the bed into the bedroom on the second floor.

The next piece of furniture she selected was a miniature mahogany dressing table. Lilac lifted it carefully and pulled out the top drawer – nothing. The second drawer had a set of baby doll clothes in it, and the third had a small square piece of mauve paper. Perhaps it was simply a drawer liner? Lilac tried to prise the piece of paper out but her fingers were too large. She needed a pair of tweezers to get it out. She carefully put the drawer down and raced to the bathroom, where the tweezers were kept. Just as she entered the bathroom there was a loud banging noise. Someone was thumping on her back-door.

***

Astrid had run to Lilac's place via the shortcut through the alley into Korimako Street, then down the drive to her back-door. After catching her breath, she banged hard several times with the palm of her hand. While waiting for Lilac to answer the door, there was movement of some kind to the right of her peripheral vision. She looked through the gap in the hedge, where the Roydons' gate was situated.

A heavily pregnant woman was unpegging clothes from the line. Astrid recognised her immediately as being Tegan, Francine's girlfriend, already claiming her inheritance, by the look of things. When Astrid glanced towards the house, she could see the silhouette of a solid-looking man bending over something in the kitchen. She gasped. Who could he be?

She hurriedly looked away, hating that Tegan and a male stranger were now living in the Roydons' house. Obviously it had all been arranged and written into

Francine's will, that Tegan was to take possession of her new home, just weeks before the baby was due. She and Francine and their new baby would have been a perfect family. Of course, that wasn't to be. Astrid tensed and took one last look, remembering how, just a few weeks ago, she'd been pegging and unpegging the myriad of clothes for her tormentor. To Astrid, it had seemed as though Francine only ever wore things once and took pleasure in seeing her slaving away, washing and ironing everything to achieve the perfect state she insisted on. She looked towards the kitchen window again, but this time there was no one there.

Then Lilac's back-door opened and she stood there with her right arm in a sling. She was looking askance at Astrid. "What are you doing here?"

"Let me in, you fool. Hurry!"

Lilac swung the door back and Astrid flung herself in, as if pursued by a hungry hyena.

"Why have you come here?"

"Because of that interfering P.I. Listen – he's likely to visit you next and start asking a whole lot of questions. You know what he's like: a cunning wolf in sheep's clothing."

"Questions about what? I don't know what you're talking about, Astrid."

"Aren't you even going to offer me a drink?" Astrid

threw herself onto a kitchen chair, her face red and sweaty.

"I suppose so, but you still haven't told me what sort of questions he'll ask me."

"About the earrings, or maybe the fact that you've just broken into Cindy's house, a few doors from his. He wanted to know if I owned some sun and crescent-moon earrings. I said yes, but that one was missing."

"I know the missing one is what you put in Cindy's letterbox," Lilac said, "but I won't be telling him, if that's what you're worried about."

"Oh yes, I told you about it the other night. Didn't I? I think I was slightly drunk," Astrid said, screwing up her face at the memory.

Lilac smirked. "More than slightly, if I recall correctly."

"All right, no need to get hoity-toity about it. I noticed you were drunk yourself," Astrid sniggered. "What a disaster it must've been when Cindy opened the parcel. Must've scared her so bad she looked like a possum in headlights. She must've just about shat herself! I wish I'd been a fly on the wall that day."

"Look Astrid, I'm not sure you should be here. What if Benedict turns up and sees you sitting here? He'll get even more suspicious."

"Why would he? Aren't we allowed to be friends?"

Lilac hesitated. "I told him once we didn't see eye-to-eye, and never had."

Astrid's sinister smile re-appeared and Lilac sucked in her breath.

"Things change, they always do, but you're living in the past all the time. That's what's wrong with you, Lilac – you've never moved on."

"I only said it to stop him thinking we had planned anything together."

"When you wanted him to think it was only me? Thanks, for nothing."

"I had no idea what was going on then. You know that!"

"That interfering Aldo," Astrid said, her mouth a thin line. "He must've told Benedict bloody Aberthorp about the sun earring he found in the kitchen that day."

"What about the other one? Did you find that in the kitchen too?"

Astrid sighed and didn't say anything for a while. Finally, she replied "All right, if you must know, yes, I did. And I would have given it back to Miss High-and-mighty if she hadn't given me the cold shoulder – ever since that particular day. Anyway, she couldn't have it all the way she wanted it."

"Would you like a drink?" Lilac spoke softly, already opening the fridge and taking out a wine bottle, holding it up for Astrid to see. She hated to see her friend upset.

"Only if you're having one." Astrid was starting to look more relaxed now, as she watched Lilac struggling with one hand to unscrew the bottle. She didn't offer to help. Finally, it was open and Lilac awkwardly poured them a large glass each. Lilac was aware of the fact that they both needed to keep clear heads at a time like this, but wanted above all, to appease Astrid.

"Will you look at that? Just what the doctor ordered, my friend. Got any nuts?"

Lilac ferreted around in the pantry and found some salted peanuts that she poured into a bowl and placed on the kitchen table. "You don't have to explain anything to me, you know. In fact it's probably better if I don't know anything more about the earrings. Then I can't slip up and say something I'm not meant to." Lilac lifted the glass to her lips, with her left hand and thirstily swallowed a large mouthful.

"You're right about that – better you're in the dark. Anyway, I don't know what all the fuss is about. She had it coming."

Lilac took another drink. "Don't talk about it. Let's just enjoy our wine and think about happy times to come."

"Oh, yes, I'll drink to that." Astrid downed half the glass in one gulp. "Hey, these peanuts are to die for."

Her fingers groped in the bowl and came out with several.

After a few minutes, Astrid opened her purse and pulled out an old photograph. "Look at this. I found it in an envelope in one of my drawers." She passed it across the table.

Lilac stared at the photo in which a young Cindy Herskington looked back at her. "So these are the earrings you keep talking about. Why didn't you say? I recall her being so proud of them when she showed them to me."

"So you *do* remember?"

Lilac stared at Astrid who was drinking her wine rapidly and eating peanuts in between sips "Why are they important now?"

"I don't know, do I? But precious Benedict seems to think they are."

Lilac sensed that Astrid was being cagey, but decided to take the line of least resistance as Dominica had instructed: 'Play dumb. Pretend you don't understand. Don't get drawn in.'

"Well, my friend, you can rest assured I won't be saying anything. All right?"

Astrid smiled. "So we really are friends again, matey?"

She looked a lot younger when she smiled yet, despite her softened demeanour, Lilac didn't trust her one bit. "Course we are. Let's drink to it." She re-filled both their glasses and they raised them together so they met in the centre of the table with a quiet *chink*. "To us," she said, and they both drank, their eyes already unfocused with the numbing effects of the alcohol.

"Anyway, when I was at your back-door and looked over to the Roydons' place, there was someone in the house." Astrid was staring fixedly straight ahead now in concentration.

"Who was it?" Lilac said, thinking it was probably Tegan.

"A man, judging by the silhouette – a solid-looking man bending over something in the kitchen."

"What? Who could it be?"

"From the shape of him it looked to me like Charley what's-his-name from the shop."

Lilac laughed, tiddly all of a sudden. "Charley? I can't imagine why."

"Well, I can! They were keen on each other, once upon-a-time."

"You make it sound like a fairy story," Lilac said, with a dreamy, faraway look in her eyes. "I'm glad we're friends again," She got up and took another bottle from the fridge. "It's just like old times."

***

"Is it worth having a chat with Lilac about this?" Gail said, as she and Benedict ate lunch at Coffee Mania.

"The earrings? No, I'm more interested in what Lilac told us about Cindy and Charley. I didn't know anything about them getting together, and he never said a word."

"I did find out a bit about Charley for you." Gail picked up her phone and scrolled through it. "He has an 'interesting' past."

"Go on."

"He's thirty-eight, born in Seagrove. Both parents deceased. Has a sister, but no one seems to know where she is, apart from being overseas, apparently. Anyway, it appears he was once in love with Cindy Herskington, as her surname was then. But she ended up with Aldo and Charley went over the edge and robbed a bank. Had a gun on him and got twelve years. His parents were poor, although they had their own home. After they died, the house was sold to pay off all their debts. Tough for a youngster who had just left school. He was part of the group of school-leavers who used to meet at the Roydons'."

"What year did he go to prison?"

"2004. And when he got out in 2016, Francine Roydon offered him a job in the shop. They were still friends, but there could have been some underlying resentment there on Charley's part, because he didn't like the way Francine and Aldo had treated Cindy; Aldo having rejected her, and years later Francine refusing to even admit she was Jenniver's half-sister. Of course, Francine's friends had suspected for years that Andy Roydon was Jenniver's father. He probably denied it, of course."

"So how could Charley and Francine still be friends with that between them? Plus, he once went out with Cindy, and likely felt a sense of justice that the girl who had hurt him had latterly got her comeuppance," Benedict said.

"Charley was probably grateful to have a job and a place to stay, and was prepared to forget the past. After all, he didn't have a lot going for him as an ex-con."

"You're right, but who's to say he hasn't secretly borne a grudge against Francine *and* Aldo all along?"

"Could be." Gail was scrolling through her phone again.

"Anything else?"

"Nothing apart from the fact he went to prison when he was eighteen. He came out aged thirty with lots of tattoos. That's all I have."

"Okay, this is what I think happened: when Cindy arrived from Scotland, she went to see Charley. I suppose it's only natural she'd want to catch up," Benedict said.

Gail frowned. "Really? What about the hurt we were talking about?"

"Right, but as so much time had passed since then, and she too had been hurt – by Aldo and Francine – they now had something in common. There could also still have been a flicker of romance between them. Or else they're simply old friends catching up? It doesn't have to be sexual, does it?"

"Not necessarily, but there could have still been a spark there."

Benedict shrugged. "There's also another way to look at it."

"Oh no, I think I know what you're going to say…"

"They both had grudges against Francine, and together planned to get rid of her. And Cindy's grudges became Charley's too. He was still in love with her and was prepared to do anything to please her."

"So you want me to arrange an interview with Cindy?" Gail said, preparing to take down a note.

"You're ahead of me there, my friend, but yes, why not? We haven't even spoken to her yet, and I think the time is now."

Gail rubbed her hands together. "I can't wait!"

Chapter 18

Thursday 13th June

"You'd better stay here tonight," Lilac said, hoping Astrid would agree. She looked as floppy as a rag-doll.

"No, it's all right, I can only sleep properly in my own bed."

Astrid was in no state to walk home, and Lilac was drunk too, so she phoned for a taxi. When it arrived, she steered Astrid towards the cab and helped her in, then climbed in too. On arrival at her flat, Lilac asked the driver to wait and had to hold onto Astrid's right arm, helping her inside. She quickly shut the door behind them but not before she saw the curtains fall back into place at Miss Wilson's flat.

"Don't you ever do anything else?" Lilac muttered, as she got Astrid to her bedroom. The bedsheets were crumpled and there were clothes and books everywhere, which gave the room an untidy, grubby look. She pulled back the covers and Astrid flopped down into bed, fully clothed. Lilac pushed her gently so that she was lying straight before covering her with the grey-looking sheets and tattered blankets. As she turned to switch off the light, her gaze fell upon something sparkling, lying on the dressing table.

Lilac's hand reached out involuntarily, and her fingers closed around the crescent-moon earring, before slipping it into her pocket. She glanced quickly at Astrid, whose eyes were closed and her mouth slightly open, breathing noisily. Lilac smiled, turned out the light and ran to the front-door, barely making a sound.

The taxi accelerated off, the driver whistling in a friendly manner and all Lilac could think about was carrying on with what she had been doing before Astrid had so unexpectedly arrived at her house.

As she paid the driver and turned towards her house, Scamper was sitting on the wicker chair, waiting for her. Poor Scamper, he always kept out of the way when Astrid was there.

"Good boy." She picked him up and stroked his head. "It's all right, just you and me now. Good boy."

Lilac went straight to the bathroom to get the tweezers and then to the den, where she picked up the drawer from the miniature mahogany dressing table and looked inside again. Carefully she plucked out the mauve piece of paper and laid it down on the work bench. It was delicate and thin, just like the airmail paper she'd used years ago. Finally, she was able to unfold it and smooth it out flat. She began reading the letter Dominica had written to her twenty-four years ago – January seven, 2000:

Dear Lilac,

Yes, I am now gone and that's why you're reading this. Don't be alarmed because I think I've foreseen my own demise, so knew this was going to happen – just not when. My second-sight has not always been the gift some thought it was. Often it was a curse that tormented me day and night.

What you are about to read – what I need to tell you – has always puzzled me. The real meaning has never been totally clear to me, like so many other messages I've been sent. I only knew it concerned death and possibly murder. But whose? The letters DEF were shown to me over and over, and as you know, they are my initials: Dominica Evangelina Frimble. But even though the message looks so clear, I've always thought, rightly or wrongly, that it also alluded to something else, or someone else. That's all I was shown.

You know me, Lilac, and you know I only ever told you the truth. So this is one time where you need to keep an open mind. Remember these words – 'for murder, press three' and think about them, because I know you can figure it out. If there's someone you really trust, ask for their help.

Your loving partner, Dominica.'

Chapter 19

Friday 14th June

The bus careered along the bumpy country road, heading for the women's prison. Cindy, who was sitting near the front, was undergoing a painful internal struggle. She wanted to see Jenniver on her own, because she had things to tell her, and once Gregor arrived, this wouldn't be possible, because he'd want to accompany her to the prison.

Gregor wasn't part of her youthful past, or the internal world created by it – a world Cindy had been carrying within herself for twenty years – and living within for the majority of that time. The most precious person in her life and who had changed everything was not Gregor but her daughter, Jenniver. She didn't deserve to be rejected by the family she had been born into, no matter how tawdry her conception had been perceived due to the age difference between Cindy and Andy Roydon. That wasn't right.

"She says she's not my half-sister, Mum," Jenniver had said when she'd phoned that day of Francine's rejection. Cindy had hurt as much in Scotland as her daughter hurt from the other side of the world.

"I'm coming over," she'd told her daughter, when Jenniver had rung again a few weeks later to say she was in trouble with the police. Within a few days, Cindy was on a flight, and the hours spent travelling had given her plenty of time to think about how to avenge her daughter's fate.

Yet even as she put her false persona to good effect, Cindy feared she could never win. She didn't listen to the other small voice; the one telling her this wasn't necessarily correct as her true self was still there – just buried in a quagmire. This self told her she could win because she once had the courage to have her daughter alone after travelling to the other side of the world to give her a better life.

Despite her need for revenge, there was still a thin thread, holding her to the better, calmer and accepting version of herself, that she'd discovered in the years since marrying Gregor and living in Scotland. This same thread had made her feel guilty for what she'd done, when she'd driven past the Holy Angels church yesterday, on her way home from Charley's flat.

***

When Benedict and Gail arrived outside Cindy's house in the hope she'd be home, they found Mrs Shields who was bent over the flower beds in the neighbouring plot. At the sound of their car door slamming shut, she stood upright, a trowel in her right hand, and smiled in greeting. Benedict smiled back On his way to Cindy's front door, Mrs Shields called, "She's gone out."

"Oh? What time was that?"

"About half an hour ago."

"Do you know where she went?"

"No, but she headed that way."

"Thanks."

"I think she might have gone to the prison," Benedict said starting the car again. "We really need to see her today. This whole thing has gone on long enough."

***

Cindy pictured Charley's face and the tattoos on his fingers instead of Gregor who was arriving today. She hated the idea of going back to Scotland; her love for Charley enveloping her so. The weak link in that bond however was that stupid woman who'd started playing games with her, like that earring left in her letterbox.

She found these games irritating and distracting. She didn't want to have to deal with them. Her affair with Charley and her visits to the prison used up all her emotional energy; she had no more left for games. And now there was the raincoat placed in her suitcase the other night. How stupid Astrid Lorning was, and always had been as far as Cindy was concerned, allowing herself to be beaten up on a regular basis by that weasel of a husband. And now, trying to scare Cindy into thinking she could frame her for…

"How's your daughter coping inside?" a voice beside Cindy suddenly said.

Cindy turned to her right. The seat had been unoccupied before, but now Zoe sat there – the woman whose daughter was in prison for the third time, doing a seven-years' stretch.

She forced a smile. "Jenniver's just fine. She's a strong and confident woman, you know. A person who lives without fear."

Zoe stared at Cindy with glassy eyes. Her skin had an unhealthy yellowish sheen and her grey, greasy hair was unkempt. "My Sally's depressed. She reckons there's a lot of bullying in there and her life is like hell from morning to night."

A feeling of tightness grabbed Cindy's abdomen, but she still managed to smile. "That's no good, but I'm sure

Sally can stick up for herself."

Silence followed but Cindy sensed Zoe staring hard at her. She looked around again to see the other woman scowling. "You had me fooled," she said, her lips hardly moving and a look of contempt on her face.

"What do you mean?" Cindy tried to keep up the pretence of confidence and cheeriness, but there was something about Zoe's expression that made her falter.

"That you were an innocent mum visiting her daughter."

"I don't understand," Cindy said. "What am I supposed to have done?"

Zoe turned round in her seat and her stare penetrated into Cindy's eyes. "The word's out at the prison that you killed your ex's wife, Francine Roydon."

Cindy was floored. "What? Who the hell is telling lies like that?"

"The number one bully, so Sally says. And your Jenniver got herself pulverised by the same bully when she stuck up for you, didn't she? On her birthday too, so Sally said."

The shock of what Zoe had just said made Cindy feel physically sick; her little girl, assaulted for standing by her mum. "I don't believe you."

"Believe what you want," Zoe said, her mouth turned down grimly at the corners as she continued to fix her gaze on Cindy. "Is that what you did then?"

"Why would I? I had no reason to do that. I'm a married woman! My husband's arriving tonight from Scotland. We love each other."

"That's not what I asked though, is it?"

The bus stopped outside the prison gates, its wheels scrunching on the gravel. Zoe rushed off, leaving Cindy too stunned to even think of what to do or say next. Perhaps even going into the prison was going to be dangerous, if that was their opinion of her. She imagined the unnamed bully rushing over and punching her senseless before the guards could tear her away. Yet she reasoned it was probably just something the bully had made up to intimidate Jenniver, who wasn't a hardened criminal like most of them in there were. Poor Jenniver, whose only crime was feeding her own drug habit by selling drugs to others to get enough funds for her own. She must have been like a lamb to the slaughter. Cindy came to her senses and ran towards the exit door at the front of the bus, almost knocking the driver over in her hurry to get to the visitor's area. He was making his way slowly to the door.

"Sorry," she said, pushing past and hurrying to join the end of the visiting line.

***

Benedict and Gail arrived at the prison fifteen minutes after visiting time had begun. There were two policemen standing at the entrance with sniffer dogs and they eyed them suspiciously as they got out of the car. Benedict and Gail stood beside the car as they waited for the visitors to come out. The plan was that when they finally did, Benedict would somehow encourage Cindy to talk to him.

He went over to the bus that was waiting to take the visitors back to Seagrove. The driver was leaning with his back against the bonnet, smoking a cigarette and blowing smoke-rings up into the air.

"What time will you be leaving again?" Benedict asked.

Around three-thirty, sir. Sometimes three-forty. There's room if you need a lift back."

"No, thanks. I'm actually waiting for someone to come out and wondered if I'd have time to speak with her before the bus departs?"

"Should do. We often have a ten minutes' delay because of stragglers. They like to spend every last second with their loved ones, the poor devils."

***

Jenniver sat on an orange painted metal chair by an orange metal table, where they always sat during visiting times. All the furniture was bolted to the grey concrete floor and the chairs were cold to sit on. As Cindy hurried over, she noticed Jenniver's face and cried out. "My God, what's happened?" She leaned forward and looked closely at Jenniver who didn't smile in greeting, as she usually did. Her left eye was closed and she had a deep gouge all the way down her right cheek.

"Nothing much, Mum. Just the usual bullying. I need to keep out of her way, that's all. But don't worry, it's not going to happen again. I have supporters."

"Did you report it?"

"*Shhh*. No, and don't ask me why. Anyway, the wardens found me on the floor and I couldn't get up, so they took me to the sick-bay. I was silly enough to stand up to the rotten devil, that's all."

"Tell me why it happened, Jenniver. Please."

"You know why, Mum, but I'm not here to judge you. Just remember that. I have no business even wanting to know about it."

Cindy said nothing for a while, just looked down at the table. "I'm sorry, Jenniver, but I am not a murderer. It didn't happen the way you might think. It was something even I didn't know was going to happen. That's all I can say, and I'm sorry."

"I love you, Mum, and I always will – no matter what happens."

"How can you love me? I don't deserve it."

"You don't have to deserve it, Mum. You told me that once, remember? You told me that the love between a mother and her child is unconditional."

Cindy looked at her daughter and, despite her injured eye, could see the love she spoke of there, as well as a determination she admired. Jenniver had only just turned nineteen and had a maturity Cindy had herself learnt through becoming a mother at seventeen. "Are the meals all right, love?" Cindy asked, in an attempt to change the subject.

Jenniver tried to smile. "Yeah, course they are. Not luxury, but you know."

"Have you made any friends?"

"Sure I have, Mum. The main one's Sally and she said she'll protect me from now on. She's pretty tough, Mum, so I guess I'm lucky to have her watching my back."

Cindy's spirits rose, even though she hadn't liked what Zoe had said to her on the bus. "I think I might know her mother. I met a woman on the bus called Zoe and she was telling me about her daughter, Sally, who's in for seven years. Is she the one?"

"Yep, and Sally means what she said, though I have

to do whatever she asks. That's her only condition."

"What does that mean, darling?"

Jenniver looked away before answering. "Listen, Mum, I want you to know I'm okay and you're not to worry about me. I have some pretty tough mates in here, and they've all told me that from now on they're going to look out for me."

"I'll be thinking of you every day." Cindy didn't try to explain to Jenniver about how she'd found true love. She never thought she'd ever love anyone again, after Aldo, but when she and Charley started seeing each other on her return, it had just happened. She couldn't explain it – even to herself, it had been so unexpected. Yet of course it had happened too late. There was no going back now and putting the past into a different order. As Charley had said, "C'est la vie." All she could do was agree.

***

When the prison visitors began trailing out, Benedict and Gail were ready to take action. Cindy appeared in the first group, walking towards a purple car, parked nearby with its engine running. The driver was a balding man wearing glasses. He was smiling as Cindy climbed into the passenger seat and they drove off.

"Hey, that's Charley," Benedict said. "She's not taking the bus back after all."

"I'll drive," Gail said, already opening the driver's-door. "I'll make sure we don't lose them."

Benedict threw her the keys, knowing she had the gumption to race. They drove off at speed; the old car noisily showing its power.

"The bloody bus is just pulling out," Gail said, as she began to overtake, but it was too late – there was a car coming the other way. "So where do you reckon they're going?"

"Probably his flat, but why now?" Benedict's instincts told him something had unsettled Cindy and Charley but he had no idea what that could be.

When they arrived back in Seagrove, Gail drove past Roydons' Antiques and they saw that the shop was open. Was Cindy in there too?

"Let's try her house first," Benedict said, and Gail sped there promptly. Mrs Shields was no longer in her front garden, and when Benedict knocked on Cindy's front door, there was no answer. He went round to the back and tried again, but nothing. Cindy was definitely not in unless she was hiding out of sight.

***

Lilac's car was hidden in its usual place and she watched as a purple car, pulled up outside Cindy's house. Cindy got out and went inside, while the bald driver waited. Lilac recognised him as being Charley from the shop.

About five minutes later, Cindy came out again, carrying a bulging overnight bag. She drove her little car out of the garage and followed Charley's. Lilac watched as both cars disappeared from sight. She was convinced they were having an affair. Why else were they spending so much time together? All those years ago, she'd seen Cindy and Charley, in their blossoming youth, outside in the backyard at the Roydons', holding hands and even kissing on one occasion. Back then, Lilac was a frequent visitor to the Roydons' residence.

Then they had split up and Charley had robbed a bank and gone to prison. Cindy was then together with Aldo. They were so young, and in love with each other. As for Francine, Andy Roydon tried to rule her with an iron fist. He tried to rule Irene in the same way. He laid down laws that were seldom kept; one being no sex before marriage, that he didn't adhere to himself. Andy couldn't understand why Aldo and Cindy broke up, and he had hated it when Aldo and Francine started seeing so much of each other. He could see how hurt and confused Cindy was by this development. He befriended her but their relationship went too far and she became pregnant. Andy Roydon was a coward, and so when Cindy left for Scotland, it had solved the problem. Later he was pleased when Francine married Aldo. He didn't care about Aldo's poorer background, because he himself was a wealthy man. Everything he had would eventually be split between Francine and Irene anyway (Francine's on the condition she retained her maiden name after they were married). She agreed to this, of course.

Lilac was about to drive away when Benedict and his assistant drove up. She watched the private investigator knock on Cindy's door. With no reply, the pair gave up and drove further up the street to Benedict's house where they stopped to go inside. Lilac had an urge to talk to him then, and Dominica was urging her on too:

"Do it, go on, do it. Don't tell Astrid though."

Despite wanting to see him, she hesitated. Remembering the business card Benedict had given her, with his phone number on it, she decided to go home and call him first to arrange a time to meet him at his office in Rowan Street.

***

Benedict and Gail had seen Lilac's car, partially hidden by the trees. It had looked as though she had been about to leave, but then she must've seen them and turned the engine off. Benedict wanted to persuade Lilac to talk to them. He reasoned she'd like to do that, given that she had already been forthcoming about the earrings, *and* the recent meeting between Cindy and Charley at the shop.

"Lilac Browne has been like a would-be sleuth recently," Benedict said.

Gail laughed. "She knows what's going on in this place, that's why. But why is she always watching Cindy?"

"Because she suspects her of being involved in what happened."

"The murder?"

"Yes."

***

When Lilac arrived home, she found Benedict Aberthorp's business card on the kitchen table. She picked up her phone and dialled the number. Almost immediately, a male voice answered:

"Hello, and thank you for calling. Benedict Aberthorp is busy right now, but your call is important to him. Press three to leave your name and number. He will return your call as soon as possible."

Lilac did as the answerphone message instructed; her hands shaking as she did so. When she'd finished the call, she went straight to the fridge and poured herself a cold glass of the remaining sparkling wine (that had since lost its bubbles). She then grabbed her cigarettes and went out onto her back porch where she sat, smoking and drinking to calm her nerves. She couldn't believe she'd finally obeyed Dominica's veiled instruction and pressed the number three on her phone. But was it for murder? "Why did you have to make it so hard, my love?"

She listened for Dominica's reply, but only silence came. Then Benedict had returned her call and invited her to visit his office in an hour's time.

***

Benedict smiled at the familiar sight of Lilac Browne framed in the doorway of his office. "Come on in," he said.

Lilac followed Benedict silently and sat down on a swivel chair. Gail made her some coffee and gave her a piece of home-made chocolate sponge, with whipped cream on top and a fork to eat it with. Lilac's facial expression was one of delight as she proceeded to savour a mouthful.

Once she had finished chewing, Lilac's words spewed forth, like clothes tumbling from a washing machine with its door open.

"Cindy and Charley," she said, "have been and gone."

"What were they doing?" Benedict said.

"He parked outside her place and she went in. After a while, she came out carrying a bag – a small suitcase. Then he drove away and she followed him in her own car. I don't trust Cindy," Lilac said.

"So why is it you don't trust her?" he said.

Benedict knew from experience that Lilac couldn't be rushed. She would tell him what he needed to know – he felt sure of that now – but in her own time. She was an anxious character, and her nervous state could just as easily lead to her concealing information as it could reveal it.

Lilac continued her train of thought, ignoring Benedict's question. "When Cindy arrived back, she made friends with Astrid. I looked through the hedge one day and there they were. Aldo too."

"When was that?"

"In April. Astrid was secretive after that. That's why I don't trust Astrid or Cindy. Cindy must have been up to something, for Astrid to go all funny like she did. And now Cindy's not even friends with Astrid anymore, or

Aldo. Astrid hates Cindy now. And Charley's sneaky too," Lilac said, with her mouth full again.

Benedict's interest was roused. "In what way?"

She swallowed the last of the cake and looked at Benedict. She hesitated before answering for fear that Astrid would find out what she was about to say. Somehow, Astrid always found out everything she did or said.

"It's all right, Lilac, nothing you say will go further than this room."

Suitably reassured, Lilac said, "Astrid came over to my place and said there was a man in the Roydons' kitchen – Tegan's now, of course. She could see a silhouette of a man through the window. She said it looked like Charley, from the shop."

Benedict smiled slightly, as if Lilac's words had confirmed something that until now he'd been unsure of. "Well, that's interesting. Thanks for sharing that with us."

***

Lilac couldn't believe she'd just revealed all that information to Benedict Aberthorp – a man she'd once feared. Yet there was something about his manner that made her want to talk; a calmness that encouraged her to confide her secrets.

Now she'd begun, she wanted to tell him everything – to get the horrible weight off her shoulders – especially the crescent-moon earring, that she'd placed in the drawer of the miniature mahogany dressing table in the dolls' house where she'd found Dominica's letter. Benedict needed to know about that too. Lilac was tired of all the secrets, and the earring was one of them.

For a long time now, she'd been sinking under the secrets of the past. They had laid themselves squarely on her and now demanded to be exposed. If she didn't, she could imagine herself slowly disappearing into the earth, with the weight on top of her, until there was nothing left of her.

Lilac often dreamt of the day when she would be totally free of the past; its secrets eroding her well-being at every turn. It felt like she couldn't fully enjoy anything in life anymore; not in the way she used to when Dominica was here. Now, every day she faced an internal battle, in which no matter how hard she tried, the past always came back, circling around, like a hungry animal, searching for its next meal. And then Lilac would step back and surrender herself, allowing the memories to come rushing back and take over again. During such moments, she would go to the bedroom, where Dominica's diary still remained in its Stygian bedside drawer. She would open the pages and read the penultimate entry:

'Wednesday March 2, 2005 – Lilac and I want to free Astrid from the monster.'

Now, here she was, after eating chocolate sponge cake in Benedict Aberthorp's office and enjoying every morsel. Yet there was so much she hadn't yet told him. Her survival instincts told her to be careful now, but at the same time she was almost certain that he was the right person to tell – because of Dominica's message. The riddle still hadn't been solved though, because she didn't know yet what the 'for murder' part meant.

The flimsy, mauve-coloured letter, was inside her jacket pocket and she put her hand in and touched the fine paper with her fingers. – DEF – Dominica Evangelina Frimble. She'd tell Benedict all about it, but perhaps not yet. She picked up her coffee cup and stared straight ahead.

***

Cindy liked the way Charley was so willing to agree to anything she asked of him.

"I always felt incomplete until you turned up again," he'd said, when he first saw her again that day she came into the shop to see him.

Cindy took pride in the fact that she had the power to

make him so willing to comply with whatever she suggested or asked him to help her with. He always agreed without hesitation, as if she'd instantly become mistress of his life. They fell into each other's arms and minds so easily and seamlessly that Cindy was also complete when she was with him. The world around them disappeared when they were together and it was like they fused into one being.

And now, here she was, in his small, tidy flat while he was downstairs in the shop, serving customers, as if everything was normal. He'd close the shop at six p.m. There was nothing to worry about. Cindy unpacked her suitcase and put her clothes into the drawer Charley had emptied for her. She hadn't brought much, but had made sure to pack the sun earring, and the brown raincoat left in the spare room that night by Lilac Browne (no doubt on Astrid's orders). She'd seen Lilac running away and then limping to her car afterwards, holding her arm.

Cindy began looking for a place somewhere in Charley's flat to hide the raincoat. Somehow, she and Charley would get it back to where it belonged – to Aldo's beach-house. Yet not today, because today Gregor was arriving – in just over an hour's time – and she didn't want to see him, which is why she was here, with Charley. The earring she kept safe in her handbag. No one else was going to know about it. She still didn't know where the crescent-moon one was, although she had her suspicions.

She looked at her watch: 5:50 p.m. When Charley closed the shop in ten minutes, they were going to have a drink together and work out a plan of action. In the meantime, she had something important to do. She picked up her phone and keyed in the text message she'd thought of earlier: 'I've had to visit a sick friend to make sure she's eating. I'm cooking her an evening meal. See you soon, my love.' She didn't want Gregor to worry, at least not for a while – and so she told him where to find the spare key and said she'd be back soon.

"She used to visit me, you know," Charley said, lightly running his tattooed fingers down Cindy's cheek. "We were friends then."

"Who?" Cindy said, dreamily. She was already falling under the spell Charley cast on her.

"Francine, of course, in prison. She'd come once a week. No one else ever came."

Cindy, like a drowsy bumblebee was only half listening to what Charley was saying. She didn't want anything to spoil the time she spent with him and didn't care about anything else right now. All she cared about was being with him. His closeness was like an intoxication. They'd both had some whisky too, straight from the bottle Charley kept on the floor by his bed. He liked to reach down and swig from it, and then kiss her with his whisky-tasting lips, laughing as he stroked her and pushed her hair back from her face, planting light kisses on her forehead until she tingled all over.

"She treated you so badly," Charley said, "and I hated her for that. But at least she visited me in the clink – and when no one else did."

"What happened to your friendship?" Cindy squirmed, wondering why Charley kept talking about Francine. She didn't want to remember anything about that woman. Why didn't Charley understand that? There was so much she wanted to blot out.

"She and Aldo stole you from me, and I couldn't forgive them for that," Charley said. "But Francine was the main one I blamed, 'cos Aldo was caught in her spell, like a fly in a spider's web. There was someone else, she stole her from me as well."

Cindy's body suddenly went rigid. "What? Who was it?"

"Tegan Tresco. She used to live next to the Roydons, remember? With her parents and brother. The beauty was always protected by her parents, especially her father."

Cindy lay still and was cold all of a sudden. "Tegan used to be sent away to boarding school. She went to a private school somewhere down south. I remember that much about her. So what happened?"

"She still came home for holidays," Charley said, reaching for the whisky bottle again. He sat up and took another glug then lay on his back and stared at the ceiling as if he was thinking intently about something.

Until now, Cindy hadn't considered Tegan a part in Charley's life. Yet Charley's words rang in her mind and she kept hearing them, over and over: 'There was someone else she stole from me as well.'

Was Tegan the reason Charley finally turned against Francine? The woman who'd helped him get back on his feet after his prison stretch? Charley must have been in love with Tegan all along. Worse still was the probability he was still in love with her. Was he thinking about her all the time? This scenario hadn't been factored into anything Cindy had dreamed of. How could this be happening?

Charley was in the shower when Cindy gathered up her few possessions. She tucked the brown raincoat right at the back of Charley's bottom drawer, behind his jumpers. Then quietly, she left the flat, climbed into her car and drove away, back to her rented house.

***

Aldo's entire body grew rigid and his mouth drew itself

into a thin line, as he recalled the fact that Tegan was living in what was once his and Francine's home. Worse still, Tegan was having a baby. His mind went back to the time when they had lost their baby. And now, sitting alone in his beach-house, staring out at the night sky, Tegan's face came into his mind: the girl who'd lived with her parents and brother next door to the Roydons; the one who looked like an angel.

Francine had liked Tegan and looked forward to the day when she'd finish boarding school and come home to live in Seagrove again. "Tegan and I are going to be friends again," Francine had said on more than one occasion. However, when she'd finished boarding school, Tegan had gone to university to study medicine. Aldo remembered Francine telling him one day that Tegan was a GP, working in the South Island and that she was married to a doctor there.

When Tegan's husband had been tragically killed in a train crash while on his way to attending a conference in Australia, Tegan had given up her practice and returned to her parents' home in Seagrove. Aldo remembered this all happened around Christmastime, 2004. Francine used to go over to chat to Tegan, telling him how the two women were friends again. He never placed any importance on Francine's visits to Tegan. Besides, he'd also known Tegan, although not well, as she'd always been away at boarding school. Even after he and his school friends had all left school, Tegan had remained at boarding school, to gain higher qualifications for the university in Otago.

And now the irony – Tegan living in the Roydons' house, left to her by Francine and soon to have their baby. By the time he returned home from hospital in May 2005, he had seen the 'for sale' sign on the Trescos' property but they had already moved out. When he'd asked Francine where they'd gone to, she'd looked puzzled.

"I don't know, love. They just moved. Their house hasn't sold yet, but they've gone," she'd said.

***

"Is there anything else you want to tell me?" Benedict asked Lilac, as she finished her coffee and placed the cup down.

Lilac blinked and stared straight ahead.

"More coffee?" Gail asked, silently appearing to pick up the used coffee cup. "Cake?"

She shook her head. "No thanks."

"Well," Benedict said, "I suppose the police will be into their own enquiries by now. I hope to have my own conclusions drawn up by the end of the week. It will be good when it's all over, won't it?"

Lilac's mouth opened and closed again. She stared at Benedict, blinking rapidly but said nothing. "I need a cigarette." She reached into her jacket pocket and extracted a crumpled packet and a lighter.

"I'll show you outside."

He led her down the stairs and out into a small courtyard where there was a garden area with two chairs. Lilac immediately lit up and took two deep drags of her cigarette. Then she sat down, staring ahead of her as she smoked. There was a slight breeze blowing and the smoke drifted away. Benedict sensed there was something Lilac needed to get off her chest. He just needed to be patient.

"Of course, it would be even better if the police reached the same conclusions as me, don't you think?" Benedict watched her face for any sign of a reaction. "Because if they don't, it will mean there may be a miscarriage of justice. What a joke that would be!"

"Er, yes, I suppose so. Look, there is something I wanted to show you." She pulled a thin, mauve sheet of paper from her jacket pocket, opened it out and smoothed it with her fingers before handing it to Benedict.

He noted from the date at the top of the letter that it

had been written a long time ago. He began reading.

'Remember these words – for murder, press three – and think about them. Because I know you can figure it out. If there's someone you really trust, ask for their help.'

"Well, I trust you, Mr Aberthorp. Do you know what Dominica was trying to say?"

The letter was unexpected. "Can you come back tomorrow afternoon?" he said. "I'll need a little time to think this over – with Gail, if that's all right?"

"Er, yes, of course it's okay. Dominica said as much in the letter." Lilac may have disclosed the contents of the letter to Benedict but she had decided never to reveal what she had read in Dominica's diary. She wanted to keep one secret to herself.

'Thursday, March 3, 2005 – tomorrow we're attending a BBQ at the Roydons.'

***

Astrid searched her bedroom for the crescent-moon earring but couldn't find it. After a day of housework and ironing for the 'rich bitch', as she now called the woman for whom she did housework, she was tired.

For days Astrid had been thinking of visiting Benedict Aberthorp. She wanted him to think she was trying to help solve the case. And she wanted to tell him about the raincoat and the truth about the missing earring; to set the record straight by telling him about the morning Aldo had found the sun earring on the kitchen floor. She wasn't friends with Cindy anymore and now she both feared and hated her. She didn't know what Cindy and the evil Charley were up to but she knew the lovers weren't to be trusted.

Lilac had told Astrid about seeing Cindy going into the shop where Charley worked and lived. What if they were planning to implicate her and tell the police she'd done it? If so, then Astrid wanted to present her side first. She'd tell Benedict she hadn't said anything before, because she didn't want Cindy to get into trouble. Yet now, after thinking about it, she had to say something. Astrid was confident she could make Benedict believe her. And if he asked what kind of trouble? she would reply, "Well, you might start wondering what the earring was doing on the kitchen floor and how it had got there – maybe even on that particular day."

First though she had to find the crescent-moon earring and began frantically searching her bedroom. Then she remembered the day Miss Wilson had told her about the small blue car pulling out from the parking area outside Astrid's flat while she'd been at work.

She wanted to raise Benedict's suspicions of Cindy

sufficiently for him to justify searching her house, and when he did, he'd find the other earring and the raincoat. Maybe even both earrings? Perhaps Cindy had come to the flat and taken it back while Astrid was out working for the 'rich bitch'. Either way, Astrid wanted Benedict to make Cindy his prime suspect and then for the police to take her in for questioning. With any luck, they'd charge her with premeditated murder and subsequently she'd be imprisoned for life. However, Astrid still couldn't be sure that the crescent-moon earring was actually in Cindy's possession. She had to find out, and for that she needed to persuade Lilac to help her.

Astrid decided to tell Lilac of her plan. Lilac wasn't completely ignorant of the facts, no matter how innocent she may appear to be, and Astrid trusted her opinion as to whether her plan was a viable one. If she agreed to help her again, and they were sure Cindy had both earrings, Lilac might even agree to accompany her to the private investigator's office, driving her there in her trusty car. Having made a plan of action, she got up and put her coat back on. After one last, unsuccessful look for the earring, she left the flat and trudged through the dark to Korimako Street. She hated the dark alleyway and once through it, she ran the rest of the way.

***

Benedict photocopied Dominica's letter and gave the original back to Lilac, who put it into her pocket. "I must get home now. Scamper will need his tea."

When Lilac turned into her driveway shortly after her visit to Benedict's office, a shadowy figure was standing by the letterbox. As she got closer, she could see it was Astrid. What on earth was she doing here? Lilac's whole body went rigid and she felt on the verge of screaming.

"I'll wait while you see to Scamper," Astrid said, showing an unaccustomed kindness towards the cat she'd never liked. Lilac was immediately suspicious. Something must be wrong.

"Scamper, Scamper. Come on boy," she called repeatedly. He obviously sensed the enemy was in his territory and was hiding. Lilac persisted and eventually his hunger overtook his caution. He was now purring and rubbing his large fluffy body on one of the table legs in the kitchen. Lilac patted him and dished out a larger than usual portion for him before taking the plate out onto her back porch. She then let Astrid in via the front door so as not disturb Scamper, who would have bolted if she came anywhere near him.

"Why have you come round so late?" Lilac said, going to the sink to wash her dirty dishes from earlier in the day. She could barely disguise her annoyance at

Astrid for turning up unexpectedly like this, and she kept thinking of the earring she'd taken. Maybe that's why Astrid was here? She shivered involuntarily.

"I just wanted to see you – have a glass of wine, like old times."

Lilac carried on casually washing her dishes. "Take a look in the fridge. There's a couple of cold ones in there." It seemed to Lilac, that Astrid could do nothing these days without wetting her lips with alcohol first. She suspected, not for the first time, that her friend was an alcoholic.

Astrid hurried over and took out one of the bottles: her favourite sparkling wine. She reached up for two of Lilac's wine glasses and quickly poured them both a large measure. Afterwards she sat there, politely waiting for Lilac, while admiring the Rosé in front of her. "Come and sit down, you can dry them later." Lilac immediately noticed that Astrid's voice had a forced kindness to it. She watched as her friend held onto the stem of her glass with her gnarled fingers. Lilac had no desire to drink wine right now but she'd go along with what Astrid wanted while hating herself for being so compliant.

Astrid would normally start drinking as fast as she could without waiting for Lilac. This aroused Lilac's suspicions of her friend's motives even more.

"So, you been doing that housework today?" Lilac said, sitting down at the table. "You look knackered."

"I am, mate, don't you worry. The rich bitch left me my money though. She's good like that, she is."

They raised their glasses and chinked them noisily before Astrid took a large swig, while Lilac took a small sip to appear convivial in front of Astrid. She wanted to keep her wits about her rather than get drunk again.

"Anything wrong?" Lilac eventually said, hoping her facial expression didn't betray her guilt.

"Course not, mate. Why would there be?"

"No reason. Only…"

"I know what you're going to say – it's not like me to come round so late."

"You don't need to explain anything. We're back on good terms, that's the main thing. I don't mind when you come over, you know that. It's nice to see you."

"Here's to us." Astrid glugged down half a glass and smiled crookedly. "Boy, life can be strange sometimes."

Lilac watched her, an uneasiness growing in the pit of her stomach. She hadn't intended to tell Astrid anything about her visit to Benedict Aberthorp or, why she'd gone there in the first place. She wasn't even going to tell her about seeing Cindy and Charley. Now she wondered if somehow Astrid had found out. Yet how could she have? And there was the earring too; was

Astrid going to say anything about its absence?

"How do you mean, Astrid? Has something else happened?"

"No, but it's like this, you see: I need to see that Benedict bloke. If I don't, he won't know to search Cindy's house, will he? Think about it."

Lilac was sure Benedict wouldn't find anything useful at Cindy's. She was also sure Cindy was running scared, although why, wasn't clear. For some reason, Cindy had decided to make herself scarce, just as the net was closing in. "A good idea of yours, as usual," Lilac said, remembering Dominica's words: 'Play dumb, admit nothing, pretend you don't understand.' "What will you tell Benedict?"

Astrid, bleary-eyed, swirled the wine in her glass and studied it without answering.

"You need to word it so you don't look suspicious," Lilac said.

"I'll tell him I only pretended the earring was mine, but that it really belongs to Cindy. And if he looks in Cindy's place he'll find both earrings. That means you and I need to go to Cindy's first and make sure both of them are there. She must've stolen the crescent-moon one from my flat because it's not there anymore. My God, she's cunning. 'Cunning Cindy' – that's my name for her now."

Lilac squirmed at the thought of doing Astrid's bidding. "But what does having the earrings prove? Maybe she just wanted them back with her? Where they belong." Lilac took a long drink to calm her nerves.

"It proves Cindy was there on the day of the murder. I'll tell the smartarse P.I. what he wants to know. I'm pretty sure he's got his eye on Cindy – the eye of a suspicious detective."

To Lilac, Astrid's reasoning was full of flaws, but she'd never say that to her. "You *could* do that. You're so clever, Astrid, you really are."

Astrid looked at Lilac and smiled at the flattery she thought was heartfelt. "Got any chips, love?"

Lilac got up to fill a bowl with salt and vinegar chips and placed them in front of Astrid. It was then that she noticed the scar, just above Astrid's left eyebrow. Normally, Astrid would leave a lock of hair loose, to cover the scar, but in her drunken state, she unguardedly pushed the hair aside. Lilac could see it clearly now and it made her think of Elroy; the one who'd thrown the ashtray at Astrid's head, knocking her out and causing a deep gash in her forehead that had required ten stitches.

"What are you staring at?" Astrid said, reaching for the chips.

"Your scar, is it painful?"

Astrid put her hand up to her forehead. "Sometimes

it throbs a bit."

"He was a cruel man," Lilac said, carefully.

"You weren't there at the time. I think I deserved it."

"Of course, you didn't! I suppose he told you that?"

Astrid was quiet and, after eating more chips, took another slurp of her drink. "Andy Roydon told me I had deserved it too. In place of Elroy, *he* punished me. He told me he had to because that's what I deserved. I was like putty in his hands. When he died, I was glad. I wanted to celebrate."

Lilac laughed and they both drank together. "There's just you and I now. We're the only ones left who know what happened."

Astrid had a faraway look in her eyes. "And may it stay that way. But I want to talk to Benedict, anyway."

"What? Not about that time? We can't do that!"

"Of course not, silly. I mean Francine. I want to tell Benedict about Francine wanting the dagger. She came round to my flat asking about it. Said she had a client who wanted to buy one and that Elroy had taken it years before. She looked drunk to me, as if the booze had given her the courage to come to my flat."

"You never told me she'd done that. What kind of a dagger was it?"

"German Saxon, circa 1600. It was rare, Francine said. She asked if Elroy had hidden it somewhere, so I told her I'd look for it and then she left."

"Why hadn't she asked you about it years ago?"

"I dunno, do I? Must've been short of cash or something to suddenly want it, just like that."

"Did you find it?"

Astrid took another gulp of wine before answering. "Look, I'll tell you this, but it's to go no further: it was with the others in a box in the back of my wardrobe. But I didn't want Francine to get her hands on it."

"So what did you do?"

"I was going to tell her I looked but couldn't find it. Then I had another visitor – Charley – he said Elroy had taken the dagger."

"How did he know? Wasn't he in prison around that time?"

Astrid sighed and looked at Lilac. "So when did Charley go to prison?"

Lilac tried to remember. "I don't know the exact date."

"Well, I do – it was December, 2004 – just before Aldo and Francine were married. Elroy had bought a whole load of antiques in June of that year – he'd been sent over to England to buy them. When he got back, he brought them all to our house and showed me."

"Okay."

"That's when he told me he was keeping one of the

daggers. He reckoned Andy Roydon wouldn't even notice because he was having an affair at the time and was thinking about this girl all the time, day and night."

Lilac poured them both some more wine. "Andy had lots of affairs."

"Course he did. He liked teenagers the best. This one was seventeen. He used to talk about her to Elroy all the time, and Elroy would tell me about Andy and what he was up to. Mind you, wifey had passed the year before so I suppose he could do what he wanted."

"I hate thinking of a seventeen-year-old going with an older man like that. It's revolting."

"Just forget about it. I only told you because that's why he didn't take much notice of what Elroy had brought back from England. So, Elroy just brought it home. He used to get it out and swing it around. It scared me, I can tell you, especially when he was drunk."

"Is that what you're going to tell Benedict?"

"No. I want to tell him about Charley. He came round and said he knew I had the dagger. He wanted to see it and so I showed it to him. Then he said something weird."

"Go on."

"He said he wanted to take it home and keep it in his room. He said he'd hide it. I was pretty scared, but there was no way I was giving it to Francine. I didn't want to give it to Charley either, but in the end, I had no choice."

"Why?"

"Because Charley said Francine had told him that Elroy and I hadn't gone to Germany in March, 2005. If I didn't give him the dagger, he threatened to tell someone about it."

"Bloody hell. Is that all Francine told him?"

"Yeah, because apparently when he asked Francine why that was important, Francine wouldn't say."

"Holy moly!"

"And he used the dagger to kill Francine?"

"Hold on a minute – whatever gave you that idea?"

Lilac took a big gulp of wine and shrugged her shoulders. "I don't know, except that was the dagger that killed Francine."

Astrid glared at her. "You're too ready to jump to conclusions, you know that? Were you even there that day?"

"No, I was out shopping."

"But you came home, didn't you?"

"Yes, and I was the one who found her body, laying on the lawn, under the olive tree – as everyone knows."

"And was there anything else?"

Lilac let her mind go back to that day. "It's funny you should mention that, because when I went out to the letterbox, Aldo was just leaving the property. I knew it was him but when I called out, he just kept on going."

"And didn't you think that was suspicious?"

"Yes, and I told the police and Benedict about it. They took it seriously, they said, but since then I've been told nothing."

Astrid smiled. "*Aha!* There's your answer then: Benedict has decided not to follow it up. That's what I think. He's as weak as bloody water, just like the police. Maybe I won't tell him about the dagger after all…"

Chapter 20

Saturday 15th June

Benedict looked at Gail. "Press three equals pressing the letters DEF on a phone. So, Lilac phones and my answerphone asks her to press three to leave a message. But is it for murder?"

"It's a cry for help on Lilac's part," Gail said. "And didn't you say she has something she's been hiding for years?"

Benedict kept looking at the letter. "Okay, so Dominica E Frimble wrote this in 2000. And then in 2004 she supposedly went to Australia with a man. I don't buy that story, by the way. Nor do I buy the story about Elroy's disappearance."

He was now more convinced than ever of his previous suspicions – that there had been three murders rather than just one – two of which had occurred nineteen years ago.

Gail was gazing at the screen of her laptop. "What

about Dominica and Elroy? What say they were murdered, as well as Francine?"

Benedict smiled. "Yes, Dominica was a clairvoyant and she predicted all three murders. That's what *did* happen, even though she didn't know it at the time."

Benedict began scribbling on a piece of paper:

$D = Dominica = 3$
$E = Elroy = 3$
$F = Francine = 3$

He showed his note to Gail. "I think Dominica's second sight was spot on. But how are we going to find out for sure?

"If Dominica and Elroy were also murdered, the perpetrators have found a way to cover it up. And now we're trying to solve three murders that took place nineteen years apart."

"Oh no." Benedict raised both hands defensively. "My client has only hired me to find his wife's killer, not the other two, which, by the way, I'm sure he knows nothing about. He wasn't around in March, 2005 and when he came back from the hospital, both of them had already gone."

"Even so, surely there were rumours when he got back, or at least suspicions? It must've been strange to come home and find two people had disappeared, just like that. Was it his illness that helped him believe any stories he was told, do you think?"

"Perhaps. And of course, the Trescos had moved out and put their house on the market during that time too. Was that just a coincidence?"

***

For most of the night, Aldo had been awake, thinking about the day Francine was murdered. He kept going over in detail every moment of the morning he'd gone to have lunch with her, right up until he'd left for the dental appointment. He'd told Benedict Aberthorp everything he could think of about when he'd first arrived and had to wait in the kitchen for Astrid. He could still visualise Astrid coming into the kitchen, carrying a tray of dirty dishes. At the time, he supposed they were from Francine's breakfast but never mentioned this minor detail to the private investigator as it hadn't seemed in any way relevant. Yet suddenly now it did because by that time, breakfast would've been at least a couple of hours before, and Astrid was an astute housekeeper. Also there were numerous empty dishes and more than one coffee mug.

Benedict had asked him more than once, about his visit to the dentist. That led him to suspect that Benedict might be agreeing with what Lilac Browne had said about seeing him leaving the property, long after he was supposed to have already left. There was no getting away from it now: there *was* one small part of the day he'd deliberately left out – specifically the time after he'd finished at the dentist. After the short visit, he had gone back to the house because Francine had left something for him that he'd forgotten to pick up earlier.

When he'd returned there'd been no one home, so he let himself in. The door hadn't even been locked. The item in question would be on the desk in Francine's office, so he'd walked in, put the envelope with his name on it in his trackpants pocket and left for home. He'd only been there for a few minutes and hadn't noticed anything unusual. Later, he was phoned to say Francine had been found dead, under one of the olive trees in the back-yard. She must've already been laying there when he went back to the house. He hadn't told Benedict about his return visit because it would seem suspicious, especially having already denied it. Of course, it would look even worse if he told the truth now, but nonetheless Aldo wanted to tell Benedict he'd gone back, and the reason why.

***

"Okay, Lilac, go right ahead. Gail, can you press the

record button please?" Benedict said.

She dutifully pressed the button. "Done."

Lilac looked at the piece of paper in her hand and began: "On Wednesday, April seventeen, Scamper came over to my place and I could hear voices, so I looked through the hedge, where three people were sitting in the gazebo in the Roydons' back-yard. It was in the afternoon and they were drinking wine. I kept quiet. They seemed to be having some kind of meeting and discussing things together, but I couldn't hear what they were saying."

"Who were they?" Benedict said.

"Aldo, Cindy and Astrid. I recognised Cindy from the sound of her voice and after staring at her for a while, the way she looked which was quite a bit different from nearly twenty years ago when she used to visit the Roydons. She was only sixteen then."

"And they're all still friends?"

"Not now, they aren't but way back they were always friends, those three. But they did something weird – they all pricked their fingers with a needle and mingled their blood together. I was in a good position to see them through the hedge, but they couldn't see me. They wouldn't have liked me listening in on their conversation, let alone watching what they were up to. I stayed still and quiet. Dominica told me to watch them. She said they were up to no good."

"Pricked their fingers?"

"Yeah. Put the blood onto a saucer and mixed it around. Then they looked at each other and pressed their pricked fingers together and said together: 'By the mixing of our blood, our oath endures forever.' I didn't want them to know I'd seen what they had done, and Dominica warned me not to say anything."

"Why did they make the blood pact?" Benedict said.

"I don't know, but it was scary, and I was frightened."

"Is there anything else you want to tell us before you go?" Benedict said lightly, so as not to put the quivering woman in front of him under any more pressure.

Lilac hesitated. "There is something, but I don't know if it's important." She hesitated, frowning.

"Why don't you tell us and we'll see?"

"Okay, well it's something Astrid told me about Charley. Apparently, he came to her flat to take the dagger and hide it from Francine. It was one Elroy had kept back years before. And Charley told Astrid that if she didn't hand it over, he'd reveal the lie about her and Elroy's supposed visit to Germany in March, 2005. So, Astrid reluctantly gave it to Charley. You see, Astrid told me she was going to tell you anyway, only I think she might have changed her mind. Astrid can be like that sometimes."

Benedict remembered what Charley had told them about Elroy keeping a few of the daggers for himself, locked up at home.

***

Lilac drove home via Plover Street in order to keep up her surveillance on Cindy. As she passed number seventy-one, a tall, red-haired man climbed into Cindy's car and they drove away. On an impulse, she followed them. She was giving Benedict so much information now that she considered herself almost like a member of his staff.

It surprised her to see Cindy and the man turn into the bus station car-park, and there was the bus, waiting to leave for the prison. It looked like they were going to the prison together.

It seemed to Lilac that both her body and mind now felt so much lighter since sharing all that information with Benedict Aberthorp. She was finally getting rid of the secret baggage she'd been carrying around – some of it for years and some just a couple of months. The more information she shared, the more she wanted to continue spewing forth, like a tap that couldn't be turned off. Besides, Benedict and Gail, were becoming like friends to her, and she enjoyed their company.

***

Benedict stood at his office window and watched as Lilac drove away to join the traffic crawling slowly up and down Rowan Street.

"Come on, I think it's time to pay Charley another visit," he said.

"Yes, why not?" Gail pulled on her jacket.

Mrs Shields had been forthcoming about the comings and goings at seventy-one Plover Street, ever since Benedict had asked her to be his watchdog. He'd known her for a few years and they'd always been on good terms. She might well be perceived as a nuisance nosey-neighbour, by some, but, to Benedict, such people were a valuable asset to any neighbourhood, especially for deterring burglars. So that's how he found out Cindy had a house guest – a Mr Gregor Carollan. And that meant that right now Charley was probably on his own at the shop.

***

"Where did you hide the dagger, Charley? The German Saxon dagger you were given by Astrid? The one you said you were keeping safe for her?"

"Don't talk rubbish. I've never had the dagger in my possession. Did Astrid tell you that? She's a mental case, just like her friend, Lilac."

"You went to Astrid's flat and she gave the dagger to you, thinking you were going to keep it safe for her and stop Francine getting it. But you didn't hide it in your flat, did you? You took it to the Roydons' and put it somewhere safe, waiting for the right moment. The identical weapon was found lodged in Francine's chest on the day of the murder."

Charley said nothing but there were beads of perspiration on his forehead and his face was flushed pink. Charley lifted his glass to his lips and took a sip, his hand visibly shaking. "Where's Cindy gone? Where is she? Have you tried to turn her against me too?"

Charley's resolve was weakening now, especially without Cindy to back him up. "She's gone back to her house," Benedict said, smiling. "Her husband arrived from Scotland last night and they're going to the prison to see Jenniver. In a few days Cindy and Gregor will be flying back to Scotland." He hoped his words were scaring Charley enough for him to tell the truth about everything that had happened on the day of the murder.

Charley looked as if he was going to cry. He seemed to shrink into himself as he crouched over the table, both hands now clutching the glass of whisky.

"What are you going to do now, Charley?" Benedict said, goading him in an effort to get to the truth. "She's going away with Gregor and you'll be left here alone to face the music. Is that fair?"

"You're trying to trick me into saying something incriminating," he whined. "I know your tactics."

Benedict was amused by Charley's defensiveness but kept his expression neutral. "Why would I do that? I just want to solve this puzzle. That's my job, after all."

"Then you should ask Aldo Sherwin what happened. He knows. He pretends he's innocent, but we all know he's not."

"Aldo was hurt by the actions of his wife, and someone has seen that as a motive; someone has tried to frame him for her *murder*, Charley. And they used a raincoat to try to convince the police Aldo had done it, by planting one at the murder scene. When the police asked Aldo to show them his raincoat – the one he'd been wearing on the day of the murder – he couldn't find it, could he, Charley? The coat was stolen from his beach-house. It seems the police took the bait, just as they were meant to, and questioned Aldo for hours about his missing mac."

"What raincoat? I've never seen his brown raincoat. I didn't even know he had one."

The shop door-bell jangled as someone entered. Charley got up without a word and went out to attend to whoever had come in.

Maybe Charley was telling the truth and didn't know anything about the raincoat substitute? Was it possible Cindy had put the raincoat under Francine's hand after they'd killed her, *without* Charley's knowledge?

When Charley returned and sat down again, Benedict decided to confront him. "So, what really happened that Friday, Charley?"

"You're asking me? How would I know?" He'd somehow perfected a look of complete innocence and, if Benedict didn't know better, Charley could have fooled him into thinking he really was. Yet Benedict wasn't that naïve.

"Where were you on the evening of May ninth and the morning of May tenth? And don't tell me you were at the Bayside Lodge in Moana, because we already know you didn't arrive there until the evening of the tenth."

Charley stared vacantly ahead and raised the now half-empty glass to his lips. "All I want to know is where she's gone. I love that woman."

Gail appeared in the doorway and Benedict signalled to her that they were leaving. "Don't you be going anywhere, Charley. We'll need to speak to you again."

"He could scarper, you know," Gail said, once they were outside.

"I don't think he will. He's in love."

***

Cindy had told Gregor she had to check on her friend and then driven round to see Charley. She parked further along the street from the shop and waited to see if anyone familiar entered or left the shop. As she watched, she saw Benedict and his friend emerge. She waited again until they had driven away in his car, before going into the shop.

"Charley, it's me, Cindy," she called, knowing he would be closing early on account of it being a Saturday. "Are you all right?"

"I'm out the back, love."

Cindy walked through to where he was sitting at the small table, a half-empty whisky bottle in front of him. She felt her body grow weak with emotion. No matter what happened, this was the man she really loved. Only, he couldn't really be 'the one' anymore; it just wasn't possible.

"The P.I. told me you're going back to Scotland with your husband. Is that true?" Charley said, staring hard at her.

"I don't want to go," Cindy said, "but Gregor's come over, unexpectedly, so things are getting difficult."

"Let's go to bed," Charley said, getting up from his small table.

Cindy took his hand and desire flowed through her despite feeling sad that this was probably the last time. Once upstairs, he took his shirt off and then began undressing her. "Oh God, why does life have to be so unfair?" she said, as they lay down and Charley began stroking her forehead and then kissing her lips.

"It doesn't have to be. Just tell him you want to stay here."

Soon Cindy lost all track of time and even momentarily forgot where she was. It was such a pity this dream would soon be over, but first and foremost she was a practical woman; a woman who had planned everything.

Chapter 21

Sunday 16th June

Unexpectedly, Benedict received a call to visit Aldo as soon as possible so he and Gail went straight to the beach-house. He said he had something he wanted to tell them – about the day of the murder. Gail volunteered to take notes.

"I had to go back to the house," Aldo said. "After the dentist."

Benedict frowned. He couldn't understand why Aldo was suddenly telling him this now.

"I was the one who had to find out if you'd even been to the dentist," Gail said.

Aldo's expression was one of displeasure at this apparent snooping. "What did they say?"

"That you'd been, but only for a short visit. Just a check-up."

"It only took fifteen minutes. Then I remembered the bank card. Francine had a new one for me and had told me not to forget to take it with me. She said she'd put it in an envelope with my name on it."

"But you did forget?" Benedict said.

"Yes. It was in her office, but after we'd finished lunch, it slipped both our minds and I left without it."

"So, you drove back to the house in your car?"

"Yes, and let myself in. The whole place looked deserted. I went into her office, found the envelope and drove home."

"Lilac told us it was you, and she called out. Did you not hear her?"

"No, otherwise I would've answered her, wouldn't I? I was listening to music through my headphones." Aldo's eyes were downcast. "Look, I've been guilt-ridden for weeks now – for not telling you I went back to the house. It was really playing on my conscience." His face looked haggard and he was unshaven.

Benedict was hastily trying to work out the truth of Aldo's story. "Did you see or speak to anyone on your property, or in the house, when you returned?"

"There was no one, but the front door was unlocked, which was strange."

"Did you know Charley and Cindy were having an affair?"

"No, I had no idea, but years ago they were in love, so I'm not surprised they got together again. The mutual attraction must've still been there."

"What's your opinion of Charley?" Benedict said.

"He's all right. Francine used to visit him every week when he was in prison. They were good friends when they were at school."

"So, what made Charley go rogue and rob a bank?"

Aldo looked into the distance. "He was in love with Cindy and, as you know, she and I got together for a while."

"Charley must have taken that hard?"

"Oh, yes. Charley was hurting. There's no doubt about that. And back then he had no income to speak of other than the unemployment benefit, so I suppose he got reckless."

"Look, about your return to the house: I appreciate your honesty. Besides, we were both sure Lilac was telling us the truth."

"You were?"

"Yes. We had no reason to disbelieve her."

"All right, I take your point."

"So, what are your plans now?"

"I'm going to stay at the beach-house. It's my home now and I like it there."

***

Lilac didn't need to watch Cindy anymore, so she switched her attention to Charley instead. She'd worked out that he was infatuated with Cindy and that she was just as much in love with him. So, she wondered what he was thinking now that Cindy had gone with her husband and left him in the lurch. "Poor Charley," she said to herself, as she parked her car a short distance away from Roydons' Antiques from where Lilac watched the comings and goings of the shop. It was now ten a.m. so she supposed the shop would just be opening, as it did around this time on a Sunday morning.

As she sat in her car, eating chips and drinking a bottle of vanilla-flavoured fizzy-drink, she nearly choked in surprise when she saw Astrid go into the shop. What on earth could Astrid want with Charley? Astrid had never mentioned Charley until just recently, when she'd told Lilac about the dagger, and his turning up at her flat, telling her he'd keep the dagger safe for her. Perhaps this current visit had something to do with that?

***

"I'm off to church," Cindy called to Gregor.

He barely looked up, but smiled. "Off you go then, love." He didn't believe in God. It was all silly rubbish to him.

Once she was near the Holy Angels church, the tolling bells seemed to be drawing her in and she found herself repeating the words she'd been taught, back in Scotland: "'I am a child of God, a beloved child of the Father – and mother'," she added, getting out of the car and hurrying up the steps.

There was an elderly priest, standing just inside the door. He looked up and smiled. "Welcome," he said. "I'm Father Francis."

"Can you hear my confession, Father," Cindy found herself saying.

"Of course. Mass doesn't begin for half an hour. Come this way."

She knelt down next to a rough-looking man who smelled of body odour. She wondered if he too was going to confession, but he soon got up and ambled away. Cindy's eyes were transfixed on the plaster statue of Mary, as she waited for the light to come on above the confessional door.

Soon she was inside the small room, kneeling next to the grille, the priest a faint outline on the other side. Without a doubt, this moment would be a turning point in her life. In a sense she was coming home – to love and peace. The dark side was a lonely, unsettling place to be in, and revenge didn't taste as sweet as she'd once believed it would. Instead it ached, like an ugly, festering sore inside her. If only she could be healed.

"Bless me, Father, for I have sinned." Until this moment, she had never known how much she wanted to be cleansed of the wasteland that was her own pitiful soul.

Later, when she came out of the confessional, Astrid was entering the church. Cindy shivered involuntarily. She hadn't expected to see her. What was she doing there?

"I've seen something rather horrible," Astrid said, her eyes wide and startled-looking. As they drew near to each other, Astrid held out her hand. "Here, you might need this."

When Cindy looked down, there in Astrid's palm was a silver medal of Mary, the mother of Christ. "Thank you," she said, picking it up and closing her fingers around it. "I didn't know you came to church."

"Sometimes I do. I pray to Mary and Father Francis and I have a talk." Astrid's eyes were fixed on the greenstone pendant Cindy still wore. She'd told them once it was called a Manaia. It was slightly shiny and it looked smooth.

"What do you mean, something horrible?" Cindy asked, but Astrid didn't answer.

***

Benedict was driving towards Roydons' Antiques when Astrid rushed out of the shop. She didn't notice him parking his car and going inside. There seemed to be no one there, so he called out, "Charley, it's Benedict. Can I talk to you please? Charley, open the door, for God's sake."

There was no answer, so Benedict went through to the back of the shop and towards the stairs leading to Charley's flat. He had a feeling that something wasn't quite right, and then he saw him. He gasped as the upside-down figure of Charley lay before him, his feet resting on the steps while the rest of him faced downwards, his head at an awkward angle. Benedict gingerly walked over and tried to find a pulse, just below the angle of Charley's jaw, where the carotid artery was located. His skin was cold but he was still alive when Benedict dialled the emergency services.

While waiting for the medics to arrive, Benedict hurriedly climbed the stairs to Charley's flat and almost tripped over the wire that had been pulled taut across the second step. So, that's how it was done, he noted, gingerly placing his feet onto the next step and going doggedly on, to open drawers and look in cupboards. In a bottom drawer there were a few crumpled clothes and some jumpers. He pushed his hand right to the back, just as he'd done with all the drawers, and groped blindly around. This time his fingers closed on something slippery. He quickly pulled it out and stared hard at a brown raincoat.

"What the...?" Benedict shook out the coat to find the label to be sure, and there it was: 'Quelrayn Bri-nylon. Wash in warm soapy water. Rinse thoroughly in cold water and allow to drip-dry. If the coat needs pressing use only a warm iron. Do not dry-clean.'

Now he had concrete evidence to show to Aldo as well as Detective Finnegan who would no doubt put up barriers and need convincing that this was really Aldo's. Benedict would tell him that neither Aldo nor his raincoat had anything to do with Francine's murder.

Chapter 22

Monday 17th June

When Gregor had turned up so inconveniently, Cindy smiled to herself at the thought that she too could have it all: a husband, the satisfaction of revenge, and eventually her daughter's freedom. The priest told her peace only came with forgiveness:

"God will forgive you, my child, and we too must forgive."

Cindy had tried forgiveness but that hadn't worked for her. The idea of power and revenge made her think of the difference between strength and weakness. Power could be turned into an abuse of strength, and weakness could be either succumbing through fear or rising up through payback.

She'd once cowered like a broken doll, but when it came to Jenniver, everything had changed. Revenge had brought with it a sense of short-lived freedom. Finally, the church had reeled her in, like a caught fish, and she'd told the kindly priest everything. He was Christ's earthly representative, and that brought a little comfort.

If only Charley hadn't mentioned Tegan – how much he'd liked her – because that had meant his love was being shared, although he hadn't exactly said he was in love with Tegan. Even so, it was Tegan who had it all – a baby, a house, and her freedom. Yet despite everything, Cindy's confession had purged her of her sins, even though she had no remorse when she lied to Gregor, telling him she'd missed him and loved him with all her heart.

Cindy and Gregor had already been waiting for two hours at Seagrove Airport for the fog to lift and Cindy was growing impatient. She could see the small plane they would soon climb aboard, and after an hour in the air, would touch down at International Airport in the city. From there, in just a few hours, they'd be on their way back to Scotland, and Cindy looked forward to reaching the safety of their isolated home where she could at last breathe freely again. However, her mind was full of jumbled thoughts, and she hated waiting like this. The fog didn't look like lifting any time soon so finally, she had to excuse herself and went to the restroom.

Once inside the toilet cubicle with the door locked, reality hit her like a hammer. Memories of Jenniver and

Charley began whirling through her mind, until she had to hold onto her head with both hands to still her thoughts. Jenniver had understood why her mother and Gregor had to go back to Scotland, but Cindy had promised to return in a few months to see her daughter again. Of course, that was a lie, but she'd had to try to stop the panicky look in Jenniver's eyes, the last time she'd visited the prison.

Now she couldn't get Charley out of her mind; his tenderness and his tattoos. Perhaps she was wrong and he really did love her? If only he was here with her now, instead of Gregor.

"I'm sorry, Charley. I'm so sorry, Charley. Charley, I love you." She said the words over and over again, crying until she was exhausted. Eventually, she splashed cold water on her face, came out and went back to sit with Gregor, who was quietly reading a book.

"You okay, sweetie?" he said, looking up.

"Yes, I'm fine," she said, looking away quickly.

***

Gail, whose task it was to watch Cindy, phoned Benedict with an update on the fog. "It hasn't cleared yet," she said. "And they've announced the flight will probably be cancelled. What do you want me to do?"

"I'm already here," Benedict said. "Don't look round now, but I'm standing behind a large potted plant near the entrance to the cafeteria. I can see you, hiding behind your newspaper."

Gail was sitting three rows back from Cindy and Gregor. All eyes were on the sky, where the dense fog refused to dissipate.

"Meet me in the cafeteria and we can discuss it," Benedict said. "Now."

Gail neatly folded her paper slowly, taking her time so as not to arouse suspicion. She tucked it casually under her left arm, picked up her handbag and went to meet Benedict.

Once Benedict and Gail were seated in the cafeteria, she paid particular attention to Cindy and her husband, who were still facing ahead, their eyes scanning the murky sky with hope. Benedict and Gail's chairs were angled so they could watch the entrance and see when their targets finally left the airport.

Benedict looked at Gail and tapped his watch. "The airport will make an announcement any time now about the flight cancellation, and I still haven't asked Cindy what her movements were on the day of the murder. It's got to be today. It's imperative we hear what kind of alibi she has, if any. So, my friend, be prepared to get up suddenly and then follow me out."

Gail smiled impishly. "Of course. This sounds rather exciting, especially for someone like me who usually deals with nursing dramas in the Australian outback."

***

"Poor old Charley," Astrid said.

"What? Has something happened to him?" Lilac's forehead wrinkled into a frown.

"Yeah, he fell down his stairs at the shop. Broke his neck, they say. Poor old bugger. I suppose a fall like that would've killed him."

"He isn't that old. But how come? Was he drunk or something?"

"Dunno. What I do know is that Cindy's gone back to the Highlands. She left a note in my letterbox."

"Why? Did you two become good buddies again after all?"

"Not really. Anyway, I'm glad she's gone. Silly tart."

"You mean the earrings?"

"Never mind about them. Looks like the killer's dead, don't it?"

"Charley? He couldn't have killed Francine."

"Why not, with Cindy's help. I wouldn't put it past him."

"What are you on about, Astrid?"

Astrid poured them both a large glass of wine. "C'mon, my old mate, let's have a drink, why don't we?"

Lilac pursed her lips and watched as Astrid's mouth transformed into the smile that always made Lilac feel uneasy. "Here's to us," Lilac said, drinking down half the glass in one go.

"You look thirsty, girl." Astrid tittered and drank fast too.

Lilac watched Astrid's eyes, behind the gold-rimmed spectacles. They were already looking glassy as they gazed vacantly across the room. However, Astrid was thinking of Charley, when she'd seen him at the antiques' shop, laying at the bottom of the stairs. He looked dead, and she hoped he was, then he'd never be able to say anything. She remembered how he'd looked all those years ago, when he came out of prison; a hardened criminal with shifty eyes.

***

When Cindy finally walked slowly past the cafeteria entrance with Gregor trailing behind her, Benedict felt tense.

"C'mon, fellow sleuth," he said to Gail conspiratorially out of the corner of his mouth.

However, Gail was already on her feet with bag in hand, ready to follow. They hurried outside, where the couple, both wheeling their suitcases behind them, headed for the taxi rank. Within a few seconds, Benedict and Gail were standing behind them. Luckily there were several others waiting, no doubt all from the cancelled flight.

"Hello, Mrs Carollan," Benedict said, already holding his private investigator's badge in his hand, ready for the moment he'd need to show it. "I'm a private investigator – Benedict Aberthorp. I'm doing some work on the Francine Roydon murder case. Would you mind if I asked you one or two questions regarding your whereabouts on the day she died?"

Cindy's face blanched and she looked pleadingly at her husband, who immediately fixed Benedict with a stern stare. "Do you have the right to do that? And in a public place?" he said, frowning, as he took Cindy's arm protectively.

Benedict held up his identity badge for them to see. "I'm working on behalf of Aldo Sherwin. I won't take more than a few minutes of your time. If you'd like to sit down in the airport lounge?"

Gail stood back, watching proceedings and ready to step in if needed.

"It's all right, Gregor, I don't mind saying what I was

doing. What day was that, exactly?" Cindy's face was now calm and her manner unassuming.

"Friday, May ten," Benedict said, watching her face closely, and assessing her body language for signs of a reaction.

"Oh, yes, I remember now," she said, as if a light had suddenly gone on in her mind. "I had a bad migraine and stayed home. Most of the day I was in bed with the curtains closed to keep out the glare, which always makes the migraines worse."

"Thank you, Mrs Carollan," Benedict said humouring her. "Were you alone, or can someone vouch for your being there that day?"

Gregor was about to protest, but Cindy held up her hand. "No, I lived alone there, but it's possible my neighbour, Mrs Shields, who is normally outside gardening, would remember if she'd spoken to me that day."

Benedict noticed the smirk on Cindy's face. "Thank you so much," he said, "You've been most helpful."

He made a mental note to have a word with Mrs Shields without delay. Cindy and her husband were obviously keen to leave the country as soon as they could.

"Saffron Motel, please," Gregor said, as the driver stowed their cases in the boot of the taxi. "No flight for two days, I'm afraid." He glanced Benedict's way as he spoke. "We've had to re-book."

Chapter 23

Tuesday 18th June

"He didn't die after all," Astrid said, raising a wine glass to her pale lips. "And now Cindy's in trouble."

Astrid found out that Charley had woken up the next day and had told the police everything, but luckily, hadn't mentioned her name. She knew he'd always pitied her – the way she'd been treated by Elroy and then later, by Andy and Francine Roydon. Good boy, Charley. At least he'd protected her.

Lilac watched Astrid's lips moving as she took a large swig of her wine. They were sitting outside in the back garden of Lilac's property, on two white plastic chairs, placed strategically on the round stepping-stones that were set into the dichondra lawn that never needed mowing. On the metal table before them sat a green glass bottle, still half full of sparkling wine.

"So Charley was only unconscious?"

"Must've been. But now all hell's broken loose by

the looks of it."

"Oh, Astrid. I'm sorry, but I have to ask you something I've been wanting to ask for weeks now."

Astrid gave Lilac a meaningful look. "I know what you're going to say: did I have anything to do with the death of my boss? Well, the answer is no, of course not. The police have already asked me the same thing. They wanted to make sure Charley was telling them the truth when he said I was totally unaware of what went on that day."

Lilac raised her glass and held it out towards Astrid, who was half-smiling. Their glasses clinked and Astrid finished what was in hers before taking up the bottle and re-filling it. "More?" she said, gazing to a spot beyond Lilac, the sun glinting off her glasses.

"Too right," Lilac said, breathing a sigh of relief. Somehow, she couldn't bring herself to hate the miserable wretch sitting opposite her. They'd been through years of hell, and now both their lives would be different. Freedom was something strange to Lilac, and she was unaccustomed to it.

"A Detective Finnegan wanted to know about the gottage and if anyone had stayed there around the time Francine was murdered," Astrid said, as if to herself. "I told him no one had stayed out there for years."

"Gottage?" Lilac said. "You mean the sleep-out at

the back of the garage?"

"Yeah, that's right, but the detective didn't stay long, and I haven't seen him since."

"So why did he ask you if anyone had stayed in the gottage?" Lilac was puzzled now, and suspicious.

"I have no idea, so I said, 'not that I know of.' Anyway, the detective looked as if his feathers had been ruffled, a tiny bit."

"Serve him right," Lilac said, and they both laughed.

"But you know what?" Astrid said, looking sideways at her friend.

Lilac sensed a change in mood. "What's happened now?"

"My blonde wig. I found it out in the gottage when I went out there to tidy up."

"What about the raincoat found at the murder scene?" Lilac said suddenly. "Who put it there?"

Astrid put her glass down with a slightly shaking hand. "How would I know that? There are things that happen, Lilac, that none of us can ever know how they happen. You must know that."

Lilac wanted to pursue the matter further, but decided against it. She knew what Astrid could get like if she was in a tight spot.

***

Benedict felt euphoric. He was finally starting to see a pattern forming among all the many pieces of information floating around in his head.

"Gail, I hope you're a fast typist because I want you to jot some notes down as I say them to you."

"Of course. I've had to write so many nursing reports that I've got quite good at it."

"Well, this is the way I see it: Charley Raymond missed out, basically on everything, when he left school and fell in love with Cindy Herskington. His parents were in huge debt when they died and the sale of their house was used to pay off that debt. So Charley was a very poor orphan. Yet he didn't care, because he thought love would conquer everything. He was high on love, until Cindy decided she wanted Aldo instead. Then Aldo later dropped Cindy for Francine. All the kids used to congregate at the Roydons' house, and Francine was never short of money. So, she and Aldo became an item and ended up married. Cindy found a way to forget Aldo when Francine's father helped her over her loss, and then of course she fell pregnant."

"Go on," Gail said. "I'm getting the picture."

"Yes, so am I, and it paints a picture for us of a young man who had nothing much left in his life except his current love – Cindy. But by then she had gone into someone else's arms. So Charley got desperate. Now he hated the rich Roydon family, and decided he had to get money too, so he could get his girl back. The plan went awry and instead he got twelve years inside and a string of tattoos. He eventually came out a hardened man."

"He doesn't seem too rough. Aren't you being a little harsh?"

"Probably, but I'm sure he came out a different person than he had been before. However, that didn't matter, because his friend, Francine was there to help him. She gave him a job in her shop, a place to live, and an income – hope for the future."

"I know, and then his first love turns up again, with a grudge," Gail said.

"And not just a grudge. There was still a flame there and their affair began. With it, a plan was developed to get revenge."

"Which they carried out."

"Yes, but there was a fly in the ointment, so things went awry."

Gail looked at Benedict with a frown. "What was that?"

"Charley was in love with two women – the other was Tegan, whom he'd also loved in his teenage years. Francine had stolen her, and that was the final straw for Charley. Something had to be done."

"Tegan? The girl who used to live next door to the Roydons?"

"Yes. Remember I interviewed her? She gave rather a glowing report on Francine; not one that others have shared; I should add."

"Oh, I see, to throw you off track, I suppose? Maybe she also had a grudge against her?"

"I don't know if she did, exactly. But somehow Tegan and Charley devised a plan, to be carried out once the house and money for the future had all been written into Francine's new will. Then, and only then, could Francine be 'despatched.'"

"And Tegan's living in the house, which now belongs to her."

"Yes," Benedict said, flicking through his notebook. "Tegan told me Francine wanted to do that sooner rather than later, in case anything happened to her."

"Like Francine knew she was in danger?" Gail said, raising her eyebrows.

"That's exactly what I said." Benedict smiled wryly. "Now I think she must've been quietly persuaded by the woman she loved and who was having their baby."

Chapter 24

Wednesday 19th June

"Did I notice if my neighbour went out on May ten?" Mrs Shields said, as she placed three mugs of tea on the glass-topped table in her dining room.

"Yes," Benedict said, adding milk to his tea. "In confidence of course. You see, we're getting alibis from a number of people – just to rule them out of our enquiries – and Mrs Carollan is one of them. She's already told us she stayed home that day, because she had a migraine. So we're just wondering if you noticed her at all, or anyone visiting her. Anything unusual?"

Mrs Shields pushed a mug of tea in Gail's direction.

"Thanks," Gail said, opening her notebook to a blank page.

"But why her? Did she know the murder victim or something?" Mrs Shields said, looking puzzled.

"Yes, although it was in the past. But we have to look at all possibilities, you see."

"Gosh, it seems so long ago," Mrs Shields said, rubbing her forehead and blinking rapidly. "But now that I think about it, I recall being so shocked to hear about Ms Roydon's murder, that I found myself thinking hard about that day. As Seagrove is a smallish place, the police wanted anyone who'd seen anything unusual to come forward. I hadn't of course, otherwise I'd have noted it down and told them. It was funny though, because if it had of been the night before, I could've told them I did notice something rather unusual. But of course they didn't want to know about the day before, did they?" She shrugged and took a sip of tea.

Benedict almost dropped his mug. "The day before? Something unusual, you say?"

Mrs Shields leaned forward conspiratorially, and spoke in a hushed tone. "It was eleven o'clock that night, May nine. Just as I'd turned my bedside lamp off and was snuggling down to sleep, there was the sound of a car door being shut, just outside the house. I got up to take a look. I hadn't heard a car pull up so this sound was strange. I peeped through a crack in my curtains and saw someone, bending over, getting into a car, on the passenger's side. It was as if they didn't want anyone to see them. Just across the road, it was. Then the car drove quietly off up the street but the driver didn't turn on the headlights until they were a few houses away."

Gail was scribbling fast into her notebook.

"That's very interesting, Mrs Shields, it really is. Did you notice the colour of the car by any chance?"

"It was a bit hard to see, but I think it was a purple or mauve colour. I don't recall seeing one like it round here before."

***

Lilac Browne stood at the back-door of her house, surprised by the visitor who was standing in front of her. The young woman had smooth skin and curly, glossy, brown hair that rested just above her shoulders. She smiled in greeting. "I'm researching my family tree and want to find out about my aunt, Dominica Frimble. She stopped replying to the letters I sent to Australia, and this is her last known address in New Zealand," the smartly dressed woman said.

Lilac stared at her for a moment, wide-eyed. "Yes, she lived here, but has been gone for twenty years, dear. I'm her friend, Lilac Browne."

"I've lived in England since I turned twenty-one," the woman said. "I'm Zena Frimble-Harris." She held out her hand.

Lilac shook it; the skin had a silky feel. "Do you have children?" Lilac smiled.

"Yes, two girls, aged ten and eleven."

After several hours spent talking to Zena, Lilac had learnt so much about Dominica's extended family that she hadn't known about before. Likewise, Zena was delighted to hear about some of the antics her aunt had got up to in her youth. Zena was Lilac's last living link to the woman she still loved and so it seemed fitting that the dolls' house should be passed on to her and her children. Lilac had no need of it anymore.

"There's something I'd like you to have. It was made by Dominica before she left for Australia in 2005. Come and take a look."

Zena followed Lilac into Dominica's den and stood before the dolls' house. "Oh, how beautiful. My aunt made this?"

"Yes." Lilac smiled warmly. "She even made each tiny piece of furniture and all the tiny clothes, sheets, towels – everything. I'm sure she'd love you to have it."

Zena gazed adoringly at the dolls' house and its contents. "Do you ever hear from her now?"

"No, but we parted as friends. She did write once to tell me she was happy and hoped I too would find true happiness."

"You've become a good liar," Dominica whispered. Lilac wanted to tell her to shut up but instead helped Zena to carry the dolls' house to her car.

"Thank you so much, Lilac."

Tears filled Zena's eyes as she shut her car door and drove away. Lilac watched, knowing a part of her was going too. Yet it had to be like this. Her life was moving forward now, and she no longer had to carry the burden. Of course, Dominica's supposed last known address in Australia was actually that of a close friend of Lilac's who had once lived there. When Lilac had visited her, many years ago, she'd sent a letter to the Seagrove public library, pretending to be Dominica, telling them about the missing library books in an effort to make Dominica's disappearance less suspicious. The friend had even indulged Lilac's wishes for a while by sending typed letters to Zena, until the friend said she couldn't do it anymore because it was just too hard to be complicit in the lie.

Lilac turned back towards the house, realising, with a sudden tightening of her chest, that the crescent-moon earring was still in the tiny chest of drawers where she'd hidden it in the dolls' house. And then she laughed. "Oh my God!" she said, "It's gone for good now.

Chapter 25

Thursday 20th June

Benedict found Lilac outside in the garden, where she was weeding her vegetable patch; Scamper lying on the grass in the sun.

"I'm so glad you came," Lilac said, because there's something more, I have to tell you. Let's sit down."

They sat in the plastic chairs in the sunshine.

"What did you want to tell me?" Benedict said expectantly, thinking Lilac was at last going to tell him what had really happened to Dominica and Elroy.

"It's about Tegan. She came over here yesterday, through the gate in the hedge. She was crying her eyes out, poor thing. When I asked her what was wrong, she said she was upset about Charley – about what had happened to him at the flat and how he'd been arrested for Francine's murder."

Benedict looked right at Lilac. "Upset about Charley?"

"Yes, and when she said she was naming her baby boy Charles, I just about fainted."

"Go on."

"Poor Tegan, I'm going to give her all the help I can. She's got no one else, not since her parents died," Lilac said.

"What happened to them?"

"They died in a car accident in 2005. They were coming round a bend when the brakes failed. The car plummeted straight over the cliff into the sea."

Benedict shuddered. "Was it after they moved out from their house in Korimako Street?"

Lilac looked at him. "Yes. That was the strange thing. It wasn't long after they'd suddenly moved out and put their house on the market."

"I see." Yet Benedict only had his instincts and hunches to guide his thoughts rather than hard evidence. His intuition would have to do for now.

"Anyway," Lilac said, taking an envelope from her pocket, "I want you to read this. You see, I am finishing altogether with my old life. I want to move on now." She handed the envelope to Benedict. "Please take this home and read it."

***

The weak rays of the late June sun filtered down, as Benedict walked along the waterfront. He had just finished reading the letter from Lilac Browne and it was only now that he was starting to feel that the mysteries of the case were finally being resolved:

Dear Benedict Aberthorp,

I'm compelled to tell you what really happened to Dominica and Elroy. You must have wondered why I act as if Dominica tells me things? But it's not an act – she does. She talks to me because she, just like me, could find no peace until her prediction had finally come true and been laid to rest. These clairvoyant predictions had haunted Dominica all her life.

And so, it came to be that on Friday, March four, 2005, six of us were having a BBQ at the Roydons' place: Mr Roydon and his daughter, Francine, Astrid and Elroy Lorning and Dominica and I. It was something we did, from time to time.

But on this particular evening, things got out of hand. We were all drinking and had eaten our sausages and chops etc. when Elroy began abusing Astrid. It was common knowledge that he was a wife-beater but not so well known that Astrid was suffering from battered woman syndrome, a form of post-traumatic stress disor-

der. Dominica and I had figured out she did have it, although she was in denial, of course.

But still, there they were, Elroy pushing Astrid, grabbing her wrist, twisting her arm. I told him to stop. He ignored me, so I pushed him hard and he fell and hit his head on the corner of the BBQ. He didn't wake up. He was dead. When Astrid saw what had happened, she started screaming, picked up a steak knife and rushed at me, holding the knife straight out in front of her. She was going to stab me.

And that's when Dominica ran forward and blocked Astrid's attack. She stopped her all right, but with her own body. Astrid plunged the knife into Dominica's chest and killed her instantly. That's when the panic set in and Andy and Francine, decided what to do. They were going to make everything all right again.

Later that night, Elroy was buried under one of the olive trees in the Roydons' backyard and Dominica was buried in my garden. I cut my hand trying to pull the knife from Dominica's chest and of course, once she was buried in my garden, I needed to disguise the grave with some appropriate plants and pavers. That's why I borrowed those two books from the library. The first aid manual and the one on planting ground cover.

Dominica had no children but she did have a niece and nephew. I used to get my friend in Australia to send them both presents, just like Dominica had done. The youngsters never knew it wasn't her. Her niece, Zena, lived in England, and Sam lived in France.

Astrid told everyone Elroy had died while saving a woman from being raped.

So, you see, Mr Aberthorp, the truth had to be told, otherwise I could never move on. I just couldn't bear the weight of secrecy any longer. Whatever you do with this confession, is up to you.

Thank you for all you've done for us.
Lilac Browne (and Scamper)

Chapter 26

Friday 21st June

Aldo Sherwin looked pale and thin when Benedict opened his office door at ten a.m. the following morning.

"I've come to tell you what happened in 2003," Aldo began. "I've held onto it all this time, but now is the time to come clean. It was only fear that kept me quiet. I realised there was no substance to what Cindy told me. Besides, I was only sixteen then, and pretty naïve."

"Come inside." Benedict said. He had no idea what Aldo was talking about, but after reading Lilac's letter, it might be something along the same lines.

"I've written it down and want you to read it," Aldo said, passing Benedict a sheet of paper.

So it was that at ten fifteen a.m. Aldo Sherwin sat drinking instant coffee while Benedict read the note he'd just been handed:

'I was so frightened when we did the first blood-pact in 2003, and also amazed at how easily Astrid (we called her Mrs Lorning in those days) had fallen in with Cindy's plan. Much later I became aware of how much Astrid had hated Morag Roydon (known to us then as Mrs Roydon.). Apparently, Morag had treated Astrid with disdain and condescension; patronising and humiliating her in front of others in small ways, so that Astrid was being subtly yet constantly 'put-down' by her.

I remembered clearly how Astrid had come out of the upstairs bathroom just after Morag had tumbled down the stairs and lain still at the bottom. First of all, Astrid looked really panicky, then later had a half-smile on her face. There were only three of us there. It was ascertained by Cindy that Morag was actually dead. We were all so shocked and upset – or at least pretended to be. Then Cindy said the three of us had to meet up and describe what we'd seen – so that our stories matched when the police inevitably interviewed us later.

Hurriedly, in the laundry, with our fingers dripping blood over the tub, after being pricked by a safety pin we found in there, Cindy insisted on the pact which she said was a promise that could never be broken, on pain of death. She made us all say together: 'By the mixing of our blood, our oath endures forever,' as we held our bloody fingers against each other's on the spot, where the skin had been pricked.

Astrid passively agreed yet I had been terrified because Cindy had instilled in me what could happen if I breathed a word of what I'd seen. We all looked each other in the eyes and repeated the words several times. By then we had an unbreakable bond for life. Somehow with the blood seeping out of our index fingers, that made our three-way bond seem rock-solid.

Once we'd all washed our hands and made sure the bleeding had stopped, Astrid said in a low voice, "Morag Roydon was a spiteful woman. She was snobby too and thought she was superior to everyone else."

Cindy had killed Morag because Morag was wearing a greenstone pendant, called a Manaia, that had once belonged to Cindy's mother. Her mother was dead now and the fact that Morag was wearing it, made it worse. And I had been a witness to it.

Then in 2024, Cindy came back and Astrid and I were once again held to account. Both of us tried to resist, but Cindy was persuasive and so we were drawn in to renewing the pact. Cindy insisted on it, or things would go very bad, for all of us, she said.'

When Benedict looked up, Aldo had finished his coffee and was standing by the window, looking out. The sky was blue, and Benedict imagined the waves, crashing onto the pebbly shore of Seagrove's Bay where, more often than not, the sea was white-tipped and rough.

Aldo turned and a sudden sadness overcame Benedict when he saw the unshed tears in Aldo's eyes.

"It's okay," Benedict said. "You've nothing to be afraid of now."

***

In the early afternoon, at his office in Rowan Street, Benedict stood in front of the whiteboard and turned to Gail. "More typing, I'm afraid. But I think this will be the final one. It's firstly going to be my report for Aldo and then, after that, one for Detective Finnegan at Seagrove police station. Ready? We don't have much time, as you know. Their flight will be leaving soon."

"Sure, I'm ready." Gail's fingers were poised over the keyboard of her laptop. Benedict began.

"It was a complicated story, the whole of which I did not discover through my own undertakings; some facts given to me in written form, after I had summarised the outcome of my own enquiries. Either way, the fact remained that it was only when I had received these written testimonies that I was able to make my final conclusions.

For the help I received with the tying up of several

loose ends, I would like to thank Lilac Browne and my client, Aldo Sherwin, without whose help, I would never have discovered the finite details of the wider intrigue surrounding the case for which I was tasked to solve: the death of Mrs Francine Roydon. It was only once I'd been privy to all the facts that I could say, with utter certainty, that my own conclusions were undoubtedly valid and above reproach. Incidentally, both Lilac and Aldo, were completely innocent of any crime relating to this case, and remain so to this day.

The information in this report was gathered through interviews with the persons named therein. Other evidence came from interviews with third parties, photographs and CCTV footage.

I was approached by Aldo Sherwin with a request to find his estranged wife's killer. She was Francine Roydon, owner of Roydons' Antiques in Seagrove, and had been murdered just over two weeks previously. Aldo had sought me out through desperation, when he became convinced of the fact that a Detective Finnegan of the Seagrove police-force believed him to be the prime suspect.

After agreeing to take on the case, I went about gathering evidence and analysing it. Sometime later, I came to the following conclusions:

Charley Raymond and Cindy Carollan, both planned

the murder, although Astrid Lorning was also an accomplice, owing to the fact that she allowed Cindy and Charley to secretly stay in the gottage on the Roydons' property. Whether or not Astrid questioned them about why they wanted to stay there, I have not yet ascertained. Obviously, the couple had thought themselves safe from detection (by all except Astrid), the idea being that they could take Francine by surprise the following day, when Charley had already made it known that he was supposedly already away on holiday. Cindy pretended she was at home with a migraine all the following day.

But the Roydon's neighbours, the Seyners', were kept awake by a light and the sound of voices coming from the dwelling.

Astrid hoped to exonerate herself from playing a part in the murder, by leaving for home before the crime had been committed.

Both Charley and Cindy had motives that culminated in the ultimate act of revenge. I believe both persons saw themselves as the victims of Francine Roydon's actions whom it would seem took what she wanted, no matter the consequences.

For Charley, his motive for murder was firstly on account of his love for Cindy and then latterly Tegan. For both women, Charley had lost out on their affections through a Roydon. Andy Roydon seducing the young Cindy and Francine later becoming Tegan's lover.

For Cindy, her hatred of Francine ran even deeper. Firstly, Francine, her then best friend, had stolen Aldo's affections from her and eventually married him. Then it was her gullibility in sleeping with Andy Roydon and becoming pregnant, leaving for Scotland in shame. The final nail in Francine's coffin, as far as Cindy was concerned, came years later when her daughter, Jenniver, was cruelly rejected by Francine, her half-sister.

Once Charley and Cindy met and began their affair, they planned the murder together. Charley had an alibi – of sorts – as did Cindy. Yet neither of them had planned it well enough to avoid detection. There had been observers, and third-party witnesses who'd seen and heard things. All the information and evidence left me in no doubt that Cindy and Charley were responsible for Francine's death.

Cindy Carollan is also responsible for attempting to murder Charley Raymond, by placing a wire across the stairs to his flat. This action was caught on the CCTV Charley had set up as security for the shop and for the entrance to his flat above the shop. I believe Cindy wanted Charley out of the way, thinking that Tegan was the one he really loved. Also, it would prevent Charley saying anything about Cindy's involvement in the murder of Francine."

***

Cindy felt hollow inside, knowing it was soon going to be over. She was sure that Benedict Aberthorp had now fitted all the pieces of the puzzle together with the help of his assistant. Cindy had always known it was only a matter of time before there was a knock at her door. If it hadn't been for the fog, she and Gregor might now be back in Scotland, and she'd be safely out of the country.

She remembered how horrible it had been – sneaking back to the murder scene as soon as Charley had moved the body outdoors (and pushed the dagger in still further) to its place under the olive tree before returning to the gottage. Cindy had the raincoat Astrid had given her, so that it could be used as a distraction when it was found. The idea had been Astrid's and Cindy had taken it on board as being a good idea to divert the police from the real killers. Cindy had snuck out to place it under Francine's right hand. She'd almost fainted at the sight of the lethal dagger protruding from Francine's chest. She had to lift Francine's upturned hand, where she placed the raincoat, askew on the ground, to make it look like Francine had ripped it away from her murderer in the struggle for her life. She and Astrid had decided not to tell Charley about the raincoat as he probably wouldn't have agreed. He'd come to see Aldo as a victim, even though he'd once stolen Cindy from him. However, Astrid had already told her that Lilac was going to steal Aldo's raincoat and stash it in her house – that had been part of her and Lilac's plan originally. They had nothing against Aldo, but saw that as a convenient way to get the police distracted and even to blame Aldo for the murder. What did it matter, really? Aldo would be none the wiser, although later, Cindy and Lilac regretted they had thought that way.

But Astrid told Cindy that Lilac wasn't cut out for anything more than that, so she was no longer to be included or know about what was going to take place. Cindy had liked the idea of the raincoat, because, for her, it was like wielding a double-edged sword: the sky was going to fall in on Aldo as well as Francine; something which neither of them had foreseen.

Her hand went to the greenstone pendant around her neck – the Manaia. She wanted to ask it to protect her as she stroked the three fingers carved into the pendant, representing birth, life and death. Then she remembered the medal of Mary, the mother of Jesus, that she'd placed in a small leather purse to carry everywhere with her. If only she could hold it. Father Francis had said all she needed was simply faith. That did not require her to touch or even wear the medal. All the same, with the medal in her pocket and the Manaia round her neck a sense of peace now surrounded her. It was like two worlds combining to give her the strength she needed to face whatever was ahead.

Yet where were the earrings? Who would have known they also held an inestimable amount of power? Cindy loved symbolic items she could hold and look at. That's why she'd been so devastated when she'd seen the Manaia hanging round Morag Roydon's neck. "That was the day my heart broke," she whispered to herself. "That was the day my world flipped and I landed upside down, suddenly able to see truth in everything."

After Cindy's mother had died, her father must have had an affair with Morag Roydon and that day Cindy realised her father must have given the greenstone pendant to Morag, who was probably unaware of its origins. Yet Cindy had known because she remembered exactly what it looked like, and after her mother died, she searched for it but could never find it.

Cindy hated the fact that she'd allowed herself to be seduced by Andy Roydon. She'd fallen for his charms because of her own vulnerability, and now, when she clasped the Manaia and felt its shininess, her shame was replaced by the memory of her mother. "The Manaia will always remind me of you, Mum."

***

Later that night Aldo washed his raincoat in warm soapy water, rinsed it thoroughly and hung it in the shower to drip-dry. He wondered if he would ever wear it again. Probably not, he decided. He felt at peace at last, his equilibrium finally restored. His mind had been troubled for so long that he'd forgotten what it felt like to truly feel at peace with himself. Finally, he had unburdened himself by telling Benedict everything; his agonising thoughts silenced at last.

***

The hospital in Seagrove was Benedict's next destination. After parking in the visitors' car-park, he was soon walking down the corridor towards Charley's room in the surgical ward. He noticed there was someone walking ahead of him, carrying a bunch of flowers. It took a few moments before he saw that the visitor was Tegan. He slowed his pace so as to remain at a discreet distance. Once she had gone into Charley's room (wherein he'd been told the patient was in halo-traction), Benedict walked on until he reached a chair just inside the door on which sat a uniformed policeman, looking bored. Benedict smiled and breathed a sigh of relief because he knew the police had finally caught the right person and were keeping an eye on him. He turned back in the direction he'd just come and walked to his car. He phoned Gail before driving away.

"Come to my place for tea," he said, knowing they needed to close the case satisfactorily. There was so much to tell her and so much to discuss.

"Sure, and I'll bring some wine – your favourite one."

Tomorrow he'd be free to breathe in the salty air and dream of the longed-for summer, when once again he could sit out on his deck with a book and relax in the sunshine. He still struggled – some days – just to leave the safety of his house, but there were always those long walks along the seafront, where he could experience the special kind of peace it seemed only the sea could bring him (besides the truth of any matter, of course).

He would roll the word – 'truth' – around in his mind as he trudged beside the sea, with its noisy waves and threatening undertow. Facing the truth about his own vulnerability, changed his life after Bryony died. He'd finally learnt how to cry out his grief and he'd paced and he'd sometimes cursed. Yet that was just the way he was. And now he knew it was all right to be like that – because crying meant he had a heart, not that he was weak.

Acknowledgments

My special thanks go to the following people who helped me in different ways in the writing of this book: Laura Dean (Book Editor); John Dean (Crime Writer); Tina Shaw, my tutor at NZIBS, and the editors at Cranthorpe Millner Publishers.

CPSIA information can be obtained
at www.ICGtesting.com
Printed in the USA
BVHW041209051222
653467BV00005B/105